AN EXMOOR

Moving to Combe Tollbridge

ROSEANNA HALL

This edition published in 2023 by Farrago,
an imprint of Duckworth Books Ltd
1 Golden Court, Richmond, TW9 1EU, United Kingdom

www.farragobooks.com

Print ISBN: 9781788424615
Ebook ISBN: 9781788424622

Cover design and illustration by Patrick Knowles

Chapter One

The rhythmic patter of her keyboard fandango fell silent. Susan Jones frowned at the computer screen. Hadn't the heroine already moaned with ecstasy during her previous seduction? But did her pulse bound with indescribable pleasure, or…? Susan scrolled rapidly back through the text.

She chuckled. The young woman had expressed wordless rapture by whimpering. Not with a bang, but with a whimper? Well…

Susan sipped at her mug of hot chocolate and settled once more to her typing. Silken sheets, velvet ropes and a peacock feather fan were being deployed in a charmingly unorthodox manner when the roar of an approaching motorbike began to intrude on the creative mood Hot Pink Press's bestselling author had worked so hard to establish. She muttered something. If that was tourists in search of somewhere to park, they'd taken the wrong road into Combe Tollbridge. The village's precipitous main street led only to the little harbour and the few shops, with attendant dwellings and one pub, that huddled about it.

A few enterprising residents might squeeze space from cottage gardens for their own vehicles, but if the general public ever came calling it was encouraged to park on the far side of the valley. At the end of a rough track stood a field opening to the headland that boasted fine views of Tollbridge itself, of the Bristol Channel beyond and, on a clear day, the south coast of Wales. Once safely down the steep Coastguard Steps and across the ancient footbridge that spanned the rushing River Chole, only then were visitors able to explore the little fishing village seemingly ignored by the twenty-first century.

Susan heard the motorbike rumble along narrow lanes and shadowed alleys, the engine echoing deceptively off walls and cliffs. With another sigh she took her fingers from the keys to pick up a dainty silver fork. She speared a small cube of Turkish delight, dunked it in her chocolate, and slowly ate it. Susan wasn't ashamed of her curves but had no wish to bulge. Every time she brought home a box of her favourite sweetmeat the first thing she did was quarter each cube with a sharp knife, rolling the pieces in icing sugar so that she couldn't use stickiness as an excuse for eating two together. She sipped again at the chocolate, shut her eyes, and waited for the noise, still swelling, to fade as the bikers at last realised their error and drove away back up the valley to the main road and proper signposts.

The rumble grew louder. The motorbike was heading in her direction.

No. What made her think that? Echoes were deceptive. The bike could be going anywhere. Anywhere!

But...

Susan set down her empty fork. The motorbike drew closer. Why her heart should sink she had no idea. The bike drew close – very close. Right outside Corner Glim Cottage, it stopped. Susan leaped from her chair and rushed to a convenient window. Cautiously, she peeped out.

She caught her breath. A Triumph Bonneville! How that took her back! Those happy days when she and Andrew had the world at their feet, their whole lives ahead of them... But that was long ago. So much had happened... She blinked.

She blinked again as two figures – two young women, stretching and yawning in black leather – dismounted from the Triumph and began to remove their helmets. Susan's eye was first drawn to the short green stubble streaked with pink through which the driver ran her fingers. A black helmet seemed out of character. She'd have expected purple, or…

She gasped. 'Angela!'

A mother's fond eye could recognise her child even before the second helmet was properly off and the wearer could start shaking out her long dark locks. A mother's apprehensive eye could recognise motorbike panniers that looked… full. Suspiciously so. Full to overflowing. Angela's mother tried to suppress her growing qualms as she hurried down the narrow stairs and outside.

'Angela, what are you doing here?'

As her daughter stared, Susan realised this hadn't been the most tactful of welcomes. Being disturbed from the depths of her latest manuscript was no excuse. She corrected herself quickly. 'I mean – what's wrong? Why aren't you at the library? What's happened?' As Angela continued to be silent, Susan pulled herself together. 'Oh – I'm sorry. Who's your friend? I – I don't believe we've met.'

Angela looked dumbly at her green-and-pink companion, who laughed and moved forward, hand outstretched.

'Come off it, you know you'd remember the barnet if we'd met before. My hair's my trademark. How d'you do? I'm Andy Marsh. I've known your Ange a few years now, so when she felt she simply had to come home I said I'd bring her – well, more than happy, to tell the truth.' She gestured with pride towards the Triumph. 'A high-powered beast like this needs a good blast-through every so often to flush out the system. A motorway detox – but within the speed limit, natch.'

Susan was unable to respond as anticipated to Andy's wicked grin. Her attention had been caught by one ominous phrase. 'Come home? But – but – Angela's never lived here! I didn't move to Combe Tollbridge until ages after she—' Briskly, she shook herself. 'But I forget my manners. Do come in.' *What kind of mother isn't delighted to see her only child? Why do I suspect there's worse to come?*

And how can I even think such an awful thought?

'Until after she moved in with Paul,' Angela finished bitterly. 'Paul and I are history, mother. I threw him out – no, I left him – no, we – I – I mean, right now I don't want to talk about it. I can't. I'm worn out and my head's spinning and I'm so angry I could scream!'

'You'll make your headache worse if you do.' Andy urged her friend indoors, following her mother. 'Now sit down, shut up, and breathe. Breathe deeply. Mrs Jones – Susan? – cool – could I use your loo? It's not that we didn't take comfort stops at regular intervals, but the proper soft stuff would be luv-er-ly and with the biggest possible L. Public loos never seem to have enough decent paper and hankies just don't cut it, do they?'

Susan indicated the tiny downstairs bathroom she'd had built to the rear of the original cottage, and Andy nodded her thanks as she whisked herself inside, leaving mother and daughter together.

'Angela, I'm... lost for words.' Susan couldn't yet bring herself to say she was sorry. From the start she'd had doubts about her daughter's relationship, but hoped she'd kept them well hidden over the years. 'Thrown him out? After so long? I won't ask why—'

'I told you I can't talk about it now!'

'—but – well, you poor thing. I'm so sorry.' Sorry that her cherished only child had become such a pale shadow of her normal competent self. 'I – I don't know what to say,' said Susan. *Or what to do.* She brightened. 'I'll put the kettle on. You'll feel better with something warm inside you after driving all that way.'

4

'We... stopped at regular intervals.' Angela dragged herself upright at the table, resting her chin on unsteady hands. Hair ignored for several days drooped across her pale face; it was an obvious effort for her to push it away. 'Andy insisted. No more coffee, thanks,' as Susan began to bustle about the small galley kitchen that had once been a lean-to wash-house. 'I don't need the caffeine now. I haven't slept properly – haven't slept at all – since – since it happened, and she said she didn't want me falling off the back of the bike and her go driving on without spotting I'd been run over by a lorry...'

'Sensible girl,' returned Susan. 'But you don't need to stay awake now you've arrived. No caffeine, then – which rules out tea, too, as I don't have herbal – but how does hot chocolate sound?'

'Ooh, yes please!' Andy Marsh had emerged from the bathroom looking bright-eyed and ready for anything. 'You haven't any of those diddy little marshmallow sprinkles, by any chance?'

As she hunted in various cupboards and set tins on the narrow worktop Susan grinned, rejoicing at this kindred spirit. 'Sorry, no. But there's carvy cake if you fancy it – caraway seedcake, a local speciality – or would you prefer gingerbread? That's another secret recipe and very popular. I'd call it heavy on the black treacle, myself, and it doesn't go overboard with the golden syrup, but it's absolutely delicious.'

'Scrumptious, yum.' Andy shot a quick look at the weary Angela. 'Both for me, please, if you can spare them. I could do with a sugar boost after all that driving.'

'It was very kind of you to bring Angela such a distance on the spur of the moment.'

Andy dismissed this with a wave. 'Good for the bike, like I said – and what sort of friend would I be if I let poor Ange come down by herself on the train? Has she told you she hasn't slept a wink for days? She'd have made herself ill again – she looked ghastly when I first saw her—'

Susan pounced. 'You've been ill? Something he did to you? Not – not a hospital job?' Angela, eyes closed, began shaking her head. 'Have you seen a doctor? Do you need a doctor now? Angela, say something!'

Angela half-opened her eyes. 'All I need is sleep, Mother. Peace and quiet – and sleep. I – I couldn't sleep in the flat – the memories… I'm so tired…'

'And angry and disappointed and empty,' put in Andy. 'Empty in more ways than one, Susan. She wouldn't eat a thing on the way here, though I made her drink lots of coffee to keep her awake – but she's right, what she needs most, after a slice of cake or whatever, is to get her head down somewhere she can relax. Your spare room?'

'There isn't one.' Susan smiled as she bustled about the little kitchen. 'Or rather, not in this cottage. I had the place remodelled from the original two up, two down and a bit at the back so that now the second bedroom is my workroom. It's crammed full of bookcases and filing cabinets and my desk, of course. When visitors come to stay I book them into the Anchor – the pub – at my expense.'

Andy appeared at her side and seized one loaded tray as her hostess collected the other. They headed back to the one large room that did duty for both living and dining. Susan set her burden on the table, and pointed.

'There's the sofa and cushions for you to fight over, but with two of you I'm a bit low on blankets – though I don't think that's a problem. In the short term,' she quickly added. Andy grinned. Angela said nothing. 'Get that down you, girls.'

'Ange, you heard your mother.' Andy poked a finger in her friend's ribs as Angela's head began to slump towards the table. 'Boost that blood sugar of yours right now!'

She splashed cold milk in a mug of hot chocolate and stirred, before pushing it under Angela's nose and sliding a plate of gingerbread within touching distance. Susan watched instinct slowly take over from exhaustion, and looked her gratitude at Andy as Angela picked up the mug and sipped, sipping again before crumbling a small portion of gingerbread and tasting it. The taste seemed to please her. She sipped and crumbled again; and again. She tucked her hair neatly behind her ears, and spoke.

'Liquorice,' she announced. 'Just a hint of it – but that's your secret ingredient.' She took another sip of chocolate, another mouthful of gingerbread.

'You could be right,' said Andy.

'She probably is,' said Susan, with pride. 'Angela was always good at cookery.' She watched as a smile flickered for a moment in her daughter's dull eyes, and exchanged with Andy Marsh another glance of relief.

The two addressed themselves to their own plates, and as Angela ate and drank on automatic pilot spoke quietly together of the journey from London, the variations in scenery, the busy-ness or otherwise of different stretches of road, and the way a high-sided vehicle was invariably in just the wrong spot when an essential signpost needed to be read.

Susan, sated on Turkish delight, was the first to push back her chair. 'You finish your snack while I drum up more blankets.' She moved across to the telephone. 'Do you both like eggs? I thought, once you'd both had a nap, perhaps omelettes, or scrambled on toast – for a protein balance after so much quick-fix sugar.'

'Either would be great, thanks.' Andy cut herself more gingerbread. 'As for taking a nap, I'm not in need of forty winks the way poor old Ange is. I've lived a normal life these past few days, apart from yesterday when she pressed the panic button.'

Angela managed another smile. 'If you ever ate one of mother's omelettes you'd panic, too.' Susan chuckled, acknowledging the hit and delighted that her daughter was emerging

7

from her trance. 'Oooh!' Angela tried to stifle a yawn. 'But I agree scrambled egg on toast would be lovely, when the time comes… Only not just yet, thank you.'

Susan tapped out the familiar number on the handset. She waited.

And waited, while the ringing tone rang on. Miriam Evans had never come to terms with answering machines and argued that if people wanted her and she didn't answer, they'd call again. Susan frowned with an effort of memory. 'I wonder if— Oh, Miriam, there you are at last. I'm sorry to have disturbed you. I didn't think you were dying today.'

Andy's mug paused halfway to her lips, and Angela blinked. They could just make out the tinny laughter coming down the line. It sounded lively enough.

'That was yesterday,' said Miriam. 'Today it's a wrestling match betwix me and a roll of gift-wrap and the sticky tape to make up the parcel. You know how it is, midear. The sticky tape's putting up a good fight, but I'll beat it in the end – but what's to do, Susan? Not like you to be phoning in the middle of the working day. Everything all right, is it?'

Susan, conscious of her audience, decided on a censored explanation. 'Unexpected visitors – my daughter and a friend – in urgent need of sleep. The Anchor… isn't suitable this time, so I wondered if you'd agree to lend me a few blankets – I promise we'll take the greatest care… You would? Oh, thank you! And a dozen eggs, if possible. I haven't much in the fridge right now – I was going out to the shop later… You're a lamb… No, I wouldn't want to put you to the trouble. I'll leave the girls to finish their gingerbread and pop along in a few minutes… Yes, then you can get back to your wrestling match. Bye!'

Andy laughed. 'Your friend goes for brawn rather than brains, does she?'

Angela opened her eyes. 'Tell her they're both a waste of time. I should know.'

Susan went to a discreet cupboard. 'Blankets: the first instalment. You'll have to toss for who gets cushions on the floor and who has the sofa, but as you see there are plenty of cushions.' She went to another cupboard, equally discreet. 'Spare towels. I won't be long – it's only a short walk to Miriam's place.'

Andy jumped up. 'I'll come too. Let Ange take the sofa and as many blankets as she likes – I'm not sleepy, and I could do with the exercise, never mind helping you carry the stuff safely back. Broken eggs wouldn't go too well with borrowed blankets.'

As she began to assemble a hurried couch, Susan shuddered. 'Perish the thought! Miriam's a full-time hand spinner and weaver, and she makes the most beautiful things – so beautiful that people pay a small fortune for them and her waiting list is a mile long. She understands this is an emergency, so she's taking the chance, but I'd hate to let her down and if the stock gets damaged in any way, the only person she could sell them to would be me. Living on my own as I do I certainly don't need any more blankets! Apart from anything else, I haven't the room.'

'Hey, I'd find it somehow.' Gently, Andy spread the final blanket. 'A gorgeous feel – and those colours! Light as a feather, too. Your friend Miriam's a genius.'

As the pair made for the front door, Susan looked pleased. 'She is, though I'd have thought her colour sense rather on the muted side, for you. Angela, we'll leave you to settle yourself in your own time. This way.' She led Andy from the cottage round to the narrow Three Square Passage and into Stickle Street. 'Miriam dyes all her own yarns,' she went on, but paused as her companion burst out laughing. Realisation had dawned on Andy Marsh. Susan's phone call hadn't, after all, disturbed someone at death's door.

'Yarn, hair, these days anything goes,' she gurgled. 'Let's hear it for individual choice!'

'Miriam's choice is the natural look. She's not too keen on artificial chemicals—'

'Is anyone?'

'—and she likes to know what she's handling. Making her own dye's an obvious step, even if it takes time from the spinning and weaving – and she gives full details of every dye on every label. It's not really risking her livelihood because it will never come out exactly the same way twice, even for Miriam, but people who buy her things like to feel they're in on a trade secret.'

'And might try it themselves one day,' supplied Andy, 'if they only had the time, which they never have – but it makes them think they could do it.' She nodded. 'It's a good gimmick. Like my hair. It pays to advertise! Back-to-nature artisan craft has come into its own over the past few years, so you need to stand out from the crowd.'

'It's not exactly my colour, but I think your hair's great fun.' Then Susan sighed. 'It's rather nice that you're Andy, and Angela's friend. Her father was another Andy – she hardly remembers him, he died so young – but he'd wanted to call her Andrea and I thought it might be a bit too much like staking a claim on the poor child. Angela was an acceptable compromise. Still, I've sometimes regretted—'

'Don't! I wish my parents had been as considerate as you. If you think I'm Andrea, you're wrong. It's A for Andromeda, would you believe?'

After a pause, Susan said that she would.

'Ange told me you've got a serendipitous sort of mind that picks up general knowledge from all over, for your books. Remember my surname is Marsh?' Another pause. 'My middle name's Rosemary. My parents… are both keen botanists.'

Susan guessed some keen deduction was expected. She concentrated. Andy waited, walking in silence beside her.

'Andromeda,' said Susan at last, sympathy and triumph giving equal weight to her tone. 'Bog or Marsh Rosemary, you

10

mean? My botanical Latin's never recovered from when half the plant names in creation were changed a while back, but I seem to remember—'

'You remembered, all right. And did I hate it at school! Andromeda! Oh, I cursed my parents for years – but once I got out in the big wide world, I realised it was a great gimmick. The downside is, it was my name that first attracted my ex – he was a science fiction geek.' Andy laughed. 'Maybe still is – no idea, and don't care – but extremely ex, believe me. I guess that's why it was me Ange called when things went wrong for her. She knew I'd been there myself – gone through it all and come out the other side, though it was money with me, not itchy underpants.'

'Ah.' The news of his betrayal came as no surprise to Susan: she'd always wondered about Paul. It had been a (secret) relief when he and Angela chose to live together rather than marry. There was vague talk of *One day, when we can afford it* but Susan had been only too thankful for modern expectations. These days the young seemed to require a lavish (and expensive) ceremony after equally lavish, expensive hen and stag nights – no, weekends – in exotic locations followed by a honeymoon in a location even more exotic and expensive. Susan had grown up believing that money saved by a couple who planned to marry should be put towards buying a place to live, rather than on what she couldn't regard as anything but an unnecessarily theatrical performance. Her own wedding…

But she accepted that times change, if not always for the better. Death had robbed her far too soon of Andrew Jones and at times her heart still ached, but for much of the younger generation it seemed that losing, swapping or even divorcing a partner was almost routine. Whether Angela would prove as robust as many of her peers Susan didn't know. All she could do was think positive.

'My congratulations,' she said now to Andy. 'You came out the other side pretty well, it seems to me. I just hope it didn't take too long.'

'Pretty well, yes, even if it got a bit ugly at the time.' Susan's air of genuine interest encouraged Andy to enlarge on this. 'We had a joint bank account, you see, saving for a deposit on a flat—' Susan nodded approval – 'and that bastard, pardon my French, only went and emptied it one day to buy himself a sports car! A real boy's toy with a zillion cylinders and an organ-loft of exhaust pipes. He said it'd dawned on him almost too late that he was actually a free spirit and couldn't bring himself to settle down just yet, if ever. Said he needed his space, and the open road – so I told him what I thought of him, waved him on his way and phoned the bank.'

As Stickle Street turned into Harbour Path, Susan was enjoying the lively narrative. 'It's only halfway down but we'll go as far as the turning bay at the end, by the cliff.'

'Fine by me. Give poor Ange more time to herself.' Andy wasn't slow to catch on. 'Well, it didn't take long before he missed his home comforts more than he expected, but I wasn't having him back and told him so. Main reason, I could never trust him again, plus I'd realised he wasn't the only one who'd found out just in time they wanted to be a free spirit, though it was a motorbike I bought, not a car. Told him he could take off on his travels again with my blessing because I could absolutely see his point of view.'

'The biter bit.' Susan was full of admiration. 'Could he see yours?'

'Bit good and deep – and no, he couldn't. Didn't even try. Wanted me to pine for him and make a scene, I guess. Male vanity.' She snorted. 'Told me, when I didn't crumble the way he wanted, he accepted he'd behaved badly, but everyone deserved a second chance. Asked, if he paid back the money, would I give him one?'

'Of course you didn't.'

'No way, José! Not after it cost me the top-flight coffee machine my parents gave me for my birthday. Could even have killed me.'

'He tried to electrocute you?' Susan toyed with the idea of suggesting a crime fiction imprint to Hot Pink Press, for whom she wrote as Milicent Dalrymple. She'd have to find a more suitable pseudonym, of course, for... Blood Red Books? She chuckled.

Fortunately, Andy laughed with her. 'Nothing like that, though it was bad enough. Made me realise I'd had a lucky escape. Sometimes these things can turn seriously nasty. Stage One gaslighting, you could call this. Dead creepy. I rushed home from work one day gasping for a drink, charged into the kitchen, went down with an almighty wallop – grabbed at the counter to break my fall, which is how the coffee machine came down with me – and hey, are those tiles *hard!* I hit my head as I fell, and the coffee machine was smashed to pieces. When I came round all I could see was chunks of glass and metal and plastic – and all I could smell was lavender. I thought it must be brain damage, until I realised the bastard had sneaked back in with a tin of furniture polish and made a death-trap of the kitchen floor. Like I said, dead creepy. I'd had no idea, before.'

'Dead creepy,' echoed Susan, aghast. 'What did you do?'

'Phoned the locksmith, gave my landlord notice and a spare set of keys, found another flat and decided on a change of career. Men may have muscles, but so have women and you can't deny we can do a hell of a lot more for ourselves than we think.' Susan, who'd been forced to learn this the hard way, nodded. 'So I took a few courses, picked some useful brains, and now I call myself a J.O.A.T. – it was Ange thought that one up for me. We met on one of her part-time library days, when I was checking through the DIY section.'

'A – a shoat? A piglet?' Clearly, modern slang had passed Combe Tollbridge by.

'Sorry.' Once more Andy laughed. 'J.O.A.T. – Jill Of All Trades. Catchy, right? All trades within reason, that is. I don't heave sacks of cement about, or climb ladders to fix loose tiles or clean gutters – I don't like heights – but I'll tackle most of those small jobs most people would get a man in to do. There's a few females would much rather have another female around their personal space, like when it comes to bathroom plumbing or unjamming their knicker drawer when it sticks. The minute your Ange calmed down enough to tell me what Paul had been up to, and asked for my help, I was able to change the lock of her flat right away.'

They had reached the breakwater at the end of Harbour Path, and the unofficial turning area. Andy neatly hopscotched a lump of gravel halfway to the foot of the cliff and back. 'So that's my story! I'll leave Angela to tell you hers. It's none of my business, except as a friend. Talking of which, shall we go back now to your friend Miriam's house to borrow the eggs, and the blankets?'

Chapter Two

They strolled away from the breakwater. 'Here's Harbour Glim.' Susan stopped by a whitewashed cottage whose deep leaded windows gazed out upon the harbour and the Severn Sea beyond. 'Perhaps you noticed I live in Corner Glim? For *glim* read *gleam*: of light, that is. Centuries ago the two lamps in line together, here and up at my place, were built to show incoming boats the one safe passage through the chezell – the shingle – banks out there.' She pointed. 'Then after the tidal surge in 16-something – or tsunami, or whatever – anyway, the chezell shifted far more than it normally does, with two streams flowing into the harbour and Bristol Channel tides the second highest in the world – and the glims couldn't be relied on any more as aids to navigation. Defoe's Great Storm of 1703 finished the job. These days they're plain live-in cottages, the pair of them.'

'Houses with real history. Cool! I love it.'

Susan rapped on the door. The polished brass knocker was in the shape of a fouled anchor. 'That's how Miriam and I first met. I'd only just moved to Tollbridge, and a courier muddled the address and delivered the page proofs of my latest book to Harbour Glim without stopping to ask anyone to sign for it who could have sent him back to Corner Glim. He saw what he thought was the right house, rang the bell, left the package on the step...' The door began to swing open. 'When she tripped over it Miriam guessed what had happened and brought it up to my place and said hello—'

'And she says hello again.' In the open doorway stood Miriam Evans: wiry, dark and quick of movement. She nodded to Andy. 'Now I don't remember Angela too well, but from your looks you're no daughter of Susan's. Come along in, Angela's friend. Come in, both!'

Smiles were exchanged, introductions made, shoes dusted on the mat.

'Did you win in the end?' enquired Susan, as Miriam closed the door.

Miriam stared, then winked, patting a brown paper parcel waiting by the door. 'It was a close enough fight but yes, I taught that sticky tape a lesson and I'll be off to the post first thing tomorrow. It's my own fault, mark you, for being in such a rush when I did really ought to know better. It's the same every year, never able to recall if my cousin Annabel's birthday is the 12th or the 21st.' She made a comical face. 'It's far too long now for me to ask outright, and young Jane may be my god-daughter but I don't care to ask her, either. She'd be telling her mother something needs to be done about Mad Old Miriam going off her head!' She laughed again. 'But it's the thought that counts, and I hope she'll be pleased. You'll not be so pleased,' she added to Susan as she led her guests through to the kitchen. 'I've only ten eggs, I'm afraid. We didn't make the dozen – but there's three rugs from my seconds box for you, and no hurry to return them while you have need of them.'

'That's wonderfully kind, thank you.' Susan let Andy take up the blankets and stroke them in admiration. 'I'll drop the basket back later, once things are – are a bit more settled. We'll be on our way now. I don't want to leave Angela for too long.'

Miriam saw her friend's worried expression, and guessed at some acute domestic crisis, but said again that Susan had no reason to hurry on her account. After all, once she herself had sent off her cousin's birthday present she'd start choosing yarn for her next project and be settling down to warp the loom, which Susan knew took all her concentration. She'd have no time to bother with second-best blankets or empty baskets or anything else, for a time.

'She doesn't strike me as Mad Old Miriam,' said Andy as they headed back along the Harbour Path. 'My guess is this Annabel's in on the joke and Miriam just plays along.'

'You could be right. She's organised in her weaving, certainly – with both of us self-employed she's taught me quite as many tricks as I've shown her, the way the paperwork seems to change with every blasted budget. I imagine you must find the same...'

Deep in business conversation, the two made their way back to Corner Glim Cottage.

Next morning Miriam was outside Farley's as it opened, brown paper parcel at the ready. The village store, post office and courier hub was owned and run by the family trio of Olive (née Ridd) Farley and her identical twins Debbie Tucker (divorced) and Tilda Jenkyns, relict of a local fisherman. As the door was unbolted, Miriam hurried in.

'Thank goodness,' she said, seeing nobody else ahead of her in the queue. 'This will go first into the sack and then I can get on with my own concerns.'

'Home or abroad?' asked Tilda. 'Just you pop it on the scales, midear.'

They were interrupted by the telephone. Tilda smiled weakly at Miriam, picked up the receiver and spoke in her official voice. 'Combe Tollbridge Post Office... Good morning, vicar... Oh.

Oh, dear oh dear.' Officialdom faltered, and rapidly blinked. 'It comes as no surprise, o'course, but…'

As she listened she blinked again, fumbling for a handkerchief. Debbie and Miriam exchanged knowing glances. They had little doubt what news had been imparted by the vicar to make Tilda Jenkyns cry.

'Oh, yes.' Tilda sighed. 'Yes, you can leave it all to us. Would – would you yet have any notion when the funeral might be? I see…'

'Old Prue's gone at last, then,' said Debbie as her sister replaced the telephone and put the paper hankie to her eyes.

It was neither twin telepathy nor a lucky guess. Prudence Budd, since the death of her husband Elias ten years ago, had been the much respected village elder. After a hip-breaking fall and admission to a nursing home in the nearby town, Tollbridge had prophesied that Aunt Prue would never thrive so far from home. It wouldn't be long; and indeed, the prophets had been right. Eight months compared with more than a century wasn't long. The loss was inevitable – and inevitably sad. Tilda blew her nose; Debbie shook her head; Miriam sighed. All three stood silent for several reflective moments.

Tilda threw her tissue in the waste paper basket. 'Mr Hollington said the home saw she was failing and phoned him to be with her, on account of the tide about to turn and her being the widow of a fisherman.' As was Tilda herself. Those who were bred on the coast knew that seafaring folk and their kin were always happiest, when the time came at last to sail into eternity, for that voyage to begin on a falling tide. In the case of Prudence Budd the outward voyage had been a long time coming. It was the aftermath of Prue's one hundred and fifth birthday party, riotously celebrated in a crowded village hall, that had caused the fatal fall. Tollbridge agreed it was the way Aunt Prue would have wanted to go.

Tilda extracted another tissue from her pocket and blew her nose again.

'I should have known.' Debbie rallied her forces. 'I dreamed last night of a wedding, and that can often mean a funeral to come.'

Tilda brightened. 'Or maybe a wedding! Could be Mickey Binns will put the question to Susan Jones after this long age – and wouldn't that be lovely?'

'Only if she accepts him,' pointed out Susan's best friend.

There was a ripple of laughter. Michael Binns Junior (son of Mike) believed his feelings for the comely author were hidden from the rest of Tollbridge, but the only Tollbridge resident unaware of his silent worship was Susan herself. Or so it seemed. Miriam never discussed the matter with her friend, but she sometimes wondered whether Susan simply had too kind a heart to allow Mickey to commit himself to an emotion the busy Milicent Dalrymple could not reciprocate.

Miriam changed the subject. 'Did Mr Hollington give any idea about the funeral?'

'She deserves a proper send-off, old Prue,' said Debbie.

'She was never the same after she lost Elias,' mourned the sentimental Tilda. 'And at her age your bones don't knit so well.' She sighed, then smiled. 'Even if they'd let her come home she'd not have been happy on crutches, not happy at all.'

She exchanged speaking looks with her sister. Miriam grinned. Olive Farley, mother to the twins and, though long past retirement age, still the official postmistress, had put up a spirited fight against the use of even one walking stick.

'A wheelchair would have been worse,' said Miriam. With a furious river to one side and a lively stream on the other, Combe Tollbridge boasted very little flat land apart from the central harbour area. The surrounding cliffs were in places almost vertical, muting to merely precipitous as the white torrent of the Chole widened to the harbour, and the little Rindan poured straight into the sea. The rivers plunged from Exmoor a thousand feet above, rushing between narrow rocky walls where sometimes only the region's small but nimble goats moved with any confidence. From time to time there came to the village naturalists equipped with mountaineering tackle and expensive cameras, in search of rare ferns and scientific fame, but Tollbridge left them to it. Let those who'd a mind to, go clambering the heights! There were hazards enough and to spare at sea, never mind asking for more trouble on dry land when it wasn't necessary.

'There'll be a grand turnout, whenever it is,' said Debbie. 'Wanted to be cremated, didn she? Jerry Hockaday will doubtless drive the minibus for them as don't have cars, the taxi seating so few when I reckon everyone will want to pay their respects.'

'But in the church first,' Tilda began, when a rattle at the door and a jangle of the bell heralded the arrival of Louise Hockaday.

Louise was the wife and mother of fishermen who'd learned the hard lesson that driving a taxi in the twenty-first century could be as good a source of income as putting out to sea. With interest she now contemplated her neighbours as she leaned on the thumbstick she used to help her move about the village. Her son Jerry had painted the stick bright yellow 'in case of fog' and her brother-in-law Mike Binns, father of that Mickey who so admired Susan Jones, whittled a new handle for the stick so that one arm could be hollowed to hold a small flask of brandy. Suppose (said Louise) she fainted while out alone for her daily walk? By the time an ambulance found her it might be too late.

'You all look as if you've something to say,' she remarked.

'The vicar's just told us dear old Prue has gone.' A third paper hankie appeared from Tilda's pocket. 'He said to let everyone know, and we were talking about the transport that's sure to be wanted for the funeral and how your Jerry would arrange who's to go in the minibus—'

'—and who'd rather share a car,' finished her sister, as again she blew her nose.

'She wanted to be cremated and scattered at sea, same as Elias.' Louise was thoughtful. 'The crem's more than half an hour's journey from here. Could be not everyone's wishful to come – nor able, neither.' She straightened from her thumbstick stoop. 'And how is your poor mother today?'

The twins said as one that she kept very well, thank you. Miriam hid a smile. Tollbridge didn't forget that the young Louise Jerome (now Hockaday) and Olive Ridd (now Farley) had once been inseparable, from their first day at school until they fell out over whose turn it was to clean the blackboard with the new wooden-backed sponge. Hair had been pulled, shrill words exchanged. In theory the quarrel was repaired after a stern talking-to from the young and pretty schoolmistress they both adored, but eight decades later an undercurrent of rivalry remained. With the coming of great age had come arthritis, though so far only Olive had needed replacement joints. While Louise could stride (cautiously) about the village still, Olive found it impossible to walk up the hill to visit her old friend, and had to sit down to do the ironing. Mike Binns designed and constructed a special stool to fit under the post office sink for her to wash the dishes in comfort – but as he also designed and brazed the narrow brandy-flask that fitted so neatly inside the yellow thumbstick's special handle, honours were adjudged even.

Louise pondered. 'Jerry will want to know how many people there'll be before he can decide if our own vehicles will suffice, or whether he'll be needing to ask someone else to help out.'

'We'd best put up a list and collect names.' Debbie nodded towards the notice-board beside the post office counter. 'Where people can set down their preference.'

Tilda was for once quicker than her twin. 'Behind the counter would be better, with names given and us write them down to keep them from general sight. You read such shocking things in the papers.'

Miriam nodded as Louise said, 'Burglars. Best ask the vicar what he thinks. He can say something in church next Sunday.'

'The place will be packed,' said Miriam. 'Everyone knew Aunt Prue. Bring-and-buy sales won't be the same without those peppermints of hers.'

They all smiled. Debbie paid tribute. 'Making them right to the end, she was, even with her broken hip. Every time she knew we'd be over to the cash and carry she'd ask us about a bottle of extra mint liqueur…'

Tilda emitted a little sigh, lamenting the final bottle they'd bought that surely no one else would want, now. 'And she so proud of her peppermints, too!'

'Then the secret must die with her.' Louise was brisk. She nodded to Miriam. 'Same as your fowls and their seaweed, midear. Only you know exactly how much, and when.'

Miriam laughed. 'Hardly a secret! The whole village knows my birds happened to find a taste for kelp when I put out a strand or two for telling the weather. And it's good exercise for them, jumping up and down after they've pecked the bottom off – and what's more, the eggs pickle so beautiful.'

Even Tilda joined in the gust of merriment that followed. 'Remember when Aunt Prue forgot which was what and used your eggs in a carvy-seed cake?'

'Weedy cake, she should have called it!'

Miriam smiled. 'She fed it back to my hens, so nothing was wasted. It's an ill wind.'

'D'you remember—' Louise had begun, when again the doorbell jangled.

Captain Rodney Longstone, R.N. glanced about him and doffed his quiet tweed hat. Tollbridge wits insisted that the spray of feathers pinned to the band was from the albatross he'd once shot on the high seas – didn't someone write a poem about it? 'Good morning, ladies. You have a solemn look about you. Nothing too serious, I hope.'

A flurry of explanation assailed his ears, but an officer of the Royal Navy is trained to cope with anything. 'Mrs Budd's funeral? That's sad news, though not unexpected. What a remarkable age. We exchanged few words, but I know she will be missed.' Since Captain Longstone came to live in Tollbridge he had made many acquaintances, but no particular friends. He would explain, when encouraged to socialise and declining every opportunity, that he'd spent far too much of his service career close-quartered in submarines and had dreamed for years of the quiet life when he retired. Tranquil Combe Tollbridge, so far from the madding crowd, was the ideal place for a peace-loving sea dog to drop anchor. His chosen anchorage was Baker's Cottage, at the far end of Meazel Cleeve, deep in the tree-hung valley of the little River Rindan. He was said to be writing his memoirs, but no sign of a finished manuscript was ever seen.

Tollbridge was too tactful ever to hint that he need not worry that the scandalous end to his marriage, which had made national headlines one August silly season, would embarrass either himself or the village. Everyone knew the facts as reported in the tabloid press and nobody thought the captain a penny the worse for them. Tollbridge viewed this innocent party with a great deal of sympathy...

Which, had he known, Tollbridge guessed would have embarrassed him all the more.

'...and I doubt if one among the great number of mourners sure to attend the funeral would be missed, either at the church or the crematorium.' The captain coughed. 'I believe I could both pay my respects and play a far better part by keeping watch around the village while most of the houses are unoccupied. A fine memorial to such a splendid old lady it would be if Tollbridge was ransacked by opportunist thieves while her friends and family were bidding Mrs Budd a dignified last goodbye.'

'That's just what we were saying,' said Tilda.

'You'd be doing us a real favour, Cap'n.' Debbie beamed at him. 'Most folk are sure to want to go, and now we can set a list on the notice-board for all to see and sign up without worrying. Thank you. Will you take your usual?'

'Please.' The captain bowed. Part of his regular exercise was to walk every day to Farley's and buy, with his newspaper, what had come to be known as a Captain's Twist of four pepper-mints to Prue Budd's ferocious recipe, rolled and secured in greaseproof paper. 'Or perhaps on this occasion I'll take two.' He sighed. 'I suppose these will be the last, although…' He hesitated. 'Somehow they haven't been the same since Mrs Budd went into the home. Perhaps the shock of her accident…'

'She never wanted to go,' said Debbie. 'Always swore they'd have to carry her out feet first before she'd leave Clammer Cottage.'

'It broke her heart, poor love,' mourned Tilda. 'Moving from Combe Tollbridge where she'd lived all her life – and her spirit too, I reckon.'

'Her spirit will be easy once she's back for the funeral,' said Louise. 'As will the rest of us with you on the watch, Cap'n.'

'We'll keep back the rest of the mints,' promised Debbie, handing him his ration for the day. 'Never mind a secret recipe, we'll have a supply put by special, just for you!'

Once more Captain Longstone tipped his hat, murmuring that it was very kind of Mrs Tucker but he had no wish to take advantage of such kindness. Debbie brushed this aside, smiled, and handed over his newspaper. He thanked her, nodded to the others, and made a dignified exit.

'A real gentleman, the Cap'n,' observed Mrs Hockaday before the bell had jangled itself quiet. 'And a rare piece of luck for the village he idn one for crowds! Jerry and my Gabriel can arrange for a dozen minibuses now, if required.'

'Always settles his account on time—' Tilda began, then stopped. 'I wonder who'll pay to put the notice in the paper? Prue and Elias never had no children, remember.' Once more her eyes brimmed with unshed tears. 'There's family connections and to spare here in Tollbridge, o'course, but even Barney Christmas can't claim being closer cousins than anyone else. The home, I suppose it'll have to be, seeing that's where she died.'

'Barney?' Louise Hockaday was scornful. 'Why, the families never got on from way back, his mother being as she was – and after Elias died and Barney tried to buy the cottage saying he worried Prue couldn't manage on her own – well!'

Miriam thought this unfair. 'Come now, Louise, he didn't press the point when she turned him down. Said loud and clear it was her right, and he wouldn't argue, and so he didn't. He bore no grudge. There was a card and a present every birthday...'

'He paid for all the drinks at the party,' put in Tilda as she weighed Miriam's parcel and printed the stamp. 'Both parties!' she added.

Everyone laughed. 'When she turned a hundred,' Debbie reminisced happily, 'and five years later, too. She kept saying she wanted no fuss and he said she never meant it, and just went and done it, didn't he.'

'And she had a lovely time,' sighed Tilda. 'Both times. If only she hadn't tried so hard to dance on the table – oh, dear...'

'Barney Christmas,' said Louise, 'for all he means well is a sight too fond of his own way. Wants to be *someone* in Combe Tollbridge and always did, from the moment he come back with money in his pockets to burn.' She challenged her companions with a look. 'Not that you can blame him, I'll grant, with his family so poor and his mother left with six to rear on her own, and him the eldest having to leave school and not take up the scholarship, bright though he was.'

The others nodded. The story was familiar to them all, but the death of Tollbridge's Aunt Prue had been sad news. At times of stress, reinforcement of the familiar can bring great comfort.

Miriam, paying for her parcel, added a metaphorical penny-worth at the same time. 'She always said they couldn't afford the uniform and the books and all the extras.'

The sniff emitted by Louise entirely lacked the sympathy of Tilda's. 'Which was maybe true… maybe. But small use she had for the truth in a general way, such as how she bamfoozled the authorities over his age and had him out of school and out to sea, when fishing was what he never cared for, as well you know.'

'Not that anyone in these parts would have reported her,' said Miriam. 'Remember how hard things were for everybody, after the war.' As with all fishing communities, in Tollbridge there had been many families whose fathers, sons and brothers did not come back, having no known grave but the sea. Sweeping for mines was dangerous work.

Minefields had been laid by both sides in many seas during the Second World War, and once the war was over they'd all had to be cleared. Time alone does not render a mine safe. As metal rusts and chemicals decay it can become even more of a hazard than when it was first primed and laid. No explosive device can be judged harmless until it has exploded.

Louise regained the initiative. 'So soon as his mother was underground he was off, just like the younger ones who'd already got away, Barney having near enough paid by himself for them to have the book-learning she'd made him miss. And nobody could blame him for going. Only, since he's been back…'

'There's been no doubt he made money while he was gone,' Miriam said.

The twins spoke as one. 'And never let on how he made it—'

'—nor how much.' There was a thoughtful pause.

'Enough,' said Louise, 'to buy the ship's chandlery when old John Ridd retired, and young Jan away in the police not wishful to take it over – *and* the old coastguard place—'

'—and the school,' supplied Miriam, 'when it was closed. I've heard him say that all stock's profit, if you wait long enough.'

'Hah!' Louise was scornful. 'He's near enough the same age as my Gabriel – he'd best not wait too long!'

'Near enough the same age as Mike Binns, too.' Miriam glanced at Mike's sister-in-law. 'I was thinking, Mike and your Gabe might be Prue's closest relatives, except of course – funny how we forget – Mike's only by marriage, not being Tollbridge born and bred.'

'But lived here from an evacuee during the war.' Louise spoke with the voice of authority. 'So now, me and your mother,' with a nod to the daughters of Olive Farley, 'with Gabriel – and, yes, with Mike Binns – will be next as nothing the oldest inhabitants, now Prue's gone at last to be with Elias, and the rest...'

The silence of memory was interrupted by the rattle of an inside door heralding Olive Farley on two walking sticks, a red and a green held in the appropriate port and starboard hands. Like her daughter Matilda, Olive's husband had been a fisherman. Like Tilda her loss had occurred years ago, but even now, as Tollbridge's official postmistress, she was duty bound to check at least once a day on what her daughter-assistants might be doing. She and Louise fell at once into routine skirmishing, while Miriam, having seen her parcel safely deposited in the post office sack, said she'd best be on her way to start spreading the news about Prue.

It was a slow walk home to Harbour Glim Cottage. Miriam exchanged greetings with every neighbour she met, telling them what she could. It took her almost an hour to travel a few hundred yards: everyone had a memory of Prue Budd, and wanted to share it.

But Miriam wanted to share the news with someone else. Once indoors she hurried to the telephone. 'Jane? Jane, midear! How's my favourite god-daughter?'

'Miriam, hello! I'll try to find out and ring you back, soonest. All okay at your end?'

The pleasantries over, Miriam came to the point. 'Last time your mother and I spoke, Annabel told me you and Jasper had thoughts of leaving town. Said you could both work from home a lot of the time and fancied somewhere in the country. Plenty of fresh air, room for a garden. Done anything about it yet, midear?'

'Nothing definite, what with one thing and another. You'd have been sent a change of address card, if we had – but we're still keen. Jasper fancies more of a back-to-nature lifestyle with our own vegetables and maybe soft fruit too, in time. He says the right-sized place might have room for a separate studio for me.' Jane Merton was an artist, establishing her career; Jasper owned a small but successful advertising agency. They'd met when Jane had to deliver some artwork in person to the agency when unable to send the usual email attachment. A power cut at Jasper's end lasted longer than expected, and pressure was being applied by an important client.

'Remember how you and Annabel used to visit me down here?'

'Oh, yes!' Jane was enthusiastic. 'When I was little it was as much of an adventure just travelling to Combe Tollbridge as it was to spend the rest of the week in an honest-to-goodness fishing village. I always pretended we were setting out to find the source of the Nile, or the jungle temple that guards the green eye of the little yellow god.'

'Clammer Cottage will likely be on the market very soon,' said Miriam.

'Miriam! Oh, dear. I knew old Prue had gone into a home, but... I can't believe she's gone at last. She seemed indestructible.'

'Very long last, I'd call it. She was past a hundred and five, remember.'

'And the cider went to her head at her party and she tried to dance on the table – yes.' Jane laughed. 'She'd never have given the proper rats-in-the-barrel scrumpy to a child, but I do remember Elias letting me have a sip or two when she wasn't looking, from that double-handed mug of his. My head was always a bit swimmy afterwards. And the stories he used to tell – him, and Ralph Ornedge, and Prue's sister Prill – she knitted me a beautiful pair of mittens once, and I gave them to my teddy bear when I grew too big to wear them…'

Jane had erratic but happy memories of childhood holidays in the little fishing haven and the many friends she'd made, village elders Prudence and Elias Budd foremost among them. Knotted with arthritis the old man could no longer fish, or achieve much in either of the gardens of which he'd been so proud; but he was always ready with home-made sweets for youthful visitors, or clandestine sips of cider, and exciting (and, she'd realised years later, heavily censored) tales of Tollbridge's past.

'Clammer Cottage,' she said slowly. 'At the top of the village, isn't it? Not right at the bottom like you. How's mobile reception at sea level?'

Miriam laughed. 'I hear tell it's reasonable in the right place with a following wind, but most of us rely on an ordinary land-line, or the telephone box by the pub.'

'The Anchor. I remember.'

'The Anchor, yes. As for this broadband of yours, they say it can be sluggish, though I'd not know, but you can always ask someone who *does* know when you come along down to take a look, midear. Have I the right of it, that you're interested?'

'In Clammer Cottage? You bet. We can investigate further at this end…' Jane's mind was more than half made up. 'It would be lovely. On the very edge of Exmoor, on the coast of the Severn Sea – and Lorna Doone country, too. It all comes back to me. We'll check things out online before we come, but please keep us in the loop if you hear anything.'

Her godmother promised to do so, and gave as many additional details as she could. Jane made notes, reminisced some more, and eventually, with heartfelt thanks, rang off. She hurried to find Jasper.

'Busy?' she asked.

'Taking a breather.' Her husband closed his laptop, and smiled. 'Who was that?'

'My godmother, mother's cousin Miriam. The one who wove us that gorgeous tapestry picture for a wedding present.'

'Oh, yes. Lives in some West Country backwater where you used to go on holiday, and the old chap would fill you with sweets and get you tight on scrumpy when his wife wasn't looking, and tell you ghost stories about shipwrecks and tin mines.'

'Close enough. It was silver they mined, not tin. His name was Elias Budd, and he had the strangest back garden I know. It was the other side of the river from his house, and you had to cross a private bridge to reach it – a little wooden affair, with a gate at each end – and I seem to remember he grew the most amazing vegetables.' She glanced quickly at him. 'Cabbages taller than me, peas and beans in great wigwams of bamboo canes…'

She sensed his interest, and smiled to herself. 'Of course, I was only a kid. They'd probably be ordinary size if I saw them as an adult.'

Jasper had reopened his laptop, typing busily as she spoke. 'Combe Martin in Devon, right? Seriously mined for silver from the Middle Ages to the Tudors, but the best seams were worked out and there's been nothing much doing ever since.'

'Not Combe Martin, Combe Tollbridge, but they don't dig for silver any more in Tollbridge, either. I forget the details. There was a landslide of sorts and all the miners were killed, I do remember that. Someone called down a curse on the lord of the manor, and he – or his son – ended up being run out of town...' She frowned. 'Or that might have been another story – but it's not important, either way.' Her eyes sparkled. 'Miriam says the cottage – Clammer Cottage – will soon be up for sale!'

'Clamour Cottage?' Now it was Jasper's eyes that sparkled. 'Ah yes, the ghosts of the miners clanking their silvery chains all night, filling the air with hideous groans and nobody's able to sleep a wink. The peaceful life of the countryside!'

'Idiot. Clammer.' Jane spelled it. 'Or clam. The local word for a plank bridge – just chop down a tree that's tall enough, and your feet need never get wet again.'

'Oh.'

'Elias died years ago, but Prue stayed in the cottage almost to the end. She only went this morning, and there's nobody to inherit. It was the dearest little place, and you know you fancied growing our own veg – and what fun to have our very own clam!'

'Or clammer.' Jasper had googled the word, and looked pleased with himself. 'You're right, not many people have a house with a bridge of its own. If we get unwelcome visitors we just trot across the clam and lock the gates. Sounds good.'

'Jasper, you think we might go down and take a look?'

'We'll look right now. Postcode? Full address?' Jane dictated from her notes. Jasper grinned as he typed. 'Hempen Row? You said the old boy grew cabbages and peas, not cannabis. I'd no idea life was so exciting in your godmother's part of the world. No wonder they talk about the wild west.'

'Double idiot.' Jane shook her head. 'The vegetable patch just happens to be where the hemp gardens were, before they stopped growing hemp. Years ago people made rope from it, and cloth for sails. Tollbridge is a fishing village, and pretty isolated. People found it easier to make as much as they could for themselves rather than buy it in from outside, and have to wait ages and pay ten times the normal price when it finally arrived. It's right at the bottom of a valley on the edge of Exmoor. Communication used to be dreadful until the internal combustion engine came along. The hills were far too steep for railways – well, still are. Even the coal was brought across by boat from Wales.' She smiled. 'Elias told me he remembered the stagecoach when he was a boy, and how passengers would get out and walk if the horses were tired. I never knew whether or not to believe him.'

Jasper was tapping again at the keyboard. 'Last stagecoach run, Lynton, 1920. Your Elias might have exaggerated, but he certainly wasn't kidding. It sounds wonderful. Let's take a closer look.'

'Found it?' asked Jane, after more keyboard tapping.

'Could be. See here.' She went to look over his shoulder, and they studied the laptop image together. 'We've found the road, at least. You didn't say which number.'

'Oh, I think it's all names, not numbers – or people don't use numbers if they have them – but I seem to remember it's right at the end of Hempen Row. There's a bend in the river… We won't be able to see the bridge, though. It's round the back.'

'Clammer,' amended Jasper, busy with the mouse. 'We can see it from the air – but you're right, it won't give Tower Bridge sleepless nights.' He switched back from the aerial view to street level. 'Clammer Cottage. I like the look of it, Jane. There's potential there. I could become a real Man With A Shed in my vegetable patch, and you could have a garden room and call it your studio. Facing north, of course.'

'The headland might be in the way.'

'Don't be a wet blanket. I have a good feeling about this. Peace and quiet and creative space – you'll become famous round the world. There's already the Newlyn School of art, and the St Ives School. Well, Jane Merton can go down in history as the founder of the Tollbridge School!'

Chapter Three

Jasper grew as keen as his wife on the prospect of leaving their London flat for the wide open spaces of Exmoor, and the possibilities of Clammer Cottage. Miriam had told her god-daughter she would send a selection of the tourist booklets and pamphlets written and printed locally; her promise was soon kept. These slim publications could be bought in Widdowson's Bakery, in the Anchor's entrance lobby, and in Farley's General Stores. Sam, a Farley cousin, had inherited the small Tollbridge Printery from his father. From time to time he talked of updating the old-fashioned information for those few modern tourists who came to the village: because they were so few it was merely talk, and nothing was ever done.

Miriam warned Jane not to expect too much when the package arrived, and Jane duly warned Jasper. She needn't have worried: he was thrilled. He read every word, researched as many facts as he could on the internet, checked black-and-white photographs against Google Streetview. He enthused over quaintly crowding cottages with their tall, bold chimneys that stood proud and massive into the street, narrowing further the already narrow lanes and footways.

'You can tell they were added years after the houses were originally built,' he told Jane. 'You start with your basic cottage – a cooking-pot over the fire, smoke going out through the thatch, though not until it's had time to kipper everybody inside first—'

'Ugh.' Jane's eyes began to water in sympathy.

'Then some genius invents the chimney, and the hearth. Just look at the shape, the size of those chimney pots! And the way the upper brickwork is stepped...'

Jane was pleased by his enthusiasm, and rather amused. After all, it was she who was the artist; yet it had been his imagination that was so dramatically fired. His deflated look when Miriam suggested they should leave their proposed visit until after Prue Budd's funeral was almost laughable. Jane wouldn't let him tempt fate by booking too early into the Anchor, and he fretted over online photos of harbour views, hoping it wouldn't be long to wait.

It cannot be denied that Combe Tollbridge is an undistinguished little village, served by a spirited but unimportant river, the Chole, and on the far side of the harbour by the even less important stream of Rindan. Both rivers drain from the moor, but only the most determined fitness enthusiast or fern-hunter would ever track one or other modest torrent on its rocky descent from source to sea. Tollbridge does not inspire large numbers of casual day trippers. The views, however, in the right place can be magnificent.

A touch of magnificence was guaranteed whenever Gabriel Hockaday and his brother-in-law Mike Binns were down by the harbour, being picturesque. Both had splendid 'Old Salt' whiskers, Gabriel's of such splendour that every year he was first choice for Father Christmas at the parish party. Mike was in competition with his son Mickey as to which Binns beard would first show signs of grey. Mickey's mother, of Huguenot descent, had bequeathed to her son her dark, dramatic colouring; Mickey's father, the carrot-topped cockney Mike, ignored all teasing about dye and cobbler's wax, and kept the key to one drawer of the bathroom cabinet well hidden.

Mike was mending lobster pots; Gabriel was knitting expertly with eight shining needles. In seafaring communities it isn't only the women who create those idiosyncratic upper garments of oiled, water-repellent wool worn by local fishermen to keep them comfortable at sea. Each locality has its own distinctive pattern for purposes of identification should the sea decide to claim its own. Further along the coast Appledore is noted for its 'frock' but in Tollbridge the garment is a 'jumper', and Gabriel was locally famous for his skill, patience and speed of jumper production.

Both old gentlemen were wearing their newest jumpers with knitted pull-on beanie hats, also new. The previous sunny day had brought a hire car of Americans who found driving on the wrong side of the road a problem when told by the satnav to turn sharp right. The shock of their escape from sudden death chilled them to the marrow. The evident warmth of the dark blue jumpers encountered as they went in search of restoratives hinted that a fair and profitable exchange might be negotiated: as it was. After the Old Salts had performed their regular welcoming routine, accepted generous tips, and directed the Americans to Widdowson's for a cup of tea if they thought it too early for the pub, Gabriel pulled out another hank of yarn (spun and dyed by Miriam Evans) and cast on for another jumper.

As they sat now enjoying another bright, busy day, a strange voice addressed them. 'Um – excuse me. When we drove in we kept looking, but we couldn't see the toll bridge…'

'Ah,' said Gabriel, fingers flying without pause as he glanced up. 'You wouldn.'

'So – is it on this side of the river we have to pay?'

'You come by car?' Mike Binns showed white teeth in a wide smile.

'Yes, we did.'

'And parked up on the headland—' he gestured in that direction – 'and walked down the Coastguard Steps?'

'I suppose so, if that's the stairs with a wooden handrail that come down from a bumpy sort of field. They're very steep.'

'We looked, but we couldn't see anywhere to pay up there, either.' The middle-aged woman seemed as concerned as her husband.

'Ah,' said Gabriel again. 'You wouldn.'

'Parking in the Watchfield's free,' said Mike, 'and if that's where you come from you've already crossed the river to get here, so there's nothing at all to pay.'

'Nor hadn been these five hundred years.' Gabriel chuckled. 'There's no toll bridge now in Combe Tollbridge, not anywhere. You can stretch your legs all day and you'll not be charged a penny.'

Mike Binns knew his cue when he heard it. 'The lord of the manor was the last person to try, but he didn't get away with it for long…'

Gabriel took up the tale. 'Far backalong this would be, in the days when kings rode in armour on horseback, needing money to pay for foreign wars. They cared little how they got it, and the people suffered something cruel under taxes and similar.'

'Huh! Tell me about it.' The middle-aged man had received a disturbing letter from the Inland Revenue just before departing on his West Country break.

'In these parts the very rocks bear riches, if you know where to look.' Gabriel's tongue was as quick as his fingers. 'There's gold, though not much…'

'There's uranium,' said Mike. 'It's rare – but 'tis there, all the same.'

'There's tin, in Cornwall, and lead over to Mendip—' Gabriel brandished his knitting – 'and, long ago, there was silver. Silver in this very Tollbridge valley.'

'It's still there,' said Mike, 'but nobody will ever dig for it.' He paused. 'They wouldn't dare. Not after what happened.'

The fascinated audience breathed the obvious question.

'There's a curse,' said Gabriel with relish. 'A bible curse on the old silver mine.'

'A curse,' breathed the wife, with delight. 'How – how dreadful.'

'A curse,' echoed Mike Binns. The attention of the visitors fairly caught, he settled back to let his friend deliver the full tourist experience. 'But Gabriel knows the tale far better than me.' And Gabriel was a more memorable name than Mike. The tips were always bigger if Mr Binns managed to work it early into the conversation.

Mr Hockaday, fingers still flashing, launched into his tale. 'That King Edward of seven hundred years ago, he had miners brought here from Derbyshire, and from Wales across the Severn Sea; conscripted them, he did. Forced them to dig and delve for riches that would enrich no more than himself and his barons, with nothing spent for the good of the people whose taxes grew heavier and heavier while the wars went on and on.'

As time passed (said Gabriel) the easiest seams were worked out. From then on, lords of the manor must pay a fee to the monarch for the right to have their own people dig ever more deeply for their own silver on their own land, as well as paying a share of that hard-earned silver in further taxes. These taxes one lord of Combe Ankatell (as the village was then known) thought unfair. He made good some part of his perceived loss by charging a fee from those villagers who daily had to cross the Chole to work in his silver mine. He set heavy fines on those of his people who dared to find other, less extortionate ways to earn their bread.

'The good old days,' said the middle-aged man, as Gabriel paused for breath.

'What happened?' his wife wanted to know.

Gabriel's solemn tone grew portentous. 'One night there came a sudden great storm. Up on the moor, the wild winds blew. The rain poured, fair puddling the ground, loosening the roots of trees. One gurt specimen – an oak, some say – being top-heavy in leaf, down he come and fell in the Chole. The river was full, and flowing fast. The oak tumbled through the white waters making for the sea, when it was trapped against rocks by the bank, and caught. Then the villagers took ropes and dragged it out, and set to work with axes to trim off the branches and leave a long, bare stem.' He paused, as if trying to decide whether his next row should be purl or plain.

'What happened?' demanded the wife of the middle-aged man as the decision seemed too hard for Gabriel to make at the same time he was talking.

Gabriel winked at Mike: his turn to win the customary bet. Mike always tipped the male partner to crack first. Gabriel happily resumed his story. 'Further up the Chole there lies Combe Ploverton, bigger and busier'n us down in Tollbridge, with a grand house occupied by the bailie of the lord of the manor, the lord maintaining his right to occupy when visiting, which was seldom. Now that bailie, he received report of a fallen tree and guessed what use our village might make of it. He come hurrying down with a band of men to thwart our purpose, but we was ahead of him – and we threw the whole boiling lot in the river.'

His audience applauded. Gabriel nodded. 'So then 'twas too late. The oak was cut in half by length, both halves being used to bridge the Chole where 'twas of sufficient size for good support but well away from the Ankatell bridge by the harbour – while them as wadn busy shaping the clammer, which is to say, the other bridge – ah, they'd long since laid their plans against just such an occasion and were quick to carry them out. There was nought the bailie nor any of his men could do.'

'They must have done something!'

Gabriel chuckled. 'Climbed back out of the river. They could do nought else, as I said.' He grinned. 'But the village, they set to work as one man to build an overnight house right there beside the clammer, for guarding. Betwix dimpsy and daylight they had the walls up and the roof on, and water boiling in the pot so that none should dispute the right of it. And from that same day no toll was paid to any Ankatell for crossing the Chole... until, long years after, there was little need to cross, on account of the silver mine being lost when the land fell down and the miners died their terrible, lingering death.'

Mike took up the story. In the very year (he said) of the Spanish Armada's defeat by storm and tempest there came heavy rain on Exmoor, unceasing for five nights and four days. It soaked and saturated the ground above the mine, and invaded shafts and galleries, and weakened tunnel walls. When the sodden land could hold no more there came a low roaring rumble of destruction. Few of those underground escaped with their lives. Shock waves burst with such force that the land above gave way into a deep, wide hollow that could be seen to this very day. There was a wild commotion in the sea beyond the headland. Broken pit-props and bodies floated in chaos to the surface.

Mike paused. Gabriel said nothing. The wife shuddered; the husband looked over his shoulder as if an icy finger had rasped down his spine.

At last Gabriel spoke. 'There were others still less fortunate, buried so deep there could be no reaching them. The parson read the service over that scene of ruin as over a true churchyard grave, and spoke most eloquent on the unholy greed of men who tried to wrest more from the land than the land was wishful they should have. He preached that for ever after, that land was hallowed. If any showed lack of due respect for the resting-place of the victims of Ankatell wickedness, then a curse would lie on him and his for all time. Nature was let gather to herself what had been lost… and to this day there's none in Tollbridge, nor Ploverton neither, who'll have doing with any timber from the old Silver Wood.'

There was an awestruck silence broken at last by Mike, who knew when tension should be relieved. 'But the overnight house didn't collapse. It's there to this day – and with its own clammer, too, though tidn the first to be built in that spot, wood not being what you'd call permanent when left in the open air so close to the sea.'

'Follow your noses up Stickle Street,' Gabriel directed them, 'and past the church turn right, into Hempen Row. Clammer Cottage sits at the far end.' He sighed. 'Backalong you could have knocked at the door to meet our oldest inhabitant, Prue Budd. Eighty years or more she lived there, come as a bride and never left – only she died, just last week.' Again he sighed. 'One hundred and five years old, and her memory sharp to the end.'

The middle-aged couple expressed suitable regret at missing this remarkable opportunity to meet with living history.

'O'course,' said Mike, 'it's private property now, but Prue would have allowed you sight of the clammer and the taking of a photograph or two – and asked not a penny from you.'

'Nor she wouldn have charged you to walk across,' put in Gabriel, 'should the fancy take you, but the Chole runs deep at that spot. After her man Elias died she hadn so great a wish to reach the far-side garden, the result being I'd say these days the planks must be in a sadly cockling state. Myself, I'd be disinclined to make the attempt, but should you feel the risk a price worth paying, well…'

The husband didn't need his wife's nudge in the ribs to respond to these subtle hints. 'How much,' he enquired of Mike, 'for one of those pots of yours?'

'And where can I buy one of your woolly hats?' Gabriel was asked by the wife.

An appropriately generous amount was eventually handed over, with accompanying thanks to both old gentlemen for a fascinating narrative. Could a guidebook tell them even more? Booklets in the pub? They'd go there at once – and drink their new friends' health, and by the way...

Coins clinked, and the brothers-in-law beamed their gratitude. 'Lucky you come today,' said Mike in farewell. 'The Anchor will be private tomorrow, on account of old Prue's funeral. She'll have a grand send-off...'

She did.

So many talked of attending the obsequies that the vicar made a tentative proposal for the funeral of Prudence Budd, Tollbridge born and bred, to be held in the larger church at Combe Ploverton. It was, after all, only a short distance up the valley; everyone in both villages knew everyone else – most of whom were related! What did it matter, when the forecast seemed set for rain? What kind of tribute to Mrs Budd would it be if half her neighbours, friends and relations succumbed to colds – or influenza – or pneumonia?

'No, Theodore,' said Frances Hollington. 'They won't like the idea at all – and they'll think nothing of the rain. There are such things as umbrellas, don't forget.' He was a good man, a wonderful parish priest, and in harmony with all he met – but she'd always been thankful that his bishop had never even hinted at an inner-city appointment. This might well have shattered his illusions. 'Prue Budd lived her whole life among her neighbours, friends and relations in Tollbridge. She'd want to be among them to the very end.'

'But Tollbridge church is smaller,' lamented the vicar of both parishes. 'To have people standing outside – for there's sure to be a crowd: she was a remarkable old lady. The owner of the nursing home told me he will have to employ agency workers that day, because so many of his staff wish to be there – a great compliment after a comparatively short residence – but with no close family, how will the decision be made? And by whom? As to who goes inside the church, that is, and who must remain in the open air. We cannot easily restrict entry to the house of God. We can hardly issue tickets.'

'Most unsuitable, for a religious service. I do see your difficulty, but a way must be found around it. The funeral really couldn't be held anywhere else.'

He sighed. 'I worry there could be a – an undignified scramble.' He thought back to a recent Ploverton jumble sale. 'Elbows. Shrill voices. Bad feeling.'

'I'm sorry, Theo.' Frances was firm. She brightened. 'Ask Mike and Mickey Binns to overhaul the summer fete loudspeaker system – after all, they designed and built it. Ask if they have any thoughts on how to upgrade the waterproofing, and leave them to it.'

His eyes shone. 'Bless you, my dear! I wonder why I didn't think of them before? That pair do so love to tinker...'

'Well, vicar,' said Mickey Binns on hearing the visitor's request. 'I'd say what you need is reliable socks, cut to size and fixed with greenhouse tape.' He looked across at his father, and grinned.

'Reliable socks. I see.' The Reverend Theodore didn't.

Mike Binns roared with laughter. 'He'll never let me forget that, vicar! *Rubble sacks* is what I wrote, but in a hurry, and long ago – still, the old ones are always the best, eh?'

'Indeed they are.' Mr Hollington smiled upon father and son, so comfortable together, sharing a home without apparent friction, relaxed and teasing. Mickey, like Mike, deeply loved Combe Tollbridge and hadn't really been happy away from the place. Growing up with the legend of the lost mine he had studied to become a mining engineer, married a fellow student, gone questing after gold around the world – and never settled. It was sad but inevitable that the world-wide quest should end in divorce.

The parting held little rancour, both parties accepting that over time they had become different people, with very different aims. Mickey returned to Combe Tollbridge, moved in with Mike, and gradually became unofficial skipper of MV *Priscilla Ornedge* – unofficial because Mike, like Gabriel Hockaday, Olive Farley and many others, would defy official retirement to the end.

The strong plastic rubble sacks were bought, snipped, shaped, and secured to various parts of the public address system. Supervised by Gabriel, Mike held the ladder and Mickey climbed it. Mickey's cousin Jerry supplied hammers, nails and hooks as appropriate. Both Hockadays offered advice the Binnses chose to ignore. The four argued all the time, congratulated themselves on a job well done… and the church was ready.

Mobility-impaired mourners decorated walking sticks with large bows of sombre ribbon. Louise Hockaday trimmed her yellow thumbstick with a black rosette fashioned from a length of wartime blackout material dug out of a drawer crammed full of stuff too good to throw away. Waste not, want not, had been the British motto for years after the war. Olive Farley's red and green sticks sported smaller rosettes of similar design, made by Louise from the Hockaday surplus.

The coffin was borne into the church, and the service began.

There were mournful hymns, there were joyful hymns; there were words of praise and words of consolation. Barnaby Christmas claimed cousinship to deliver a brief eulogy, then with a glance at his watch sat heavily down, mopping his brow. The Reverend Theodore Hollington gave the final address.

He spoke sincerely and powerfully. Many who had until now scorned handkerchiefs began to fumble in their pockets. He reminded the congregation that Mrs Budd, although a regular worshipper in Tollbridge church, had wished for cremation and later scattering at sea, as had been the choice ten years earlier for her husband Elias. Without close heirs to maintain any grave unto the third and fourth generations, the devoted couple had resolved to enjoy eternity as one with the sea whose presence had been part of their lives from birth.

'But Prudence Budd's thoughts remained with the village that sheltered her good self and her Elias for so long. This is a sad occasion, but I hope to lighten the sadness with the glad news that this true daughter of Combe Tollbridge left everything, apart from a few personal bequests, of which she died possessed to be sold by trustees and, at their discretion, used entirely for the benefit of the village community.' He allowed a general rustle of astonishment and speculation time to die down. 'We will now sing the Sailors' Hymn.'

The organist thundered into 'Eternal Father, strong to save' with its plea for those in peril on the sea. No Tollbridge funeral ever omitted it; no Tollbridge resident ever mumbled the words. The service sheets – produced at no charge (a last compliment to Prue) by local printer Sam Farley – were abandoned. The congregation both inside and outside the little church could have been heard a mile away.

'Well!' Miriam Evans stood with Susan Jones by Susan's car, waiting for Michael Binns (*père et fils*) to join them for the trip to the crematorium. Jerry Hockaday was to drive the minibus; Gabriel, the taxi carrying Louise and the Farley twins. Because of her knees Olive, like several of the less active villagers, would go straight to the party in the Anchor.

'Mmm,' said Susan. Observing the whole church sit up in unison had sent her writer's imagination into overdrive.

'For the benefit of the community, the vicar said. Ever fond of chillern was Prue, and Elias too. A shame they never had any, nor any chance to adopt, the way Prill and Ralph did with

44

Mike.' Miriam sighed. 'Pretty much the last of the Christmases, Prill and Prue. There's none but Barney left now.'

'For all you know,' said Susan wickedly, 'he might have acquired a dozen children while he was off making his fortune. It's possible,' as Miriam stared. 'Someone could have married him for his money: besides, I thought he was as fond of kids as anyone. It's been good of him to allow them access to the school grounds all these years.'

'He'd no other use for the place, once the development work never went ahead.'

'But it was – is – his property. He'll do something with it, in the end – but in the meantime, didn't I hear he arranged extra insurance in case of accidents? It was good of him to do that. Once he'd locked the gates and secured the fencing there was no legal obligation to take more than routine precautions.'

Miriam chuckled. 'Oh well, I reckon you've the right of it, midear. Gabriel Hockaday can call him a scrawling old hunks if he likes, but Barney's no miser, just... careful more than most with his money. Trouble is, he's never let on how he made such fortune as he has, which naturally makes folk think the worst.'

'Human nature at its best,' said Susan, wondering again if, under another name, she might write for Blood Red Books. 'Talking of which,' she added, 'it's a shame the idiot minority has ruined things for the sensible majority. It doesn't seem at all fair that Barney should have to pay for repairs when the damage was nothing to do with him, but unless we can find out who it was...'

Miriam sniffed. 'Ploverton can say what it likes, but if that idn where those young tearaways on motorbikes came from they assuredly were no distant strangers. How would strangers know about the playground being empty?' Motorbikes. The word reminded her. 'And when do you expect your Angela back?'

'When she's finished in London, I imagine.' Susan tried to sound unconcerned. 'Her friend Andy's hiring a transit van, and she's organised a gaggle of girls to help clear the flat of Angela's belongings. They mean to pack all Paul's things into storage and pay a month in advance and send him the details... Andy's organising that, too.'

'She's no slouch when it comes to organising, it seems.' Miriam sensed the anxiety behind the words, and patted Susan's shoulder. 'Good people find good friends, midear. This Andy's a friend in a thousand. Angela will be fine. Just give her time.'

'And me,' murmured Susan, but Mickey Binns hailed them from closer than they might have expected, given that they'd been waiting for him and his father.

'Well, you clitter-clattering twosome! Always a deal to talk over after a burying, eh?'

'Save it for visitors,' advised Miriam. 'You're fooling no one here. You were a pest and a nuisance at school, I recall, and for all your higher education you're no better now.'

Hurriedly, Susan opened the car door and motioned her passengers inside. 'We were wondering,' she said as they settled themselves, 'if Barney Christmas might ask the parish to help contribute to the fence repairs round the playground equipment, to keep it separate from the asphalt those motorbike idiots tore to shreds doing wheelies.'

Mike Binns, brother-in-law and closest friend of Gabriel Hockaday, took the automatic view that if there was a way to save a penny and profit by tuppence, Mr Christmas was the man for it. Mickey, feeling that an amicable squabble over a relatively unimportant matter could lighten the half-hour journey to the crematorium, disagreed.

'Old Barney's not so bad. It's been at his expense the youngsters have had free access to the playground all this time, remember.'

'That's what Susan thinks,' said Miriam.

'Ah,' said Mickey. 'Twin souls, that's what we are.'

Susan laughed, and drove on.

Hat in hand, Captain Longstone watched from a courteous distance as the impressive cortège departed. He bowed his head as the final car vanished up the hill out of Combe Tollbridge, sighed, replaced his hat, and resumed his self-appointed patrol. He went further up to check again that all was quiet in Hempen Row, again saw nothing to disturb him, and marched back down to the main part of the village.

He walked through narrow lanes huddled with cottages that lurked under roofs of thatch or slate protecting thick colourwashed cob walls. As he walked he cast appraising looks over windows and doors, noting which gates were open (few homes in harbourside Tollbridge had room for a garden) and which were firmly latched. He went twice past the post office, where the blinds were down and there was cash in the till. He stood, listening, and smiled to hear muted laughter from the Anchor, where the wake was already under way.

He continued past the pub down Harbour Path, going as far as Trendle Cottage by the breakwater, where he saw no obvious signs of life apart from a scurry of turnstones on the shingle beach. A whirl of overhead gulls screamed to their cousins below to peck faster and deeper among the chezell as it washed, chattering and rattling, to and fro in the waves. The captain turned back and climbed steep Meazel Cleeve, which led to his own quiet home at the far end. Everything was shipshape and secure, just as when he left it.

From somewhere came the rumble of a motor vehicle. He cocked his head to one side. Not a large vehicle, and moving with confidence; no outside visitor, then, but someone who knew his way. Outsiders approaching Combe Tollbridge for the first time were always too busy checking road signs to move with speed. He hurried back down Meazel Cleeve and scanned the harbour area. He walked back along Harbour Path, but still saw nobody.

He was almost at the post office corner when the engine rumble suddenly subsided. There were too many echoes to be sure where the car had paused, but before he could turn into Stickle Street it had started up again and driven off. An unlikely pattern for burglary. He glanced across to the Anchor – landlord Jan Ridd was a retired policeman – but decided he should investigate further on his own rather than disturb the party. No doubt a casual visitor, not realising there would be no one at home today, was driving away intending to make a return visit on a more suitable occasion.

The car drove on up the hill. The echoes now were less misleading. It stopped.

Captain Longstone put on speed. Doubling up Stickle Street was good exercise and didn't take much effort, thanks to his daily newspaper-buying and, yes, purchase of peppermints… He smiled as he jogged, thinking of the Farley twins and their kindly promise. He would miss Prue Budd as much as would anyone in Tollbridge…

At Hempen Row he slowed; stopped; listened. Voices? With the Chole rushing past behind the cottages it was hard to be sure. With brisk caution he moved partway down the narrow side road.

A small grey van with an as yet unidentifiable logo on the door stood outside Clammer Cottage, former home – empty home – of Prudence Budd, whose funeral and cremation almost every village inhabitant had that day attended. Captain Longstone wondered if he might have been a little hasty. One man in (admittedly, early) middle age against… who knew how many?

Warily, he drew closer. Close enough to observe the driver of the small grey van helping his passenger to climb out.

Helping Barnaby Christmas to climb out and stand by the gate of Clammer Cottage.

Chapter Four

The captain hesitated. The man, like so many in Tollbridge, was her cousin. He'd heard it said that more people in the village were related to other villagers than people who were not: it was certainly hard, sometimes, for an incomer to remember who was who. But what he did remember was the Farley twins telling him that Barnaby Christmas had claimed kinship with Prue close enough to delivering the final eulogy before the vicar spoke.

After a moment, the captain drew nearer. Now he could make out the logo. The little grey van belonged to – the driver must be employed by – the district council.

'And then?' demanded a general chorus, as Captain Longstone made his report to the handful of mourners already in the Anchor.

The captain looked towards big Jan Ridd, ex-police sergeant. 'My knowledge of legal matters is slight.' He smiled. 'With the obvious exception, that is, of *QR and AI – Queen's Regulations and Admiralty Instructions*, which as the name suggests concern themselves with matters naval. My understanding, however, is that on land the law of trespass can only apply if damage to property has occurred. Mr Ridd?' Even after several years' residence Rodney Longstone did not easily embrace informality.

'Not sure,' Jan said honestly. ''Tis a long time, now. But let's just say, if you'd tried a citizen's arrest you might have found yourself with a case against you, Cap'n. Someone from the district council... I can't say. He'd be at least halfway official. Might be argued he was – was assessing the place for, I dunno, death duties or similar.'

Olive Farley tossed her head. 'If anyone's elected Barney Christmas to the council that's the first I've heard of it.'

'That'll be why he was in such a hurry to get away,' put in Tabitha Ridd, wife to Jan.

'Why he checked his watch,' offered Sam Farley. The young printer had escorted his elderly cousin with her walking sticks very carefully from the church, and refused to abandon her once she was safely ensconced in the pub. 'For fear he should come late to meeting this man, councillor or whoever.'

Captain Longstone was thoughtful. 'Mr Christmas took great care to remain at all times on the public highway,' he said slowly. 'And the man from the council showed some reluctance to enter the property once he realised the gate would need to be opened—'

'Hah! Barney will have claimed kin and opened it for him,' said Olive. She'd known Mr Christmas her whole life.

The captain looked surprised. 'Why, yes, he did – open the gate, that is. But, as I said, Mr Christmas stayed outside in the road at all times.' He frowned. 'From where I stood he appeared to – to encourage the other man to... investigate the property on his, that is Mr Christmas's, behalf. Several photographs were taken, for instance, and he made copious notes on a clipboard, though I couldn't see much more from where I was standing.'

'So where was that?' asked Tabitha. 'If you saw them but they didn't see you...'

'I don't believe they did, though I could be mistaken. Once I guessed there might be a – a legitimate reason for their presence I ventured into the front garden of what I believe is the Binns' cottage. I thought, with Mr Binns having been related to Mrs Budd he would forgive this minor trespass if he knew it was to keep watch on the property of his late aunt.'

Prudence Budd, née Christmas, had been twin sister to that Priscilla Ornedge who with her husband Ralph took in the young evacuee Mike Binns and allowed him to stay for the rest of his life, although the adoption was never formalised. The ties that bound Mike Binns to 'Auntie Prill' and 'Auntie Prue' were of pure affection, which can so often outweigh the ties of legality or blood.

But they all understood the captain's reasoning, and nobody argued against it.

'It do indeed sound official, to me.' Jan Ridd rubbed the tip of his nose. 'Rather above halfway, what's more. And taking photos and making notes idn a crime, so far as I'm aware. You did right in letting us know, Cap'n, but as to what can be done about it – though mayhap there's nought needs doing – we'll have to wait and see. We'll ask a few questions of the council, for sure. But you did the right thing,' he said again. 'Have a drink.'

'Thank you, no. I should be getting back on watch.' Having reported to the appropriate village authority, with a nod and a quick salute the captain returned to his solitary patrol.

Jan continued to ponder aloud. 'Could be Barney will tell us himself what he's been about, should we put the question direct. Or he might let something slip accidental.'

'That'll be the day,' said Tabitha, 'when Barney Christmas lets slip something he's not wishful you should know!'

Again Olive tossed her head, but Jan had been trained to weigh evidence. 'Natural he would have an interest, being already a man of property as we'll concede – hey, Sam?'

'So he is.' Sam Farley laughed. 'While I was giving consideration to the old coastguard place, the windows being far bigger than my own, he was quick enough to agree with me my house wadn so suitable for printing, and said he'd be happy to take it off my hands.'

'Hah!' burst from Sam's cousin Olive.

'He did offer a lower rent in exchange for a favourable price,' Jan reminded him, with a grin. 'And a quick sale, there being no chain, and him able to buy your place outright.'

'Like the coastguard station.' Suddenly, Olive was sad. 'A black day for Tollbridge, the day they cancelled the coast-guard.' Her daughter Matilda might not now be a widow, had somebody still been employed to watch the seas for unexpected storms. 'The lifeboat gone, too. A cruel loss.' The lifeboat that did eventually attend the sudden foundering in which Matilda Jenkyns lost her husband had come from too far away to arrive in time.

'If there's money enough from Prue, could be we'll see the lifeboat back again.' Jan felt a less gloomy note should be struck. This was, after all, a celebration of one hundred and five well-lived years. 'For the benefit of the village, the vicar said. Doubtless he'll be one of the trustees – but, whoever they may be, what say we warn 'em Barney Christmas, if showing an interest in Clammer Cottage, should be asked thribble the normal price, for the good of the community?'

General amusement greeted this suggestion. Glasses were raised to the possibility of a new lifeboat, though Sam Farley remarked that if the money ran to a coastguard as well, the coastguard must find a new watch-house. He himself had come to terms with Barney Christmas and would be moving in at the end of the month. He would not, moreover, be selling his own house to anyone, but putting it up for rent.

Further amusement, renewed toasts. Nobody disliked Barney: everyone knew he'd had a hard start in life, forced to support his entire family, and himself had been the last of them to make good: extremely good, Tollbridge was given to

53

understand. But Tollbridge resented the fact it didn't know for sure, and always wondered how the making had been achieved – and how great, financially, that achievement was. The only mysteries approved by Combe Tollbridge were those it devised on its own terms. And it dearly loved a good gossip...

When the door opened, cheerful mourners stayed their chatter to express surprise that the return from the crematorium had come so soon. But it opened to admit Barney Christmas, by himself.

'Greetings to all,' he said with a grin. 'Speak of the Old Gooseberry and in he comes!' He winked at the little group for whom he guessed he'd been the main topic of conversation only a short while before. By the time he appeared, however, they had moved on to discuss Jan Ridd's request for another short run of Sam Farley's local booklets, and Olive Farley's feeling that they might sell in greater numbers if the illustrations were of better quality.

'And the words.' Sam sighed. 'My dad and me, we rustled something up betwix the two of us backalong and it did for the time, but we're neither of us scholars. These days I know folk want rather more for their money.' He swigged deeply from the cider in his mug. 'I've half a mind – no, best call it one-fourth – to ask Susan Jones if she'd be willing, only I fear to trouble a book-published writer like herself. She'd doubtless think it beneath her, and take offence.'

'You can only ask,' someone began just as Barney entered.

'Have a drink,' invited Tabitha, as Mr Christmas looked round at everyone, chuckled, and sat down. 'So you didn go to the crem, then? Or – you're back early?'

He grimaced. 'You know full well tidn the case, Tabitha Ridd. Whoever it was – these old eyes aren't so young as once they were – I'll be bound he told you I'd a council surveyor along to Prue's place for an idea, just an idea, of what might be a reasonable price to offer once it's put on the market.' He laughed at the general confusion, and raised his glass in salute. 'Thought so. But I'm not here now on business. I'm here to drink to Cousin Prue, grand old soul that she was and the last of her line, bless her. I give you Cousin Prue Christmas as was born, Prue Budd as she lived nigh on eighty-seven years!'

They all joined him in this heartfelt toast.

Once more Barney glanced around the group. 'I'd hoped to find the vicar here, the crem having its own for that part of the service, but I see he's not.'

'Mrs Hollington told us he'd a christening up to Ploverton,' said Olive. The vicar's wife had stopped by their pew to admire the discretion and style of the black rosettes she and Louise Hockaday sported on their colourful sticks. 'He'll try to be along later, she said, but you know how it is with wetting the baby's head.'

'Going to get your offer in first, Barney?' But the mockery was gentle.

'I said I'm not here on business, Sam Farley. Or...' Mr Christmas chuckled. 'Well, could be I'll just put the thought in his mind for later consideration – but if he idn here it can wait, for I won't stay long.' He gazed into his empty glass. 'A sad day it's been for me, lamentable sad, bidding farewell to Cousin Prue. Now I'm the only one of us left. Doubtless I'll be gathered next, and then the Christmases will be gone from Combe Tollbridge.'

He sighed; and he meant it. No one cared to mention the five brothers and sisters who had prospered (it was supposed) away from home. None had ever returned to Tollbridge to keep faith with the old days, and it was believed that once their mother was dead, and Barney able at last to make his own escape, all contact had been lost with the brother who gave the younger ones their start in life. If Barney was now a little too tempted to let the village know he'd made money, they could excuse him because he spent so much of that money to village benefit. Tollbridge was not a lively place. Cottages, once empty, tended to remain so as younger inhabitants moved away. Since his return Mr Christmas had bought up some of these properties and renovated them using only local labour (though paying only a minimum wage) and advertising them, once transformed, as bargain holiday lets.

It was partly thanks to Mr Christmas that the Anchor sometimes had to employ an extra barmaid, and held a wider range of tourist booklets than in the past – that Olive Farley and her twins talked of commissioning picture postcards and jigsaw puzzles – and that their cousin Sam had resolved on the old coastguard station to extend the range and possibilities of the small printery first established by his father.

'So what plans might 'ee have in mind for Clammer Cottage, Barney?' Olive, an old schoolmate, was prepared to argue if he wouldn't say.

''Tis all according whether or not the vegeble patch across the Chole must be counted with the cottage garden – which I'd hoped to ask the vicar. The council wouldn be definite as to building land or agricultural, not yet.'

'Building valuation for the cottage, agricultural for the vegetable patch,' suggested Sam. Everyone knew that upon the decision of the man from the council would depend the price Prue's trustees might eventually ask.

'Another drink all round,' said Jan, whose quick ear caught the arrival of a minibus and several cars. 'Before the hordes descend. More glasses, Tabitha!'

'Oh, Jasper. Miriam here. Is Jane to hand?'

'Sorry, not just now. She's out in the park photographing leaves in close-up for a jungle idea she's working on. If it's important I can give you her mobile number, but—'

'No, no, you'll do fine. It's just, Prue Budd's funeral was today, and I wondered if you'd given further thought to Clammer Cottage and when you might be along to view.'

'That's splendid! I mean – well, you know what I mean.' Miriam laughed and said she did. 'Well, then, the sooner the better,' said Jasper. 'We googled your village on Streetview and Jane gave me the full guided tour, using those pamphlets you sent to jog her memory. The more we've found out the more interested we are.'

'Yes,' said Miriam, 'and so is Barnaby Christmas. Jane might recall the name. Barney left Tollbridge a poor man and came back rich... as Creosote, some say.'

'Good for him, if he did it honestly.'

'Oh, he's no crook. Mark you, he's ever been one to count the pennies – the pebbles, too. The older folk recall, before his father died he'd be hours sorting chezell on the beach for chuckle-stones, and selling them. He'd ask more for a set of alleys – white alabaster being worth more than coloured – and Barney knew how to turn a profit even then. But his mother made him leave school—' She caught herself up, and laughed again.

'No need for that tale now! Barney's interested too, is all. He says it depends on the asking price. When property comes empty in Tollbridge and he buys it, it's done up for rent – unless it's in Boatshed Row, where his mother had to take them when his father was dead. Four bare walls and a roof, no water... He came back swearing he'd have nobody else live there the way he'd had to do. His old home's like something from a glossy magazine, these days.' He heard the smile in her voice. 'He says if he ever gets to own the whole row, he'll burn it down and rebuild!'

'He wouldn't want to burn Clammer Cottage, would he?'

'Oh, he'd have no cause. Prue Budd was a Christmas before she married, though the families didn't get on, but it goes so far back nobody can remember the start and Barney was friendly enough with Prue, by and large. No, his talk of burning's no more than his way of showing us he could afford the loss as he never could have done before. And if you're thinking he'd bear a grudge should you outbid him, he won't. It's business, with Barney – only, don't leave it too long before you come. If he don't buy the place someone else will.'

'The Anchor, of course.' Jasper was tapping at his laptop as he listened. 'Looks good. Jane will love the harbour view. I'll check with her and we'll try for a decent room, soonest. I know she's looking forward to seeing you again.'

'And me, her – and you. It's been a longish while.'

'When we're living only half a mile from you, you might wish it had been longer.'

They were both laughing as the conversation ended.

'Good day to 'ee, vicar! Barnaby Christmas speaking.'

Mr Hollington held the telephone a little way from his ear. For his age, Mr Christmas was very hale and extremely hearty. 'Good morning, Barnaby. It was a sad day yesterday, but also a day for celebration. I think Prudence would have been pleased.'

'I reckon she is, and all.'

There was a brief pause.

'Thank you for how you spoke concerning her. Brought a tear and a joyous smile together, so you did.' Barney cleared his throat. 'She was my cousin, remember.'

'Which is why you, too, spoke with such eloquence.' The vicar coughed. 'I was sorry not to have seen you later to acknowledge your contribution, but by the time I'd left the christening you were gone from the Anchor – ah, festivities, if we might so call them?'

'The very word! She was my cousin, but I'd no mind to stay dancing hornpipes in her honour – even on the ground.' Barney chuckled, richly. 'And yet, tidn as if I can claim my age for excuse, seeing how Prue carried on to the end, and able to give me twenty years.'

'No, indeed.' The Reverend Theodore likewise chuckled. After his second mug of scrumpy in the Anchor he'd joined in a spirited jig, just as at Prue's birthday party he'd been swept into the dance and been close enough to help catch her as she tumbled from the table-top. Prue Budd had always displayed such spirit and vitality that nobody ever realised how fragile her elderly bones were. It had been a quick, clean fracture, but it forced her final departure from the cottage where she'd lived so many years by herself. Friends and neighbours were no longer enough.

''Twas the way she would have wanted to go,' said Barney, as everyone did. 'But now she's gone, there's Clammer Cottage empty and no doubt a buyer looked for. I'm minded to make an offer, if so be the price is right.'

'The price must depend on the official valuation, of course.'

'First refusal is all I ask, vicar. Once you have a price.'

'Her wishes must be respected by her trustees,' began Mr Hollington.

'True enough, ten years back she denied me, when Elias went, but that was ten years, and who's to say she hadn changed her mind in the matter? Being family, as you know.'

'Yes, I do, but her wish was that her trustees – of whom, as you rightly suppose, I am one – that we should obtain the best price possible for the greatest benefit to the village.' Mr Hollington was firm. 'The best price for the cottage – and for the land on the far side of the river. Until the entire property has been officially valued we can do nothing.'

'Beyond setting my name at the top of your list, to give me a sporting chance.'

'I will consult with my fellow trustees and mention your interest. I cannot at this stage promise more.'

'I've made a few enquiries on my own account.'

'So I understand.' The Anchor had yesterday been full of people eager to tell the vicar all about Barney and the man from the council. 'Once we know how much, if indeed any, land must be rated agricultural we will have a far better idea.'

'Ah, well. Worth a try.' Barney knew when he was beaten. 'No more than the council said, neither.' An imp of mischief prompted him to add, in a regretful tone: 'But a grand sight it would have made, all they caravans in tidy fine rows...'

The Reverend Theodore gasped, and stared at the telephone. Had he heard correctly? Caravans? He moved the receiver closer to his ear...

...and was deafened by a roar of laughter. 'Easy there, vicar! At my time of life it's too late to be setting up as Billy Butlin!'

Theodore closed his eyes and gave silent thanks.

'So long as you agree to noting down my name, and give me the chance to offer a fair price, I'll be content.' The imp returned. 'Now, should more'n one offer be made, o'course, and Cousin Prue's trustees unable to reach a decision, then you could do worse than as they do over to Chedzoy, and hold a candle auction.' His serious tone betrayed none of Barney's amusement. 'Raise the bidding – and the price – still further, that would. For the greatest benefit to the village community, remember.'

The vicar was thoughtful when he at last replaced the receiver. As usual in moments of perplexity, he went in search of his wife.

'Theo, he was teasing you.' Her tone mingled sympathy with exasperation. There were times, Frances felt, when her husband took life rather too seriously. 'I don't say he wouldn't prefer to have had you accept without argument whatever sum he offered, but Barney is too good a businessman to believe that you, or anyone else in your position, would really be so hasty in making such an important decision.'

'He kept reminding me of his kinship with Prudence. There was a clear implication that she might prefer the cottage to stay in the family.'

'Prue would know as well as anyone in Tollbridge that he, the same as she, has no family to inherit after his death. Nothing's been heard of his brothers and sisters for years – for decades! Once Barney has gone, Prue's cottage will be out of the family whether or not she would have wished it to stay with the Christmases.'

He sighed. 'The breakup of any family is always to be regretted…'

'Hardly a breakup, Theodore. I don't believe there was any quarrel, more a – a drifting apart. They haven't spoken to one another in years because it's years since they've seen one another. The worst you can say is that Barney did his best for them all, and they repaid him with ingratitude – or indifference. I'm not sure which I prefer.'

'The *best* one can say, I suppose, is that when Barnaby returned from his – his adventuring a wealthy man, his siblings didn't rush back to claim affection and a share of that wealth. I suppose,' he reiterated. 'Has it occurred to you, Frances, that all his brothers and sisters may be… dead? No wonder the poor man placed such emphasis on his kinship with Prudence Budd.'

She stared. 'Certainly not! For five – or was it six – younger siblings all to predecease him and leave no descendants? Do have some common sense, Theo.'

She gave him time to consider this, then added: 'But I still say he was teasing you – oh, not about wanting to buy the cottage, done up it would make a charming holiday rental – but about turning the Budds' back garden into a caravan site. Don't forget, he bought the school when it closed. It's true the renovations had to stop, but it's still far more convenient than the old hemp garden could ever be. The school buildings already have proper facilities – mains water, drains, gas, electricity – that would cost a small fortune to supply to Elias's vegetable patch. Nobody would waste money like that, now would they.' It was not a question.

The Reverend Theodore still looked anxious. She tried again.

'Then there's the mine. Barney was born in Tollbridge. He's bound to take history into account. While the collapsed area is more than half a mile away, it's still close enough for people – strangers – to wander by accident into places they should not. Anyone from Tollbridge or Ploverton has too much respect for the dead to encourage such wandering.'

'Surely they would notice the memorial stone at the entrance to the wood – strangers, that is.'

She clicked her tongue. 'But would they read it? Would they pay attention if they did? We can't *know*, of course, but I can guess.' As a clergyman's wife she had a strong sense of the realities. 'He was teasing you, Theo. Forget the caravan site. It won't happen.'

He tried to smile, as she clearly expected of him. 'You may be right about Barnaby, my dear – I hope so – but now... now he's put the idea in my head... I mean, should someone outbid him for the cottage – or if we are advised to sell the garden separately – they might really do it. Turn it into a caravan site, that is.'

The vicar's general benevolence occasionally stumbled over the truth of human nature. His wife had to think fast.

'A covenant! Any solicitor would know how to word it so that the land could never be used for – for any unsuitable purpose. Isn't one of the other trustees a solicitor?'

'We could hardly ask someone to draw up such a document without payment. Or even to reduce his usual fees. That would be taking unfair advantage.' The vicar paused. 'And can it be right to spend any part of the village inheritance, as we'll call it, on legal expenses?'

'To safeguard the future of the village of course it can. After all, that's the whole reason Prue left the money the way she did.'

'The love of money is the root of all evil,' he quoted, sadly.

'If you believe Barney Christmas is a money-grubber, you're wrong. There's a great difference between being Scrooge and – and simply doing all right for yourself.'

'But if his offer should be overbid by some determined and unsympathetic outsider, who sees potential in that piece of land... Barnaby talked of a candle auction. He mentioned the alternative possibility of – of sealed bids in brown envelopes.' He shook his head. 'It seems to me very like gambling. I'm not sure Prudence would have approved of that – or whether I, as a man of the cloth, should do so.'

Frances bit back, and reconsidered, her first reply. 'Prue was more than happy to buy raffle tickets, and play tombola, the same as anyone else. And at the most recent candle auction in Chedzoy the bishop himself opened the bidding, remember. And what a grand splash it made in the news! But because it was *news*, not because anyone seems to have objected that it was gambling.'

'Hmm.' He nodded. 'Yes – and the local vicar led the prayers, but... but that was for charity. For church funds, and for the good of the parish in general.'

'Exactly what Prue Budd's will is trying to achieve.'

'Oh. Yes.' He sighed. 'Yes. I will give this matter serious thought, and offer prayers for guidance. Once I have consulted with my fellow trustees I hope to have a better idea of the appropriate course of action.' Then at last he smiled. 'My most fervent prayer, however, will be that should the property not go to Barnaby, whoever buys it will show sympathy to the spirit of what we must be sure to explain were the wishes of our kind benefactress...'

Later that week Jane and Jasper Merton checked into the Anchor.

Chapter Five

They shared the drive from London and, heading across Exmoor, Jasper elected to take the Porlock Hill route to Tollbridge rather than the far less tortuous toll road. He couldn't believe the celebrated hill could possibly be as dramatic as Jane insisted. She'd been younger then, he said: lacked critical judgement. The Streetview images must give a distorted impression that only reinforced a faulty memory. With the passage of time her artist's imagination had taken flight – and fright. Making the trip in a modern car would bring it safely down to earth again, banishing all her fears.

They reached the top of Porlock Hill. Jasper allowed the engine to idle while he mopped his brow. 'On the way back we'll take the toll road,' he said.

Jane hid a smile. She knew she hadn't exaggerated when she said how the road ahead had suddenly vanished, so that all she and her mother could see in front of the windscreen was the bonnet of the car; she hadn't been mistaken about the notice halfway up the hill warning motorists to remain in the lowest gear when, at the hairpin bend, they came to a slightly easier section.

'I'll drive, if you like, while you enjoy the view,' was all she said aloud; but she felt it served her doubting spouse right when, having safely zig-zagged the precipitous drop to Combe Tollbridge and reached the Anchor, he ordered a very stiff drink.

Their luggage bestowed, they walked from the pub to Harbour Glim Cottage. Miriam was delighted to see them, whisking them indoors to display the tapestry on which she was currently working, and the length of twill she was ready to cut from one of her larger looms.

Jane's eyes gleamed. 'Thrums! You saved it for me! Oh, thank you!'

Miriam laughed. 'I'd a feeling you'd not forget, midear. It came back to me how you liked to use my special scissors, though it always fussed your mother – or could be it was *because* it fussed her, poor Annabel, wicked tease as you were.' She glanced at Jasper, who was showing polite but puzzled interest. 'Thrums is what we call the waste yarn that's too tight for weaving, at the start and finish of a length of cloth.'

'You can't do much with it,' said Jane, 'except leave it for tassels, or chop it off and stuff cushions with it, or make wigs for dolls – in some very unusual colours, I remember.'

Miriam laughed again. 'These days with hair, anything goes! Come along through.'

'Thinking of gadgets, did you ever get your inkle loom?' Jane was happily plaiting and playing with her cut-off yarn. Miriam had clipped to the remaining fringe a series of crooked hooks joining, by some neat carpentry, two lengths of wood. She skilfully cranked one piece of wood while holding the other, so that as the hooks revolved a plain straight fringe changed to a twisted one.

'Spares me the trouble of knotting by hand to secure the warp,' she explained to the fascinated Jasper. 'Mickey Binns – you'll meet him, shortly – he made it for me. Mickey and his father Mike are a grand pair for putting things together for a special need. You asked about my inkle loom, midear. Mike it was who built it for me, yonder.' She nodded.

'As thick as inkle weavers,' murmured Jane. 'You can sit so very close together.'

Jasper studied the waist-high wooden scaffold that stood on the floor, one face adorned with an arrangement of sturdy pegs. 'Bits of broomstick?' he guessed.

Miriam smiled. 'With the Binnses who knows, but doubtless you're right. In Tollbridge we'll not readily throw things out if there's a chance they might have a future use, whatever and whenever that might be. Mickey, he built me a small loom for fun, and I liked the use of it though the longest band I could weave was no more than two or three feet. His father said he didn hold with a skimped job, and built me that!' She chuckled. 'If I used every peg, the inkle bands would be yards long.'

'What happens if you don't want them that long?'

She laughed. 'I don't use every peg! Old Mike has no notion how much effort it takes to pull a long warp round the whole loom, but I'd not hurt his feelings by saying. It's bigger than I'd really like, but he made it to double as a warping board and was so pleased...'

In the road outside, a car pip-pipped its horn. 'That'll be Mickey.' Miriam paused in her fringe-twisting and set everything carefully to one side. 'He's not at sea today, but driving the taxi for his cousin Jerry. He said he'd be here once the job was done to take you up to Clammer Cottage if you'd like. His father Mike's got the keys to show you round – the vicar's agreeable, and tidn any particular trouble.'

'Is it so very far?' Jasper frowned. Hadn't Jane described trotting easily, as a child, on her own, up the hill to hear stories and be given sweets?

'Mickey thinks all townies poor, soft creatures who take no exercise,' said Miriam.

'After sitting so long in the car we could do with the walk,' said Jasper.

'Especially after Porlock Hill.' Jane couldn't resist a gentle dig. 'You're right, the walk will be good for us both – if your Mickey's up to walking,' she added.

'Not *my* Mickey.' The horn pip-pipped again. Miriam hurried to the door. 'At school together, is all. If there's anyone special it's my friend Susan, saving it's more Mickey interested in her and her… well, maybe. Or maybe not, now she's her daughter come to live with her – oh, a long story. Doubtless you'll hear all about it, but for now it's Prue's cottage you've come to see, so you'd best come and see it. Mickey, hello – meet Jane and Jasper!'

In the pub a few hours later, the little group reconvened. The Mertons had toured Clammer Cottage and been agreeably surprised. Fixtures and fittings were of course out of date, yet not so old-fashioned they could appeal to any retro ideal and be kept: much would need replacing, but the basic fabric of the building was in good heart. With intelligent refurbishment they could have the perfect work-from-home base. Mike Binns and Gabriel Hockaday, casually joining his brother-in-law to meet their prospective neighbours, explained that everyone in Tollbridge had been proud of Aunt Prue. It was a privilege rather than a duty to do things for her, well before she lost her husband.

'Whatever Elias couldn't do for himself,' explained Mr Binns.

'Or at least being nearby to help him out, as might be wanted,' said Mr Hockaday.

'Tactfully,' put in Mickey, and smothered a grin.

'My cousins,' said Miriam, a last-minute addition to the party, 'have an interest in Elias's vegetable garden. How safe would you reckon the clammer to be, after this long time?'

'Can they swim?' asked Mike.

'A joke,' said Gabriel, catching Miriam's eye.

Miriam frowned at the two old gentlemen. Just as well she'd obeyed her instinct and stopped work on the tapestry to join the Clammer Cottage expedition: Mickey Binns wouldn't dare encourage his elders to further mischief with her there to suppress him.

'It might be safe,' said Mickey now. 'You could take the risk if you wanted, but I don't know how the insurance would care for it if you tumbled in.'

Jane looked down. 'Perhaps the river's not as deep as I thought, but it's just as fast…'

'Faster,' said Mike. 'We've had some rain this past week.'

'Faster, then. I'd hate to fall in and be carried out to sea.'

'Wild swimming at its wildest,' said Jasper, his eyes bright. 'I know you're not keen, and I do understand, but I'd like to go across. Anyone else? No? Just to get a feel for the potential…'

Jasper was bubbling with enthusiasm for the potential of the old Hemp Garden as they sat with Miriam in the Anchor that evening. There was room for his shed – for a cabin studio for Jane, away from the cottage so that his own work, which involved telephone conversations and video calls, wouldn't disturb her – and he knew nothing about soil conditions but he felt sure Elias Budd must have understood them well.

'It *smelled* right,' he said. 'Everything *felt* right.' He smiled at Jane. 'If there's a ghost in that garden, I'm sure it's a happy ghost.'

'Ah.' Gabriel Hockaday, with Mike and Mickey Binns, loomed up beside the little group. 'So, you've knowledge already of the lost silver mine?' His glance at Miriam was accusing. He'd hoped for a generous tip from these tourists when he and Mike did their double act.

'Jane's my cousin,' Miriam reminded him. 'She's visited before.'

Uninvited, the newcomers sat down, confident of their welcome.

'You'll show a proper respect,' said Gabriel, serious now.

Jasper was serious, too. 'We wouldn't dream of trespassing in the Silver Wood or anywhere near it. Miriam's told us there's a memorial stone, and naturally we'd take the greatest care. Besides, it's the hemp garden we're buying, not the whole headland! We'll keep well within the proper boundaries, I promise. Why should we need to go outside them?'

'So you've the firm intention—' began Gabriel, when he was interrupted.

'I'm to be outbid, then!' Barnaby Christmas prodded Jasper's shoulder with a gnarled forefinger, and chuckled. 'No secrets possible in a pub, lad. You've a fine, carrying voice – shouting at your videos all day, no doubt.'

He pulled up a chair and sat down. 'You've building work and alterations in mind, goes without saying. You'll talk it over with your cousin, as you should, but anyone in Tollbridge will tell you there's honest workmen in these parts and you'll get a good job done if you employ the right people. In time,' he added. 'If, that is, you have someone here to oversee the work – seeing how that would help towards faster achievement than otherwise…'

The others were nodding; grinning. Only Miriam sounded a note of caution. 'Should you want an eye keeping on progress, though, I fear there's only half I could spare you. The spinning and weaving take up so much of my time—'

'—and I've the answer,' broke in Barney with glee. 'Once the cottage is yours by law, you leave your old London behind and come straightway down here.' He gestured vaguely round the bar. 'This is fine hospitality for a weekend – a whole week, maybe – but there's nought to beat the comfort of your own private place.' He fixed the young couple with a hypnotic gaze. 'Now, I've a cottage I could rent you and, given you're to be neighbours – and Miriam your cousin besides – I'll ask a bit less than the usual rate. You could be up and down to Hempen Row easy as wink, whenever you had the inclination.'

Gabriel and the Binns pair burst out laughing; Miriam smiled. Barney did his best to seem hurt by the mockery of his friends, but his grin grew wider as they all shared the joke.

Gabriel sobered first. 'Now there's a fair offer – for Barney, that is.' Mr Christmas looked sorrowful, but said nothing. 'Jan Ridd – the landlord – he might do better terms should you plan to stay a while at the Anchor, but given you're about to do Barney out of Clammer Cottage he's maybe in his rights trying for a little something in return – hey, Barney?' Behind his hand in a loud whisper he added: 'Never misses a chance, the man don't.'

'I don't,' agreed Mr Christmas. 'And no harm in that.' He turned back to Jane and Jasper. 'So what say you, friends? I'd not cheat you – we'll have no jockery, between friends – tidn good business, for one. Ask any of these daft snigglers here.' Miriam, Mike, Mickey and Gabriel suppressed their mirth to nod grave confirmation that he could be trusted.

'But – we haven't spoken to the estate agent yet,' protested Jasper. 'We haven't even talked to the trustees!'

'But you know we'd love to live here,' Jane told him, 'and you know we can afford it.' She smiled at Barney. 'Which doesn't give you permission to up your prices, but we'd be happy to pay the going rate –' she glanced at Miriam – 'and we might even give you first refusal on the renovation work.'

As Miriam showed no shock or dismay Jasper found himself agreeing with his wife. 'If we buy the cottage it's a deal,' he told Barney. 'But the purchase can't be done in a hurry. Would the offer still stand if we couldn't get it sorted in, say, a couple of months?'

Mike Binns guffawed. 'He'll wait. For the chance to make money, he'll wait.'

'I will,' said Mr Christmas. 'So we'll drink to good health and new neighbours, shall us? And you, Mike Binns, for your imperence, you'm paying!'

Over cider the three old men grew talkative, and ended up challenging one another to skittles: *skills*, they called them. Mickey was volunteered as sticker-up. Miriam said she would bring the Mertons along later. 'The alley's a clamoursome place at the best of times,' she explained as the trio, with their escort, stumped off towards a side door. 'You'll not want a headache your first night. The kittle-pins are solid wood, as is the ball, and the alley floor likewise. With a match on, and everyone shouting, we can go home deaf as haddocks.'

Jane's gaze followed the amiably squabbling group as they disappeared. 'I hope he isn't too annoyed that we mean to buy the cottage.'

'Barney? Not one to bear a grudge, if that's your concern, but it's business with Barney first and last. Keep that in mind through any dealings you have with him and you'll do fine.' Miriam smiled. 'You've read *Lorna Doone*, midear?' Jane had, years ago; Jasper hadn't, but he'd seen the film. Miriam looked pleased. 'Hereabouts is all Lorna's country. There's none these days would admit to Doone blood, but John Ridd, that's the landlord's rightful name, John or Jan he claims descent from Girt Jan Ridd of the book.'

Her smile widened. 'And there are many who say Barney Christmas must surely be kin to Jan's Uncle Reuben, who had all his money took when he was ambushed by the Doones, upalong to the moor. They caught a wild pony and tied him on its back, face down to the tail. Jan rescued him – and what he said, that's Reuben, when he could speak wasn't *Thank you, kind nevvy* so much as, Jan must remember the pony now belonged to him! Should the same happen to Barney Christmas that would be his answer, too.'

'It could explain how he made his money.' Jasper's fancy had been caught by the tale of Barney's childhood poverty and subsequent return, enriched, to the village.

'What happened to the pony?' Jane couldn't quite remember.

'Jan said if his uncle would but ride it home the same fashion he'd been found riding, he could keep it.' Miriam nodded wisely. 'It ended up at Plover's Barrows – Jan Ridd's farm.'

'Well done Jan Ridd,' applauded Jasper.

'There was a highwayman with a horse, I remember that.' Jane had been in her pony phase when she read *Lorna Doone*, being sofa-bound with a broken collarbone after a fall.

'Tom Faggus,' said Miriam at once, 'and Winnie. Jan Ridd rode Winnie to the rescue when Tom got caught up in the Battle of Sedgemoor.' Her voice thrilled. 'Why, our own Jan can show you *the very cannon-bullet* that fell in the mud between Winnie's feet... although,' with a twinkle, 'he can't explain why anyone in the midst of a battle should be caddling about after a lump of brass the size of a tennis ball when he'd an injured man to find. But yonder it rests, in that glass box over on the wall. I sent you the booklet, surely?'

'We must buy another, now we're here,' said Jasper. 'Support local industry.'

'Start as we mean to go on,' agreed Jane.

Miriam regarded her young relatives with approval. 'Maintain that thought and you'll do well, living here all year round and not only summer. I'm Tollbridge born, love the place, but can't deny we need new blood, so many young ones moving away over the years.'

'Like Barney Christmas with his ungrateful brothers and sisters,' said Jasper.

'True, they took what they could and went, but Barney came back in the end. Like me he's Tollbridge born, though you can't deny he also meant everyone here should know he did well for himself and had money to spend! It's mostly spent on holiday lets, or renting to locals – which is a start, but no more. You two will be working from home and buying in our shops – leastways, the basics. We'll agree there idn every essential to be had here, but Ilfracombe and Minehead aren't so very far... And there's always the computer,' she added, 'if needs must.' Online shopping was not a familiar concept in Combe Tollbridge, although people had heard of it. Tollbridge preferred to see what it was buying before it bought.

'Then three cheers for my dad,' said Jasper. He looked at Jane. 'It might take a while to sell the flat, so I'd say this is the time for the whisky to come into its own, don't you think? Then we could offer cash in hand to hurry the business along.'

Jane smiled at her godmother. 'Jasper was the first boy after five girls, and his father wetted the baby's head with a whole bottle of Glen Macramie.' Miriam's eyes widened. Jane nodded. 'Even then it cost a small fortune. There was another bottle for Jasper to keep, and he's done the same every birthday since.'

'Hasn't missed once, bless him.'

'He told Jasper never to drink it—'

'—which at current prices I wouldn't dare—'

'—and the collection must be worth a small fortune by now.'

'We can use it as security against a short-term loan if we have trouble selling the flat.'

'Hmm,' said Miriam. 'And what did he do for your sisters?'

'The same idea, but –' Jane rolled her eyes – 'with magnums of champagne.'

Jasper grinned. 'My father can't believe any woman, even a daughter of his, would be able to treat single malt with proper respect. He lets them open a birthday bottle on special occasions—'

'—but only because he's no idea how long fizz will keep.'

Miriam didn't know either, but she knew about Glen Macramie. One of the spirituous world's most celebrated whiskies, it was known for being 'Smooth As Silk With Nary A Knot'. Its trademark label showed a tartan satin ribbon draped with elegance (rather than tied in a bow) round a sprig of purple heather. Glen Macramie cost a gasp-inducing sum even for a single tot: only plutocrats drank doubles. The Anchor, good pub though it was, could never afford to stock it.

Miriam's approval of the Mertons intensified. 'You'll do uncommon well,' she assured them. 'Only learn to play skills – and how to hold your cider – and you'd be welcome in Tollbridge tomorrow!'

Jasper drained his mug. 'We mean to do our best. Which way to the skittle alley?'

'Come with me,' said Miriam.

Chapter Six

Next day the Mertons left Miriam in peace to her weaving, and set off on a tour of exploration. Near the river mouth they crossed the public bridge that once had been the only link between the main village and the Ankatell mine. Wider than a mere footbridge but too insubstantial for more than a horse and cart to cross, the former toll bridge led the way now past the old boatsheds to Coastguard Steps, and the Watchfield car park up on the headland. Barnaby Christmas, spotting his prospective new tenants in the distance, waved cheerily; people passing closer-to volunteered a bright *Good morning!* or *Lovely day!* and nodded or smiled at them. The Mertons happily returned the greetings.

They went back over the Chole to buy a local paper in Farley's; they prowled alleyways and narrow walks. They came upon unexpected corners where parking spaces had been squeezed, and courtyards where defiant containers held shrubs that thrived in the shade, flowering with only the reflected warmth of the sun. They climbed Stickle Street, slowly this time, observing the church, the school, and the Jubilee Hall. They turned into Hempen Row and in whispers pitied the decaying tin tabernacle, once a dissenters' meeting house, that in the twenty-first century had been voted by

Tollbridge the future home of the museum they'd never quite got round to opening in the twentieth; and still hadn't. One day, perhaps.

At the end of Hempen Row they gloated together beside Clammer Cottage, eagerly talking of fresh flowers and healthy vegetables. Jane decided the headland should pose no problem for the northern light if her studio had the correct orientation, but vetoed Jasper's proposal that he ought to slip across the old plank bridge again, just to check.

'If it gives way and you fall in, I'm too young to be a widow,' she said firmly.

'And black's not your colour anyway. You win. I won't – but it's a pity.'

Louise Hockaday, emerging for her regular walk, came up to introduce herself and explained that Mike Binns, with Gabriel, had risen at an early hour to check lobster pots:

'But Mickey has the keys and can easily be fetched, working on shore as he is today, should you be wishful to go inside again...'

'Only we didn't,' Jane told her godmother, as Miriam poured coffee and Jasper helped himself to carvy cake. 'We asked for the vicar's telephone number, and took it from there.'

'Best news of all.' Miriam's delight was evident. 'You'll not regret this, either of you.'

'Jasper's spoken to the bank, and told Mr Hollington we're serious. He's giving the estate agent our details in due course. People have been so very helpful, but – Miriam, isn't the broadband slow! And we couldn't believe the number of mobile blind spots!'

'Well, for most in Tollbridge that's been no great hardship so-far-forth, though I've little doubt there'll be something arranged one day, technology being the lifeline everyone says it is – but it costs money, midear, and takes time.' She hesitated. 'Won't put you off, will it?'

Both assured her it wouldn't. Miriam nodded. 'That's good, for I mean to introduce you to more people before you move down, in the Anchor tonight if you'd care for it.' They said they would. 'You won't be readers of Milicent Dalrymple?' Miriam chuckled. 'Thought not. It's the name used by my friend Susan Jones. Her books sell, they say, though they're not to my taste – but Susan's had experience of being an incomer to Tollbridge. She'll maybe have things to tell you.'

'If she really wants to spill the beans, wouldn't it be more tactful to meet her somewhere private?'

Miriam's eyes danced. 'My understanding is, she'd be thankful for different faces and a change of scene. Didn I say her daughter's staying with her? Susan's not said much, even to me – and I'd be about her closest friend – but she finds it hard, I know. You two are of an age with Angela. You'll talk the same language.' She was vague. 'Computers. The internet. Clever, modern stuff you all grew up with, not like us. Angela's been working in a bookshop, and a library. Even a bookshop's on computer these days, Susan says.'

'Most things are.' Jasper was apologetic. 'It's so useful, you see. Storage capacity and potential for – well, for everything you can think of, if you know how to work it.'

By unspoken village telepathy Miriam and her visitors met in the pub not only Susan and her daughter, but also Mike Binns, with Mickey. In normal circumstances the elder Binns, after securing MV *Priscilla Ornedge* against the tide, would have gone back with his brother-in-law to Hempen Row, and supper with his son. Mickey somehow learned that Susan was to be in social mood that evening, and dragged Mike straight from the beach to the Anchor for a menu special because (he said) it had been a long, hard day.

Mike was about to demand details of this hardship – after all, he and Gabriel had been the ones working at sea – when he spotted Miriam with her small party. 'Uh-huh,' was all he said, and inwardly grinned.

Miriam looked up from the tourist pamphlets she'd been discussing with Susan while Jane and Jasper did their best to entertain Susan's daughter. 'Come you here, Mike Binns! Oh – I don't see Gabriel with you.'

'Supper at home,' said Mike. 'Mickey and me, we fancied a change.' He shot a sly look towards the oblivious Susan who, after welcoming the pair, had resumed her study of the pamphlets. He winked at Miriam with the eye farthest from his son. Angela, Jasper and Jane had no idea what these contortions might mean, so they ignored them. Miriam hid a smile. 'A change is as good as a rest,' she agreed.

'We'll sit with you to have it, if you've no objection.' None of them had.

The general bustle over, Miriam explained for Mike and Mickey's benefit how Jan Ridd, Sam Farley and others had for some time talked of bringing up to date the tourist information first assembled by Sam's father, and never greatly altered over the decades apart from improved printing methods.

'I know,' said Mike. The topic had come up more than once in the Anchor's public bar although, as so often in general discussion, nobody ever did more than discuss it.

The booklets (said Miriam) might sell better if they were better written, but Sam hadn't cared to trouble a professional writer like Susan – and Susan hadn't cared to offer, though she could well see the need, in case anyone thought her a pushy incomer criticising an old-fashioned style. In many ways, Tollbridge *was* old-fashioned.

'And none the worse for that,' she concluded.

'No argument from me,' said Mike.

'My cousin Jane here's a professional artist,' said Miriam.

Mike nodded. 'I know that, too.'

'She and Susan fell to chatting, and Jan heard them, and one thing led to another and now everyone's agreed it would be a grand notion. We were looking to see which tales might be best rewritten first – Jane can think about illustrations while she and Jasper wait to buy old Prue's place – and being my cousin, she remembered best your tale of Bran and my shipwrecked relations. O'course, Angela and Jasper know nothing beyond what's written, and it would help Susan with the writing to hear it again from you.'

'Ah,' said Mike.

'It's your story more than Gabriel's, but if you could tell your part now he can do the same, should he come in later – and nothing lost if he don't.'

'From the horse's mouth,' said Susan. 'In your own words.' Farley senior had done his best, but his flat prose narrative lacked the authentic touch.

'Oh, please,' said Jane. 'I used to love hearing it as a child, but Miriam's not you...'

The others echoed her plea. Jasper offered to buy him a drink to wet his whistle. Mike blossomed at so much attention in Gabriel's absence.

'Well, now. During the war, it all began.' He raised his mug to Jasper in salute. 'In the early days there was hundreds, thousands of us city kids evacuated to safety, all shapes and sizes and me among the youngest. We all had labels on our coats, gas masks in cardboard boxes round our necks, sent off by train who-knows-where, out into the country to be safe from the bombing and the poison gas. Only when it didn't happen right away, what we called the Phoney War, many of 'em went home again. Not me, mind you. I had a cushy billet with Ralph Ornedge and his wife Prill – Priscilla.' He nodded to his son. 'Our boat's named for Auntie Prill. I adored that woman. Better than a mother, to me.'

He sighed. 'I had the best time of my life in Tollbridge. London? Forget it! Never wanted to go home. Bolted back here as soon as I could when they took me away – and here I've stayed. Enough to eat, good fresh air, places to play, nobody clouting me every five minutes – I was in clover. Ralph, he took me fishing and taught me all I've tried to pass on to my boy here.' Mickey grinned. 'When's the best time of year for what fish – how to read from the gulls where the biggest shoals might be – how to read the weather. And one night everyone said there was bad trouble coming, and not to put to sea. So nobody did.' Mike pulled again at his mug.

'But for them already out, it was a different matter. Nothing to do but run ahead of the storm or try to ride it out, and while most of 'em did, some didn. So, next morning there was wreckage along the shore, and a couple of bodies, poor devils, one on the beach and the other washed right into the harbour, both pretty well in their birthday suits, with everything torn to shreds by the sea and the rocks and the chezell.' He paused. 'And me just a kid. First time I'd seen anyone dead.'

Those who didn't recognise the local term for shingle didn't like to ask what 'chezell' might be. This was no time to interrupt.

Mike sighed, then grinned. 'Prill, she tried to stop me seeing, but kids get everywhere at the best of times, which ain't the middle of a war. The authorities had to be told first thing, in case they was German spies, but turned out the poor devils come from Wales.' He nodded to the far wall, beyond which lay the Bristol Channel. 'Fishermen caught by the storm, they were, father and son shorthanded on account of the youngest boy gone into the Navy. Just two of 'em – and their dog. Not that we knew about no dog at first, but once the bodies had been took away respectful, us kids went poking about for souvenirs. Heartless little brats, you'd call us – but there, you're old enough to know better. Not like us.

'Me and Gabe Hockaday was scrambling over the rocks under the cliff – out past the breakwater, where Miriam gets the seaweed now to feed her hens – but there wadn no seaweed then. All ripped off by the storm, blown away down the beach. Just bare rock. Couldn believe our eyes. But… it's an ill wind.'

He drank some more. 'With no kelp to slip on there was the chance to get at limpets and such, and Gabe had a good knife, so we thought we'd bring home a handful or two for the pot, or bait some hooks and try for summat bigger... and then I heard crying, higher up. Gabe said it was no more'n gulls – but I wadn so sure and I went higher – wicked scrambling that was, for my short legs – and I got closer and it weren't crying, nor yet gulls, but whimpering. It was a dog, a little black dog, part spaniel I'd say.' He smiled. 'The softest ears and the brownest eyes... She was hiding in a sort of cave, too scared to come out and all cut and bruised, we found later. Wet through and shivering, we could just about see that, but we couldn get near enough the poor little thing.'

He shook his head. 'Carried there by the storm and the tide, she was, worn out from swimming and scared half to death. I like to think it was our voices made her try telling us she was there so we could help – only we couldn't, with the rocks being sharper and steeper that bit farther from the sea. But we wasn't going to let her starve and cry herself to death. Couldn behave so callous. Could anyone?' No one it was at once agreed.

Mike nodded. 'So I stayed by her for company, being tired after my climb, while Gabe with his longer legs he went back down the cliff a damsight faster than the two of us had gone up, and found his dad and told him there was no time to be lost, and to fetch a ladder and a blanket. So they did, and the ladder was a bit shaky but I was just a nipper, so while they steadied it up I went, with the blanket tied in a sling, and brought that little dog down. Which is how we found out who'd been them two bodies, and what boat, and where they'd come from.' He looked at Miriam. 'Name of Evans, it was.'

Jasper and Angela looked at her, too. She shook her head. 'No relation to me, so far as we know, but there was the Welsh connection so, though it was before I was born, every year I put flowers on the grave – they were buried together – the same way my mother did.'

'We all do,' said Mike. 'Them that still remember.'

'At a guess, the war made it difficult to bury them in Wales,' said Jasper.

'The war made everything difficult,' said Mike.

Jasper smiled at Miriam. 'Lucky to have so many not-relations looking out for them,' he said, liking more and more what he learned of Combe Tollbridge.

'But what about the dog?' Angela found herself asking.

'Ah.' Mike smiled, then sighed. 'Bran, that was the name on her collar. Means "raven" in Welsh, her being without a single white hair. Well, Bran took a real shine to me and me to her… but then the son as was left come home on leave, and across to Tollbridge, and told us his mum fretted all the time he was at sea, and Bran having been the skipper's dog it'd be a kindness to give her back, despite she'd settled in so well with me that rescued her.' He was silent for a while. 'Made me downright miserable,' he said at last, 'and that's the truth. But Ralph and Prill, they – we – knew it wadn right to keep her when the whole crowd of us was still together and Mrs Evans, poor old girl, she'd near enough lost everything…'

There was a respectful pause.

Mike broke it. 'Then blow me down if later there didn come word of a basket on a train at Minehead, and would someone collect it for me, my name on the label and everything! And inside, a puppy, and a note from Mrs Evans to say being shipwrecked hadn't cramped young Bran's style a bit and she'd got out in an air raid one night, and, well… But this little chap, he weren't the same. He looked like my Bran, but… that was all, though the little devil took after his mum in other ways… There's a few dogs around Tollbridge still with a drop or two of Welsh blood in 'em – and he was a good little chap, but when he finally went – well, I'd not got the heart for another dog, and I never did have.'

Mickey understood his father's thinking: it was why there had been no stepmother for the half-orphaned infant. He glanced at Susan Jones, who was nodding in sympathy. There were times when Mickey felt that Andrew's death might have been yesterday, as far as his widow was concerned.

Angela intercepted that glance; heard Mickey's faint sigh; and mistook his sentiments. She herself barely recalled the father who had died so young, and having heard from her mother that Mike Binns had also been left with a small child to care for supposed a strong degree of fellow-feeling must naturally prevail between the two households.

At least in her own case the loss had not been complete. There was always a second chance. If she'd wanted it. Paul had betrayed and left her, or she'd left him, or it was mutual – but he hadn't left her for good. If she wanted him back…

But she didn't. Wouldn't. Ever. If the past few days had shown her nothing else, they'd shown her that much. She could manage without him.

She'd missed the general congratulations but quickly assured Mr Binns she had been enchanted by his story, and knew her mother could really make something of it.

'I'll do my very best, and of course I'll let Mike – and Gabriel – check the draft before I write the final version.' Susan smiled at her daughter.

'Should have been taking shorthand notes,' said Mickey. 'Final version? Why, the man never tells anything the same way twice.'

'Practice makes perfect, son.' Mike, basking in the success of his anecdote, nodded to Jasper, who'd risen to his feet proposing a second round of drinks. 'Perfect!'

The newcomers continued to learn more of the locals. Angela heard that Jasper ran his own business. 'Packlemerton's Publicity?' She whipped out her mobile phone, then put it back. 'I forgot, you have to be in just the right place to get a signal in here. The walls are so thick. Somebody fell in the fire once, leaning up the chimney to see if that might help.' Jane winced. 'Skin grafts all up her arm, mother told me.' Jane winced again.

Jasper grinned. 'Suppose I just tell you, for now? You can check us out later, in a more convenient location.' The grin widened. 'I know it pays to advertise, but falling in the fire would be paying too high a price! My mother's a Packle, or was born one. My father wasn't. The two of them together made a rather catchy name, I thought.'

Susan leaned closer to Miriam. 'I can't thank you enough,' she murmured. 'She looks relaxed for the first time since she came here. My place isn't designed for two. I can't relax, either. We're slowly driving each other mad. There'll be murder done soon, I tell you!'

'She seems to get along fine with Jane and Jasper. Every little helps.' Miriam, too, spoke in a murmur. 'Enjoyed Mike's tale, didn she?'

'The Mertons are the same age as Angela. Mike's a born entertainer – he and Gabriel could almost be professionals. Well, so am I meant to be, only right now I couldn't entertain a sausage! My publisher—' Susan pulled herself together. 'She *looks* at me, Miriam. It started when she first arrived and I was mid-seduction. You know how it is when I'm on the first draft. I was concentrating so hard I forgot I was wearing my tinted specs – these days they're so much kinder than clear glass with the glare from the screen – and even though I could see she was half dead from exhaustion she still… *looked* at me. But her friend didn't turn a hair!'

'She wouldn't.' Miriam chuckled. 'With her own emerald green striped pink, you could have worn Tom Cruise aviator shades indoors and it wouldn have worried her.'

'It seems to have worried Angela. I didn't understand at first – I didn't think she'd notice – but ever since, when she's not cursing Paul or on her laptop looking for a job, she… looks at me as if she expects me to do something else that makes no sense to her.'

'You talked of glare. Didn you explain to her, once you understood?'

'I tried, but... She asked why I hadn't altered my brightness settings – which I had, or I tried, but the balance never was comfortable and I wasted so much time fiddling with the wretched thing. So then she asked why I hadn't changed my on-screen paper from white to green, or blue. I said I didn't know how.' Susan sighed. 'I'm a writer, not a computer expert! As far as I'm concerned the thing is, first and foremost, a word processor. It delivers my manuscripts. Everything else is a bonus, no matter how useful I'll gladly admit the internet can often be.'

'Couldn you ask it how to change the colour of your paper?' Miriam didn't know how much information was available in what she would never call cyberspace; nor how easy it might be to obtain.

'That's what Angela said. Then she gave me a look and said she'd do it for me. You could tell she felt it was pointless trying to teach an old dog like me new tricks – and maybe she's right – but honestly, Miriam! You've earned your living for years without bothering too much with technology, haven't you? You prefer to spend your time with your wool. I prefer to spend mine writing... when I *can* write!'

'Did changing the colour work?'

'Well, yes. She was right about that. A gentle blue really helps, and I was grateful – but I think I overdid it, trying too hard to boost her confidence with all the upset about Paul, because now I keep catching her looking at me. Sideways. Probably assessing me for the early stages of dementia. I know she's driving me mad, but still...'

'That's what children do, midear.' Miriam was herself childless, a keen observer of human nature who found much scope for contemplation when seated at spinning wheel or loom. 'They worry about you as they grow older same way you worried about

them when they were young. Turn and turnabout's fair dealing.'
She tried to speak lightly, but she was worried for her friend.
Once back in the peace of Harbour Glim Cottage she would
have to don her thinking cap.

'—threw the whole boiling lot in the river!' It was evidently
the turn of Mickey Binns to narrate a piece of Tollbridge history,
egged on by his uncle Gabriel and a thirsty Barney Christmas,
who'd drifted across to join the little group and supervise
proceedings.

'What did they do?' Angela's eyes were bright.

'Climbed out the opposite side,' said Mike, 'and went home
to Ploverton.'

'Even the bailiff?'

'Last to be pulled out,' said Gabriel, 'but he survived. Nobody here or upalong paid too much heed to the Ankatells or
their folk. They'd been poor landlords for years, never coming
next or nigh the place but giving orders from London and screw-
ing every penny they could from the land and the workers, with
nought put back for improvements. Some folk are like that.' He
nudged Barney Christmas in the ribs, and laughed.

'The bailiff,' said Mike quickly, 'was one of the biggest screws.'

Gabriel nodded. 'And a cause for great resentment, him
being local born and bred and grown through Ankatell pride
too big for his boots. Threatened Ploverton with all sorts if they
didn't help stopping the clammer to be built – and they knew he
had the feudal right, and they had to come…'

'But,' interposed Mr Christmas, 'I'd say it was less him
losing the Ankatell oak – which any man would find cause for
annoyance, trees being good money and worth still more if
suitable for timber, as building a clammer rightly requires – and
more him losing his dignity in the Chole that overset the man
good and proper.'

'Ploverton were laughing with us,' said Mike, 'though they
were every bit as wet.'

Jasper was surprised. 'Laughing? But – I would expect this brush with the local authorities and a fight with the next village along to – to spark a serious feud, lasting through the ages.'

'You've watched too much television,' said Mickey.

'You've read too many books,' said Gabriel, as Susan smiled.

'Skittles, now,' said Mickey, 'that's a serious matter, but otherwise Ploverton's not so bad. All in the family, you might say. Susan will tell you.' He turned to her. 'You checked out the tale in some really old books, right, midear?'

Susan, a speed reader, was a born researcher. Favouring no particular historical period for her fiction she had, over the years, amassed a fund of curious and intriguing facts, legends and anecdotes to be used as appropriate. Once settled in Tollbridge she would, when unearthing anything that might be deemed of local interest, ask her friends for corroboration and, where possible, for further details. Gabriel Hockaday, Mike Binns, and Mickey were her most receptive audience.

Tollbridge elders had always known the old tales, imparting them with relish to younger generations. If the tales grew a little in the telling, what harm did it do? Sons in their turn would add embellishments of their own to the tales heard in youth – again, what harm?

Susan didn't mind if such embellishment made her original version almost unrecognisable: but she did expect the result to be plausible. Once or twice she even adapted her own text to the Binns or Hockaday version, thinking it an improvement. It was fiction, after all. If it was honest, what harm did it do?

But it had to start from an honest source, which is to say, reliable; and Susan held that nineteenth-century scholar-parsons spent too much time churning out dubious local histories without checking the facts. Victorian rustics had clearly found tourist-baiting just as much fun as did their descendants. All too often she discovered that the clerical Romantic Ideal proved mere wishful thinking. In these days of cyberspace downloads however, it wasn't hard to consult mediaeval (and earlier) authorities without leaving the house. Susan had become a skilled cross-referencer of sources, and with enthusiasm would double-check publication dates to ascertain who had cribbed what error from whom, and when.

'A feud with Combe Ploverton? Well, no.' Susan's smile was apologetic. 'No more squabbles than you'd expect in any extended family. Ploverton is what you might call the original settlement, but over the years younger sons and lads with itchy feet moved down to the sea to catch fish – the church was very strict about non-meat days – and there was the silver mine, too—'

'Ha!' snapped Barney. 'Taxes and tolls and cheatery – oh, the Ankatells did well for theirselves, right enough, though they did nothing for them that lived and worked here!'

Susan nodded. 'Or in Ploverton. Of course, you can bet the Ploverton lot didn't enjoy being chucked in the Chole – they've never been fishermen. It's too much effort to reach the sea, or rather to climb a thousand feet back up again. They're not used to water the way Tollbridge people are. They're mostly farmers, on the moor.' She laughed. 'If it had been winter no doubt the language would have turned the air blue, but the bailiff really was unpopular. You can read between the lines in some of the manor court records. In fact, in the end the Ankatells got rid of him.'

'Didn make the family any the more popular,' grumbled Barney.

'Less and less as years went by.' Mike toyed absently with his empty mug. 'And small wonder. Bad blood, through and through.' He clattered the mug for emphasis. 'Father or not, if I'd found young Mickey behaving as the last squire's son behaved I'd have run him out of town myself, just as they did with that young Ankatell!'

'Do tell,' begged Jane. As a child she'd heard whispers, but nobody ever explained; and there had been no Banished Squire pamphlet in Miriam's research bundle.

Jasper rose to his feet.

'Let me buy you another,' he said to Mike; and Mickey winked at his father, and then at Susan Jones.

Chapter Seven

Miriam went late to bed, and spent a restless night. She'd introduced Jane and Jasper to so many people she couldn't remember half of what was said, or who'd said it. The general sentiment was of friendly pleasure that Clammer Cottage would not stand empty for long. Barney Christmas accepted one drink but didn't linger: the kittle-pins, he said, were calling. Sam Farley – young enough to be his grandson! – had arrived briefly to challenge the old man – the imperence! – for a couple of days' time, once the lad had finished unpacking.

Barney's friends at once told him he needed more practice. They would come to watch, and give him the benefit of their advice. Mike went along as sticker-up because Gabriel interrupted his story of Squire Ankatell's banished son to say that wasn't the way he'd heard it from his father. Jane begged for details but was ignored. More cider was drunk. Miriam grew thankful it wasn't far to walk home.

She woke once in the night and knew she'd had some idea of how to help Susan; but couldn't remember any of her dream. She went back to sleep.

She woke early, and remembered.

'Susan, can we talk?'

'Angela's out in the fresh air, walking off last night. I'm on the black coffee.'

'Oh, dear.' Those with West Country blood seemed to have an innate tolerance for scrumpy, and sometimes forgot that others weren't so fortunate. And Tollbridge had been so very keen to welcome prospective new blood... 'But didn she seem a deal more cheerful by the end?'

'She did, so it was probably worth it. Ask me again tomorrow, when I'm awake.'

Miriam ignored this frailty. 'I've had a thought, midear. It was Jasper buying Barney a drink just as he went off with the others to the skills. Didn sink in, what Barney said before – that he's to play Sam Farley *when Sam has finished his unpacking*.'

A pause, while Susan swallowed coffee and her brain began to function.

'Called me an old man,' she quoted. 'The imperence. Yes?'

'Yes! And don't 'ee see? Sam's renting the old coastguard place from Barney – which means his own cottage in Meazel Cleeve now lies empty!'

There was a very thoughtful and much longer pause on the other end of the line.

It was broken at last. 'Oh, Miriam. Am I an unnatural mother to feel so relieved?'

'No. You work for your living, same as me, and you can't work with someone in the house no more than ever I could. When Annabel would bring Jane down I'd do nothing more fancy than plain weave. Always had to plan ahead, knowing I'd not be able for concentrating on stripes, or checks, or tapestry. Loved having them stay – goes without saying – but when you told me of settling for the Anchor as your spare room, well, I wish I'd had the thought myself, years before.'

'Contented solitaries,' said Susan, emerging from her trance.

'There's none could call us anti-social,' said Miriam. 'Not after last night.'

'Don't,' said Susan. 'But there's a time to be sociable, and other times definitely not. Jane Austen may have found it easy to write on a corner of the table with her family wandering in and out: I can't. When Angela was young it was different, but I'm long past the age when I can give a child the attention she needs all day and stay up half the night pounding a hot keyboard. I was so much more productive once she went to school – apart from helping with homework, of course. And now…'

'You did really ought to have a word with Sam. If you're fretted over her thinking you've no heart, well, you could leave talking to him until you've an excuse, like when you've done your part with the pamphlets. Only don't wait too long—'

'Wait too long? I *can't* wait! It's not just the way she looks at me, Miriam. She makes an effort with other people, which I'm sure must be good for her, but with me she's sometimes so – so angry and unhappy inside that I'm afraid, if she stays here, it'll be catching. I don't want to feel miserable! I want to write this blasted book in peace!'

If, thought Miriam, her friend felt this badly after so short a time, then it was a great pity Sam Farley hadn't spent longer in the Anchor last night. 'Would it help,' she asked, 'for me to drop a – a kindly hint on your behalf should I meet Angela out walking?'

'Could be worth a try.' Both ladies smiled at the motto of Barney Christmas; but Susan's smile soon faded. 'Less of the kindly and more of the hint would be wonderful. Angela's a better cook than me, and that doesn't bother me one way or the other – but I'd like to know how she thinks I've managed to survive all these years living on my own! The other night I woke up and she was prowling around downstairs, worried she could smell burning. I found her poking about in the kitchen. There was one of your saltmarsh chickens in the slow cooker and she'd been on her laptop all day and never noticed me fixing it – but the rattle of the lid woke her and she was afraid it might be the boiler. She was trying to find the master switch, she said.'

'Two women, one kitchen, bad news.' Miriam had once read this in a dentist's waiting room and waited years for the chance to use it.

'Two women, one cottage, worse news,' counter-quipped Susan. Letting off just a little steam had more than somewhat improved her mood. 'Perhaps I'll phone Sam and ask – oh, but I can't. Angela might be back any minute. Trying to arrange for the – the eviction of your only daughter's not easy if she's anywhere near to catch my end of the arranging.'

'Relocation,' amended Miriam. 'Resettlement. Angela needs her space, midear, as you need yours. She's wanting to build a new life for herself – you want your old life back. What's heartless about that? Where does she walk?'

'What? Oh… She likes looking out to sea. She loves the sound of the chezell in the waves. She's like me in some ways, I suppose.'

'High tide,' promptly replied the born-and-bred local. 'Then she might not have gone far. I'll find her and bring her back for coffee. A local recipe that helps lower the effects of too much scrumpy, we'll say. I'll call you with some excuse should I manage to find her, then you can call Sam. How does that sound?'

'Wonderful,' breathed Susan, and forgot to say *Thank you* – but Miriam understood.

She walked briskly down Harbour Path and spotted Angela coming from the direction of the toll bridge, Boatshed Row and the harbour's short pier. The tide was slapping its lively white lace against smoke-grey stone. Small boats were rocking in sympathy with their sisters out at sea.

Miriam greeted Angela with a friendly wave. 'Enjoying the sunshine, midear?' The sky was heavy with cloud as grey as the stone of the pier. Angela gave Miriam a look – and it was obvious what Susan had meant. 'Well,' temporised Miriam, 'and so you would, if the sun was out. Or would that have been too much for you, after last night?'

To her relief, Angela achieved a smile. 'These days my stamina's not what it was. I – I haven't done much socialising recently.'

'Come back with me for coffee – a prairie oyster, if you'd rather. My eggs give the usual recipe something extra that many folk do say picks them up very well.'

Angela brightened. 'Mother mentioned your hens before.' She fell into step beside Miriam. 'Don't they live on seaweed, or something?'

'Seaweed *and* something.' Miriam led the way back to Harbour Glim Cottage. 'For the most part it's the same as any hens will eat, but they do enjoy the taste of kelp, as I've tried to encourage. You can't always use my eggs for cakes, but when you can they do far better than adding a pinch of salt – and as for a pavlova, well!'

'Some people say the secret is white vinegar,' said Angela, and for the rest of the way discoursed on the various merits of baking powder, lemon juice and cream of tartar.

Angela heard Miriam cheerfully inform her mother that her daughter had been kidnapped for experimental purposes. She found herself smiling. 'I'll send back some eggs with her if she finds my recipe picks her up. If you feel as poorly as she looks…'

Miriam rang off, and cocked a quizzical eyebrow at her guest. Angela sipped again at the deep, rich orange concoction in the glass tumbler. 'Not bad,' said Angela. 'A Jeeves special with, you're right, that extra something…'

Miriam raised her own glass, drank, and smiled. 'We'll have coffee after.'

Angela didn't smile back. 'I'm glad I met you. You – you know my mother pretty well, don't you?' Miriam agreed she probably did. 'Do you think – I mean – do you think she's... all right? All there, I suppose I mean.'

Miriam stared.

'I mean,' Angela rushed on, free now to unburden herself without the risk of her mother overhearing, 'she never used to wear sunglasses, just a hat, when I lived with her before – and now she wears sunglasses *indoors!* She told me something about glare from the screen, and migraine – but she never used to have migraine, either. I think it was just an excuse she made up when I asked her about it.'

Miriam took a deep breath. 'Adult onset migraine, the doctor calls it,' she said. 'Susan told me about it – oh, some while since. Your mother, like the rest of us, has begun finding things don't work quite so well as they did at your age – but tidn to say she's a – a mad old bat! She's younger than me!'

'Oh, I didn't mean...' But Angela realised there was no easy way to remove the foot from her mouth. 'I'm sorry, but... You see, you're used to living alone. Mother isn't. When you're with her for a while you can't help noticing... some rather odd behaviour. She tries to turn it into a joke, but...' Angela drained her glass and set it down with a bump. 'I said I'd do lunch one day while she finished a tricky chapter, and I was hunting for heatproof mats in the dining area and – and – right at the back of a cupboard, I found an enormous, battered old saucepan.'

Miriam opened her mouth, then shut it as Angela continued to babble. 'Made of aluminium! Nobody uses aluminium these days – and anyway, people keep even stainless steel saucepans in the kitchen, where you can get at them, not in a dining room cupboard. When I pulled it out, it – it rattled, and – and inside there was a wind-up kitchen timer! Who uses clockwork these days? It's almost antique! It – it's hoarding! You see why I'm so worried?'

Miriam, turning pink, choked. Angela took her reaction for shock, and hurried on.

'Another time I did lunch – she told me your saltmarsh eggs curry well – I was hunting in another cupboard for basmati rice…'

Miriam could only nod. She was fighting for control.

'—and there was a huge storage jar half full of onion skins! Not – not live onions that could be of some use, but dead, dry papery skins in an airtight container.'

Miriam couldn't help it. She let out a whoop, a stifled shriek, and a roar of laughter.

Angela moved cautiously away from the older woman, groping for her mobile as Miriam laughed. If outside help had to be summoned the guest didn't trust her hostess's phone: like her mother's, it was a landline. It didn't move – and neither could you. If while dialling 999 you were attacked by a hysterical menopausal lunatic…

'Oh,' gasped Miriam, clutching her midriff. 'Oh!' The tears ran down her cheeks as she laughed and laughed. 'Poor Angela! P-poor S-susan!'

Angela moved further away, wondering what to do next. If her mobile phone didn't work inside this cottage, at sea level…

Miriam spluttered into silence and mopped her eyes. Even as she laughed, it had come to her that she'd been handed a splendid excuse for hinting to Susan's over-anxious daughter that she should consider a change of residence. Angela was worrying about her mother; she was thinking about someone other than Angela Jones, which had to be a good thing even though the worry was entirely misplaced. Miriam knew she must give reassurance before advice – and quickly – and then work the conversation as carefully as possible round to the hint she had to drop.

'I'm sorry, midear,' she managed at last, wiping her eyes and blowing her nose. 'Oh, that was rude of me! B-but – no, I won't start again.' She rubbed her midriff – it would ache for days, she knew – and, ignoring the younger woman's obvious reluctance, drew Angela into her own kitchen. On the floor in one corner stood a neat plastic dustbin. Miriam lifted the close-fitting lid. She pointed. Warily, Angela peered inside.

At once she recoiled. The bin was almost full of dried onion skins. It must be catching!

'For dying,' said Miriam. Angela recoiled still farther. 'All my friends save them, when they remember.' Miriam smiled. 'Your mother's very good. I love them – they give brown and tan and orange like you'd never believe – only, you need an ounce or more to every pint of water, and I like a lot more. That's a deal of onions!'

'Dyeing,' breathed Angela, suddenly limp with relief.

'Coffee, next,' decreed Miriam. 'And I'll show you my workroom. I've nothing on at present – you'd know from the smell, if I had – but there's work on my loom and you might care to see my spinning wheel, too.'

The coffee revived Angela so well – Miriam, unasked, added a dollop of honey for shock – that Miss Jones was encouraged to ask in what way she'd also been mistaken about the kitchen timer and the saucepan; and she didn't feel too silly asking.

Miriam was happy to explain. 'I'm the one as give Susan that saucepan. For years I boiled the chicken mash in it, but you're right, the health scare put me off, too, and I stopped using it.' She smiled. 'I doubt I'd call it *hoarding*, though, not to throw something out if there might still be some use in it! When Susan mentioned her little problem I gave it to her for – well, an alarm clock, almost.'

Susan's daughter was quick to pounce on just one word. 'Problem?'

'You know how she is when she's writing. Gets carried away – doesn't always notice how long she's been sat at her computer – and everyone these days,' pointedly, 'knows you shouldn't sit still too long without moving. Me, I count the rows I weave, but lines of a book is a different matter, your mother says. I said how about a kitchen timer, set for half an hour so she'd need leaving her desk and going downstairs to switch it off and on again.'

Angela was, doubtfully, nodding that she accepted this.

'So the first we tried was the battery sort that beeps, only Susan didn't always hear it.'

'I do hope she's not going deaf. She could be hiding—'

'She's concentrating!' Then Miriam forced another smile. 'Clockwork was better, but still she didn't always hear, so I said to try my old saucepan as a – a bell chamber. And that had poor Susan jumping from her chair! There's nobody can work with their nerves all of a flitter. So we tried about and above, and in the end found a timer in the saucepan, with the lid on, in the cupboard, did the business. Not that she uses it all the time, but she says it's a powerful help when she's a heavy session ahead of her.'

'Oh,' said Angela. 'I... got it wrong. Thank you.'

'Come and see what I can do with natural dyes,' her hostess invited.

Angela might voice doubts about antique equipment, but the length of cloth currently on Miriam's vintage floor loom ('my grandmother's') delighted her with its regularity, texture and colour; the range of hand-dyed hues was amazing. The pleasant hum of the spinning wheel almost tempted her to ask if she might try it herself. Miriam demonstrated the umbrella swift (for turning skeins of yarn into balls) and the drop spindle (for spinning by hand), likewise inherited from her grandmother.

'What about this?' Angela had found the two lengths of wood joined by the crooked hooks that twisted plain fringe into tassels.

'Oh, that's no more than twenty, thirty years old. Mickey Binns made it for me.' Miriam took a handful of thrums, telling Angela to hold the yarn firmly at one end while she attached clips to the other. 'See how it twirdles the warp into a fringe?' She laughed. 'I call it my tiffler, though, Susan having found that name in an old book. She says "tifflings" was what they called unweaving some of the fabric while it's still at tension on the loom – but she says it's nobody's business but mine what name I give to things!'

'Twirdle,' said Angela. 'Tiffler.' She savoured the words. 'You've been tiffling. It's my turn to tiffle.' She was alert; animated. 'You know, that's really cool. Catchy!' Her eyes were bright. 'It would make a grand trade name. Do you have a label? A website?'

Miriam's weaving, spinning and tapestry creations were sold through a handful of shops and galleries to a limited customer base: she made enough money to live, and had never seen the need for expansion. 'Well, I can't rightly sell more than I can make, but sell it I mostly do without difficulty. I'm not that bothered over technology. I can't see the why-for, with a small affair such as mine.'

'Why not? You're in business! You could expand – teach – sub-contract. You could go global! You need a website! If I checked things out for you – found someone suitable – you could…' The rest was in a foreign language, but Angela was enthusing and explaining with more confidence than Miriam had seen her display since she first arrived in Tollbridge.

While her guest ran on, Miriam was busily thinking. When Angela at last ran down, she was quick to step in. After all, Jane and Jasper had expressed similar surprise that she was so far behind the times: she'd begun to wonder if perhaps there was something in twenty-first-century ideas that she was missing, but until now had done little more than wonder. And here was Angela… 'I suppose,' she conceded, 'there could be advantages, but it sounds to be a deal of trouble. When all's said and done there might be no worthwhile benefit for money spent – and time lost.'

'It depends on what you want. Finding that out and setting it all up the way you want would be someone else's job. It can be as simple or as elaborate as you choose.'

Miriam crossed mental fingers. 'What I don't choose is a worrisome life. First for one, I'd have to learn to use a computer – I'd need to buy a computer! And a sad waste of money and time it would later prove if there was nobody to help me when the learning let me down, as it's sure to do, not having grown up with it as you have.' She gave Angela a sharp look. 'How long do you reckon to be staying with your mother?'

Angela subsided. 'I'm not sure,' she brought out at last.

'Corner Glim's no bigger than this cottage, and Susan had it remodelled for herself alone. You can't be so very comfable sleeping on the sofa under borrowed blankets—'

'Gorgeous blankets! And thank you, again.'

'You're most welcome – but there's staying beyond your welcome, midear.' Miriam forced a light laugh. 'The two of you could end up skirmishing with plates, or furniture – or saucepans, indeed!' Another laugh, in which Angela did not join.

It would be unkind to push the matter further. 'But maybe I'm seeing only the dark side. I've been a weaver most of my life, which could be a help in the computer learning. I've read books. The Jacquard loom was next to being a computer in historical times, they say...'

Angela blinked, then looked almost amused. 'But they haven't used punch cards for – oh, I've no idea. You'd have to ask in a museum, I should think.'

'You see how little I know? Nor I'm not like your mother – I never learned to type. She clatters away at her desk with her eyes closed, sometimes, while she's thinking.' Miriam shook her head. 'I don't know how she does it. I'm sure I never could.'

'I'm sure she could never make anything like that blanket, or pashmina, or whatever it will be. Everyone has different skills.' Angela smiled. 'Such as tiffling.'

Miriam smiled back. 'Want to try? Just you catch hold of this, midear, and twirdle!'

By the time they'd finished having fun with every piece of wool-working technology Miriam deemed fit for a beginner, Angela's subconscious had absorbed her new friend's words and thoroughly digested them. As she prepared to tear herself way and return to Corner Glim Cottage, she said:

'Miriam, you're right. Mother can't go on this way, with me underfoot all the time – but I think I could really enjoy living in Tollbridge. These days, if you find the right job, it's easy to work from home – anyway, I've got enough saved for a few months, at least. Do people take in lodgers? Or would that look bad for mother? Casting me out into the snow with a woolly bundle in my arms? I'd hate them to think – well, you know.'

'I know, midear. But they wouldn't. Susan's made good friends in the time she's been here. She fits in. The pair of you will do fine. Would you like me to ask around for you?' Miriam chuckled. 'One or other of my cousins is sure to know of a suitable place, whether here or upalong to Ploverton. Half the village is kin to the other half. We've no need of – of social media or computers when there's the local grapevine always ready!'

As the front door closed on Angela, Miriam was at the phone. 'She's coming back! Say nought of Sam Farley before I've the time to explain.'

'I've tried him twice, but there was no answer. He's probably still unpacking.'

'Good! Then you can act natural if she speaks of it herself, which well she might. This will all work out for the two of you, I promise, though it may take a while… I forgot to give her the eggs on purpose. You must come round by yourself to collect them, and I'll tell you what happened, and then you can act as you see fit…'

Chapter Eight

Sam Farley, with a brawny band of family connections to assist him, had been setting up all the printing equipment, manhandled in a variety of suitable vehicles from the site in Meazel Cleeve to the old coastguard station on the opposite headland. The original Ankatell toll bridge had been for pedestrians and small carts only; every subsequent bridge was built to similar dimensions. Combe Tollbridge does not gladly embrace change. The crossing stands not far inland from the mouth of the Chole, which is tidal: for centuries this made the building of a stronger, wider bridge impractical. These days all wheeled vehicles other than pushbikes, prams and children's scooters go the long way round, via the head of the valley. Sam and his cohort ignored everyone and everything – including phone calls – until establishment of the printery in its new location was more or less achieved.

Sam had started a drinks tab for his removal team in the Anchor that evening as Mickey Binns joined the party. Mickey, through his mother, was another cousin who'd been asked if he could help with the move, but he'd had to deny his kinsman. When MV *Priscilla Ornedge* left harbour she often carried anglers eager to flog the waters of the Severn Sea. A party of five, asking in a neighbouring village where conger eels might be found along that coast, had been advised by the tackle shop to arrange with Mickey Binns of Tollbridge. The arrangements were made and the five had duly spent all day fishing, encountering a ninety-pound monster that (once hooked, netted, weighed, and photographed) was returned to the waves to grow even larger. Next time it was caught it might well beat the target of a full one hundred pounds.

As a result, Mickey was big with tips and in cheerful mood. On his way home to Hempen Row he'd bumped outside the post office into Miriam, who had news to impart. He then dropped in on Susan, and could read between the lines. As he later headed for the pub, the knight errant in him was on the alert.

'You've had a thirsty day's work,' said Mickey to Sam once the amenities had been properly observed. 'You know I'd have helped if I could, though from the sound of it you'd everything sorted without me. But let me buy you a drink, to show willing – Jan! Another one here, when you can!'

Mighty Jan Ridd stooped low beneath the canopy of the bar to signal that he'd heard and understood. Mickey signalled back thanks, then turned to Sam.

'Reckon you'll find the coastguard windows suit as well as you hoped?'

'Thanks to you and your sketch plan we were able to set all down right where it should go, first time. Up and running likely the day after tomorrow – no, to be safe we'll say day after that.' Sam dug his cousin in the ribs. 'Shows what a university education can do!'

Mickey dug back. 'Cardboard squares and graph paper are easier used indoors than compasses, and surveying poles, and trusting to GPS to know exactly how things should be. Glad I was able to help that much, at least.'

'Come up and see for yourself tomorrow. Afternoon, not morning.'

'Not sleeping in the new place tonight, then?'

'I am, but there's a last few bits left to be sorted in the morning. Then it'll be finding someone to go in and do a spot of tidying, ready to rent out – unless I rent to Chris Hockaday. He thinks of coming back here full-time.' Chris was one of the many Tollbridge cousins shared by at least half the village. 'He can dust and clean the old place for himself, when he's not out taking photographs. Save me paying someone else to do it.'

Mickey raised his glass in acknowledgement of this canny stratagem. 'Thinking, or definite?' he enquired after a pause. 'He's talked before about stopping the travel to come home for good, but he never does.'

'Just because you did, don't mean other folk make up their minds so quick as you.'

'You live and learn,' said Mickey. 'Of course, if there's nothing settled a female tenant might do a better job than Chris at tidying all your clutter.'

Sam shot him a look. 'Someone in mind, have 'ee?'

'Not in the way you're thinking, but I've heard a whisper there could be someone ready to move in right away, rather than wait for Chris to make a decision. Probably keep the garden better weeded for you, see the chimney's swept on time, that sort of thing.'

'You acquainted with this young woman?'

'Well, in a manner of speaking... but not closely, mark you.'

Sam grinned. 'There's some might not care for you getting too close to young women – but I'd like to do Susan Jones a good turn. After all, they say she's going to write up my old booklets for me...'

'Who said anything about Susan?' Mickey ignored Sam's more than knowing wink. 'But, naming no names, I'm another who'd be happy to do her a good turn, should the opportunity present itself.'

Sam winked again.

Jane and Jasper Merton put their flat on the market and their possessions in store. Merton Senior's farsighted gift of Glen Macramie had indeed come into its own. Once the purchase of Clammer Cottage was complete they returned to Tollbridge and rented, for three months, Trendle Cottage from Barnaby Christmas. Between episodes of working from home one or other, or both, would go up to Hempen Row and check the progress of the renovation work. Barney's chosen team were doing an excellent job, even if it was slow.

'Hare and tortoise, town and Tollbridge,' said Barney when this observation was made one evening in the pub. They bought him a drink, and abandoned the topic.

Susan, likewise, was able to work again from home. Angela and Sam Farley came quickly to a satisfactory arrangement about the Meazel Cleeve property which Angela had asked Sam's permission to call The Old Printery. She thought the new address had style. Names were important. Mr Farley said he was flattered, and recommended a local solicitor when Miss Jones, keen to make an entirely fresh start, announced that her name from now on would be Angela Lilley.

'Stalkers keep off,' she told her mother darkly. 'Andy warned me, Paul's been saying things – but he'll never find me, or at least not easily, now I've cancelled all my social media accounts. Texts and email will be good enough for me, for some time to come! I'm starting a completely new life and I want it to succeed, this time around.'

'You know that I want it all to be a success for you, too.'

'You never liked Paul, did you?'

Susan hesitated. Angela looked at her. Susan's eyes shifted uneasily, and she thought fast. 'I didn't have to live with him, did I? What business was it of mine to like Paul or loathe him or – or be indifferent to him, which,' she perjured herself in a good cause, 'I have to admit was how I did feel, if you want to know. Be fair, Angela. How can I have strong feelings one way or another about someone I've barely met?'

Angela flushed. For some reason it hadn't often happened that Susan, visiting London on book-related business, had been able to meet up with her daughter. Hints about her spare room being in the Anchor passed Paul by on those rare occasions when the young couple came to Combe Tollbridge. He would persuade Angela they hadn't time to stay long: and they never did. With hindsight, and the brisk advice of Andy Marsh, Angela had realised that Paul had been slowly detaching her from those who should have been closest to her. He'd given her to understand that only their life together was of real importance – that she could believe he would always put her first, just as she should put him – and he had totally destroyed her trust in him one shocking, horrible afternoon.

Angela rallied. 'That's all over. Finished! You won't have to meet him now. I'm sorry you ever had to.' She forced a smile. 'I'm sorry for dumping myself on you, too.' Susan felt she ought to protest, but was given no time as her daughter hurried on: 'That's why I chose Lilley.' Susan blinked. 'As my new name. Sorry, mother, love you dearly and all that, but Jones doesn't cut it for me any longer. I mean – you wouldn't be Dalrymple if you thought it really worked for you, would you? And Susannah means lily, doesn't it?'

'It does. Thanks for the compliment.' She-whose-name-meant-lily smiled. 'Perhaps I should return it by changing Jones to Skinner.' Angela stared. Had she been right all along about her mother's mental state? 'Largest shoe-shop in the world, a century ago,' said the snapper-up of unconsidered trifles. 'Oxford Street – Lilley and Skinner.'

'Oh – yes,' gasped Angela, weak with relief. She gave her mother an unwonted hug.

Miriam Evans, encouraged by the Mertons as well as by Angela, pondered the merits of modernity and thought a slight concession wouldn't hurt. She told Angela to finish settling into The Old Printery and then come down to Harbour Glim Cottage, where she could watch her at work, learn what she did, and prepare to advise when the time eventually came to discuss having a website. 'I've shown you the niddy-noddy, and the swift, and you've played with the tiffler. Next time I'll let you cut the thrums – you can ask Jane about that...'

The Mertons were becoming further acquainted with their fellow incomer. They often met out walking: they were all agreed against sitting too long in front of a screen. To climb Stickle Street or the even steeper Meazel Cleeve in (at first) a slow trot (later, they jogged) was as good as a gym subscription, and cost nothing. Climbing Coastguard Steps to the top of the lookout headland gave them not only exercise but also a better mobile connection than could be found at the end of the little stone pier. Until their belongings were out of storage, they replaced training bars with bags of pebbles, gathered from the chezell beach.

'If we had a sewing machine,' said Jane one evening in the Anchor, 'we could make beanbags and juggle with them. Hand-to-eye co-ordination, and so on.'

'Or paperweights.' Angela had learned the hard way why Sam Farley never bothered to unstick the age-swollen windows of The Old Printery. 'Doorstops.'

'If we had the right equipment,' said Jasper dreamily, 'we could polish some of them into semi-precious jewellery. Agates, cornelians – and jasper, of course.'

Angela was coming to enjoy the peace of solitary living. 'Wouldn't it be noisy?'

'I looked it up. Tumblers are much more efficient than they used to be, and if you're clever about polishing-powder it needn't take nearly as long as you think. Sandpaper and elbow grease may be quieter, but I get the impression they're too much like hard work.'

'Varnish,' suggested Jane. 'In the fresh air,' she added quickly.

'There are mineral oils—'

'You know I hate working with oil paint.'

'Besides,' said Angela, 'who knows how disgusting something to make pebbles smooth and shiny might smell? I suppose, if you put the tumblers in your vegetable patch the noise wouldn't be too much of a nuisance...'

'Once the clammer is properly repaired,' said Jane, with a stern look for Jasper.

'No electricity.' Jasper frowned. 'I wonder if any of them work by wind-power? We could build our own windmill—'

'No we couldn't,' said Jane.

'—or a water tumbler! Harnessing the forces of nature like they did centuries ago – the tucking mills that made the cloth industry so great in these parts...'

Jane winked at Angela. 'He's been talking to your mother again. We'll ask her for a catchy name, and we could be in business!' She saw Jasper's eyes brighten.

'Like "Tiffler & Thrums" for Miriam,' he said.

Angela looked pleased. 'Not bad, you think?'

'I think! Or perhaps,' recalling Susan's comments on late-running manuscripts and publishers' deadlines, 'we could ask Gabriel Hockaday, or a Binns or two, or Barney Christmas if we catch him in the right mood.'

Angela nodded. 'It's a shame those old boys don't have a wider audience. They're wasted on casual tourists. If we could get them on YouTube they'd go viral in no time.'

Jane frowned. 'Would they enjoy that? If anyone tried filming me when I was working I – I'd seize up, I think.'

'Maybe you wouldn't.' Her husband smiled. 'Haven't you often found people hovering at your back when you've been out sketching? It doesn't usually bother you, does it, unless they crowd too close or make really stupid remarks?'

'*You won't put me in it, will you?*' said the voice of experience, with a grin. 'But that's in real life, not with a camera pointed at me. I think the old gang are at their best with a live audience and wouldn't perform to order nearly as well.'

'They'd certainly miss the tips.' Jasper thought of drinks all round, and laughed. 'How many pints of scrumpy would they think it worth losing?'

'For the chance of overnight success and a worldwide audience,' Angela reminded him.

Jane wasn't sure. 'Unless the audience visited in person and spent money locally and encouraged other tourists to come, it wouldn't be worth it. And even Mickey Binns says there's not enough here to encourage more than casual visitors.'

They pondered this for a while. Angela was frowning.

'This is a pretty cool place at night.' The Mertons looked puzzled. 'The way that Welsh lighthouse blip-blips across the channel and it's always a different effect, depending on the weather…' When unable to sleep, Angela had done a lot of exploring. She felt safer alone at night in Combe Tollbridge than with company in certain parts of London. 'And with no street lights – well, I'd never realised how many stars there are! 'Specially when there's no moon.'

'Exmoor is one of the world's darkest places,' Jane reminded her. 'And here we are, right on the edge. The silhouette of the cliffs against a background of stars…' The artist couldn't find the words: her artistry was visual, not verbal. 'Mother and I went to Llandudno once. You could see why that headland's called the Great Orme. It really does look like a dragon – a huge serpent – a great worm against the sky.'

'I'm surprised there isn't a Tollbridge serpent,' said Jasper. 'In a place like this – small, yes, but full of atmosphere…'

'Perhaps we could invent one,' said Angela. 'When mother rewrites the pamphlets for – for Sam Farley…' Her friends tactfully ignored the faint blush. True, the sheer bulk of Cliddon Hill blocked all mobile reception at Meazel Cleeve, but the end of the pier was far closer for Angela's communication needs than the top of Coastguard Steps.

Jane shook her head. 'No need to invent anything. Your mother says there's heaps of reality in Tollbridge history without making things up. Look at Widdowson's Bakery. Carvy cake – chudleighs with jam and clotted cream – gingerbread – and the legend of the fisherman's wife and the miller from Ploverton just to round things off. Susan says she can really let her writing instincts rip, when she's ready.'

'When.' Susan's daughter smiled. 'Which won't be yet, she says.'

'Mmm,' agreed Jasper. 'With her first draft finished you'd expect her to relax, but she told me, now she sees where the book needs adjusting she can't surface properly until it's sorted.' He looked at Jane. 'She said, before she starts work on the new pamphlets she needs to look further into just how they ran the squire's son out of town.'

'I hope she tells me. They never would, when I was a kid—'

'—and they wouldn't that night we tried asking, either!' Jasper laughed, then frowned. 'I forgot to ask: will she write as Milicent Dalrymple? Or is the name copyright to her book publishers?' Packlemerton's Publicity had come up against this once or twice before.

'She wants to talk it over with Sam,' said Angela, calmly. 'And with Jan Ridd, because she thought a pseudonym like "Lorinda Doone" might be catchy, but perhaps a bit OTT. She wouldn't want to offend anyone by presuming too much.'

'Someone mention me?' They'd been so busy chatting they hadn't noticed the printer make his way towards their table, glass in hand. 'Talk of the Old Gooseberry and here he comes. Mind if I join you? About your mum and my dad's old tourist leaflets, was it?'

'It was.' Angela ignored both the glint in Jasper's eye and the smile in Jane's. 'I was just saying, she doesn't want to upset local feeling by – well, setting herself up as a local expert when she hasn't lived here all her life the way most of Tollbridge has.'

'Nearly all of Tollbridge,' he amended. 'More's the pity. You ask Mickey Binns, college education and halfway round the world – or anyone else coming to us with the eye of an outsider, as it might be yourselves, or Barney Christmas who was away so many years and brought fresh notions back with him. Tollbridge is a grand place, but it's slow to welcome change. And it shows. Many of 'em our age—' with a swift glance round the little group – 'have upped and gone for lack of opportunity. I was lucky, being as there was a job waiting if I chose to take it. My dad, he set up part-time with no more than an old photocopier for the parish magazine, when it got too expensive to have it printed elsewhere.'

He nodded, and drank deep. 'Then it was mission creep, classic. Grew to printing for the parish council and such – forms, minutes, newsletters – then bingo and beetle cards for social evenings, then leaflets for the shop and the pub, for visitors – not that we had many, but still. Small-time stuff kept going thanks partly to Mike Binns, for a while, then Dad moved on to a second-hand colour machine for postcards and such. Most of the business these days is calendars, diaries, basic stuff mostly ordered from outside – plus one or two folk retired to these parts writing their memoirs, and asking if dad or me could print 'em up smart. So he learned himself bookbinding – and I did, too.'

He winked at Jasper, who was fascinated by this tale of a village entrepreneur whose business, like his own, had flourished from a one-man beginning. 'We had hopes of Captain Longstone, submarines being not in the usual way, but that man's a slow writer. Looks like we'll be waiting a goodish while before he finishes.'

'A job worth doing is worth doing well. Not everyone writes as fast as my mother.' Angela had encountered the captain more than once near her home in Meazel Cleeve. One night, as a row of lights moved slowly along the coast of the Severn Sea, he made the casual observation that a container ship was heading for Portbury Docks at the mouth of the Avon. Angela asked how, in the dark, he could tell the vessel wasn't going down-channel to the open sea, and the captain explained the difference between port and starboard lights, and the international rules about passing another vessel in narrow waters.

Angela asked if the same rules applied to submarines when submerged, and did it need radar. Rodney Longstone suppressed a smile as she quickly added that she realised she'd said something silly almost before she said it. He replied that he couldn't expect her to have his expert knowledge any more than he himself could have hers; she agreed it was unlikely he'd understand how to catalogue books by either the Library of Congress or the Dewey system ('Far beyond me, Miss Lilley!') and, after mutual apologies and some amusement, the two loners seemed to reach a distant, but friendly, understanding. As such a friend, Angela felt that if the captain wanted to take his time over his life's work, he should be allowed to do so. She knew from local gossip something of his circumstances, and could understand that he would be wary about letting slip too much information of a personal nature.

Hadn't she herself, similarly cautious, gone so far as to cancel social media, and to change her very name?

'It's a free country yet.' Sam took a lazy pull at his mug. 'As for my work – see here, young Jane, they change of address cards I'm to print for you and Jasper.'

'I said there's no great hurry.'

'We need a firm date for moving in before we post them.' Jasper smiled at Jane. 'We don't want to tempt fate.'

'Oh, yes – but this is the way of it.' Sam took another long drink. 'You'll have heard something of the sort already, I know, but being as it's me that prints 'em and my dad as first wrote 'em, this is more – well, more official, if you like.' He coughed. 'Yes. Well, now. That was a grand picture of old Prue's cottage you did to show your friends where you're to live, and it seems to me – and I'm not alone in this – well, we can use photos in the new booklets for local landmarks, as we've done in the past, only better, but – for the old tales, and for true history, I've a hankering after proper drawings. Like yours. Jan Ridd and others, they agree with me they'd add a touch of real class – if you'd be willing to help us out, midear.'

'Willing to help?' Jane was delighted. 'You really wouldn't mind? You want me to illustrate the – the legend booklets, and the history ones, for you?'

As his tentative proposal didn't seem to have offended a professional artist, Sam could relax. 'Tidn so easy, now, to take photos of a mediaeval silver mine collapsing! Oh, there's all manner of computer tricks these days, I know, but I don't want fakery – I want a true deal, where possible. Honest, so as folk can be sure. A proper drawing's got to be more honest than any – any tricked-up photo.'

Jane, although in full agreement, like Susan Jones had no wish to presume. 'I'd love to do it, if you're sure I wouldn't be treading on anyone's toes.'

'You won't. My cousin Chris Hockaday, he's a photographer by trade, but he knows what I want and knows he can't do such pictures the way I reckon you could draw 'em.'

Jane blushed. 'I can certainly try. And thank you for asking!'

Whereupon the meeting turned to consider what style of drawing might best suit the rewritten tourist pamphlets, once they had been rewritten by Susan Jones.

Chapter Nine

It was one of those now thankfully rare nights when her going-to-bed routine didn't work for Angela. When first she arrived in Combe Tollbridge, she had kept very erratic hours and (she realised) driven her mother mad; but as time passed and life calmed down – especially since her move to The Old Printery – Angela was confident the worst was over. On the whole her confidence hadn't been misplaced, but there were still occasional hiccups and tonight had brought another.

From her bedroom window she craned her neck upwards to admire the thin crescent moon in a stardust sky. Captain Longstone, discussing navigation at sea, had spoken of the shock he'd experienced the first time he saw the constellation Orion south of the equator. 'Very strange feeling,' he said. 'From an intellectual viewpoint I had to expect it, but it was still a surprise to see the great hunter upside down. Being almost symmetrical in outline, it took a second or even third look before I could really credit what I thought I saw.'

Angela searched the internet for star charts, then hunted down a basic astronomy book and now at least could recognise the Plough, the Lion and Cassiopeia. She learned that a full moon made it more difficult, a waning moon less so, to pick out individual stars; she found that in Meazel Cleeve the surrounding hills and trees forced either an almost vertical and limited view of the sky, or a departure from the house for a wider horizon.

She dressed, pocketed her phone, collected keys and a torch – Combe Tollbridge had no street lights – and left the house with the idea of walking round the harbour and perhaps over the bridge to the end of the pier. The Welsh lighthouse flashed from across the Bristol Channel; shadows jumped and retreated as the stately white beam rolled past. Angela walked with a careful tread down the steep slope of Meazel Cleeve.

She glanced over her shoulder. London habits had not completely left her. She stood still. From the other side of Cliddon Hill she saw a faint red glow.

By now she was local enough to know that even Lynton was too far along the coast for Tollbridge to glimpse the weakest ghost of distant lamps. Surely this was no time of night for a firework display? An optical illusion, then. She blinked; rubbed her eyes. The glow persisted. There was one obvious answer she hoped she'd got wrong. She found herself sniffing, and felt foolish: for once there was no breeze to carry the smell of burning from the other side of the hill.

Had the glow grown brighter?

She looked away, then back. She blinked again. It had.

Fire! She tried her phone. She knew the signal never picked up until sea level, if it ever did – but she could hope. There was always a first time.

This wasn't it.

Miriam had a landline. Run down and bang on the door? Run past Harbour Glim to the public telephone box? She hadn't brought any money with her. Was an emergency call free? She didn't know. Should she run back up the Cleeve to Captain Longstone, and bang on his door? She'd feel happier about raising the alarm if she had a second opinion. How much time would be wasted if Miriam was a heavy sleeper? The captain had talked of naval training and watch-keeping duties and being always on the alert...

Angela panted her way to the door of Baker's Cottage; thumped the knocker; rang the bell; caught her breath. A light appeared in an upstairs room. A window rattled open, and the captain's voice rang out.

'Who's there? What's wrong?'

'Me,' gasped Angela. 'I think the church is on fire – my phone doesn't work—'

'I'll be down.'

Within a very short time, he was. Angela stared at the dressing-gown he'd dragged over his pyjamas as he pushed her to one side and strode to the end of the front garden.

'Fire, yes – but it looks more like the Jubilee Hall. I'll dial 999 and then the Hockadays.' He vanished indoors before she could work out what he meant.

She wasn't sure what to do next. She waited at the open door; heard him dial; heard him speak. 'Fire, please – Combe Tollbridge, Stickle Street – the Jubilee Hall, by my reckoning, but I'm in the next valley over – post code?' He snorted. 'No idea. On the right, about halfway down, just before you reach the old school – no, I don't know the postcode for that either. Combe Tollbridge! The main street! Jubilee Hall – you can't miss it – and I'm going there now to find out!'

As he slammed down the handset Angela could hear muttering that was both nautical and eloquent. Very eloquent.

The whirr of the dial followed the slam as she finished catching her breath. 'Hockaday? Rodney Longstone. Looks like fire at the Jubilee Hall – yes, all hands to the pump, indeed. I'll be there as soon as I can – need to phone the Anchor first...'

Angela continued to wait, to watch as that ominous red glow grew redder, and to listen. Rodney Longstone roused big Jan Ridd and told him what had happened. Hurried instructions were issued and understood by both parties; the captain rang off, called to Angela that she needn't wait, and sped upstairs to dress.

He returned to find his doorstep empty and Angela waiting further down the road outside her cottage, clutching the giant can of paint she had used to refresh the Printery kitchen. In the flowerbed behind her was a large, irregular splash of white. 'It was all I could think of,' she said, trying not to sound apologetic when she saw the industrial-sized bucket he'd brought with him. 'I want to help.'

'You've raised the alarm. Well done! Now come with me, Miss Lilley.' The tone was encouraging. Without another word the two hurried down Meazel Cleeve.

They were turning left into Harbour Path when a throbbing wail echoed like the blare of trumpets on the midnight air. 'Good,' said the captain as he began to double down the road. 'They've opened the museum and set the ball rolling.'

'It sounds,' gasped Angela as she ran at his side, 'like an air raid siren.' She recognised the trumpet blare from films and documentaries about the Second World War; she found herself looking for searchlights, listening for enemy bombers. She wanted to yell *Put that light out!* as un-blacked-out bedroom windows began to show that people were awake.

'It is.' Her companion neither panted nor puffed. 'Mr Binns refurbished it rather than see it not working: and it has its uses. This area has a retained fire service. Few Tollbridge people serve because, as fishermen, they're better suited to a lifeboat, if we still had one. The nearest fire appliance is in Combe Ploverton – farmers, landsmen – where they're not so dependent on the tide. We've no room for a fire station anyway. Every second counts.'

Tollbridge was a tumult of footsteps, shouts and bustle as everyone headed toward the flames and sparks dancing high on Stickle Street. Captain Longstone's expert eye had not deceived him. It wasn't the church but the Jubilee Hall that was ablaze.

Since the night a band of (possibly) Ploverton youth had arrived on motorbikes to run riot with doughnuts and wheelies in the old school playground, Barney Christmas had kept the gates padlocked and advised Jerry Hockaday that he could no longer accept responsibility for the safety of the Hockaday minibus and taxi he'd previously allowed to park (at a reasonable cost) on his land. The insurance (said Barney) didn't think it a good idea.

He said nothing about the threatened increase in premiums should the casual arrangement continue.

Hempen Row had never been more than a wide lane. Outside parking would block it. The Hockadays asked the vicar for permission to leave their vehicles on land attached to the Jubilee Hall, and as the taxi and bus were a local asset Mr Hollington was happy to agree. On the following Sunday he preached a sermon about *Doing Unto Others as you would have them Do To You* – a well-intentioned but wasted effort, as none of the rogue bikers was in his congregation to hear it.

Tollbridge knew it would take the Ploverton appliance fifteen minutes to assemble a crew and drive down the valley; other pumps must come even farther and take even longer. As Captain Longstone told Angela, every second counted.

Gabriel Hockaday had moved the minibus to the far end of Hempen Row as his nephew Mickey Binns parked the taxi nearby. Cousin Jerry, with his uncle Mike Binns in charge, was among the doughty crew manoeuvring from the old meeting house a strange contraption that could have been a flattened wooden octopus with hedgehog spikes, squatting on a low platform. The octopus tentacles were stored in coils round huge wooden cleats fixed to a frame; the whole device rolled on lorry wheels, and needed several men to roll it.

The Octopus was another Binns invention. As a child evacuee Mike had been overwhelmed by the strangeness of country life. He'd never known that drinking water didn't come from the mains. Village pumps and garden wells were a nasty shock for many who had only ever turned a tap. Many were the young insides made unhappy by microbes to which their adult protectors had developed lifelong immunity; and Mike Binns, being one of the youngest, was one of the most unhappy. Priscilla Ornedge bought a large iron kettle and thereafter boiled every drop of water on the kitchen range, which water was taken from the village pump rather than from the garden well. Mike, a small but intelligent boy, applied this intelligence to designing a portable (if basic) pump that could draw water from the Chole, pure and fast-flowing from the lonely moor above. The prototype closely resembled the stirrup-pump on which it was based; but Mike had been born to tinker. When local fishermen spoke of bilge pumps, he listened. And learned.

Once wartime and post-war restrictions were finally eased, the money was found for Combe Tollbridge to be connected to the main water supply. While the village pump was kept as a decorative curiosity, most of the garden wells were covered over, though not filled in: it did no harm to think ahead, just in case.

Mike Binns had absorbed his foster-home's just-in-case mentality. You never knew. It might come in handy. From time to time he tinkered with what the little stirrup-pump had gradually become. As he was often joined in his tinkering by Gabriel Hockaday the invention never worked in the same way twice – but it always worked.

Mike now roared his orders. 'Let's get to the corner before we unroll the hose! Make a bucket chain, you others!'

With Jan Ridd directing at one end and Captain Longstone at the other, Tollbridge began to form a hurried snaking line across the main street. The tail of the snake positioned itself as near to the river as it could; the head crept as close to the burning Jubilee Hall as it thought it prudent to go, but there were still gaps. 'Don't block the road until you must,' said the captain. 'When the pumps begin to arrive, stand clear!'

Louise Hockaday saw that most of the village was now present, and stopped cranking the handle of the air raid siren. She stumped home to fetch another bucket.

Brakes were applied; two octopus arms were uncoiled from their cleats and lowered down the high, steep bank of the Chole. Two distant splashes; two brass nozzles, plunging deep. Two men each seized a brass handle to pull and push in rhythm.

Tentacles began to twitch. They rippled; swelled; bulged. The river flowed uphill.

Filled buckets slopped from hand to hand and, at the hall, had what remained of their contents hurled into the inferno. Nobody truly believed the fire could be put out by these puny efforts, but everyone had to try. Angela, sprinting back with empty buckets for a refill, passed her mother struggling to run in gumboots. Susan had grabbed at the first footwear to tumble from the cupboard, and now wished she'd acted a little less on impulse. Milicent Dalrymple, however, might find a use for this experience in her next book but three...

Mike shouted for another tentacle to be brought into use, and it was, but it could never be enough. By the time blue lights and klaxons heralded the arrival of the first official pump, the roof of the Jubilee Hall had collapsed.

And so had most of the bucket chain. The Octopus was allowed to dribble rather than gush. It gurgled into silence. 'No more to be done here,' decreed Jan Ridd. 'Us would only be in the way. Once that-there contrivance is safely packed away it's drinks all round for any that has a thirst – drinks on the house!'

As far more powerful hoses began to play over smoking destruction, fire captains spoke briefly with Jan Ridd and Rodney Longstone before onlookers were chivvied from underfoot. Barriers were set up. Mike Binns and his team coiled and drained the tentacles before sadly trundling the Octopus back to its meeting house lair. They then joined others planning to drown their sorrows in the Anchor. For once, few torches were needed. Glowing red and flashing blue gave more than enough light for that glum, exhausted descent.

Not everyone went to the pub. Some were just too weary: they collected their buckets and returned to bed. The Farley twins needed to reassure their mother, whose knees did not encourage uphill activity, that they had survived the excitement; moreover, the shop and post office must open at eight sharp. Their cousin Sam, self-employed and one of the Octopus crew, said pumping was dry work and he'd tell them later if anything of interest occurred. Jerry Hockaday and Mickey Binns tried to persuade their parents to go home. Louise wanted to be there early next day to tell Olive Farley all about it, and agreed to retire, but her husband and brother-in-law did not. Gabriel and Mike went with those bound for the Anchor.

Captain Longstone was another who went home once the experts took over and he'd made his report. He left most of the talking to Jan Ridd; saw that Angela was busy with her mother and the Mertons; raised a hand in salute, and melted into the darkness. His spirits were low. One of Her Majesty's naval officers – even for those on the Retired List, the Queen's commission never lapses – had no business spreading alarm and despondency. He must try his best to spread no such thing: after all, there was much to celebrate. He couldn't honestly see how the hall could have been saved even had the alarm been raised the instant Angela set out on her walk: it was an old, tired building that dated from the nineteenth century. The whole village had come together to try to save it; they'd done a splendid job, as had the fire appliances from Combe Ploverton and farther afield – but their labour had been in vain. The captain had a strong suspicion it was all going to cost Combe Tollbridge a great deal of money. With a population below four hundred…

In the Anchor, as the events of the night were recounted and embellished, the truth began to emerge. Angela became the heroine of the hour as she was heard telling Jane and Jasper again how, unable to sleep, she had seen a distant red glow on the far side of Cliddon Hill.

Miriam Evans wanted to know why Angela hadn't woken her. Angela explained she didn't know how sound a sleeper she might be.

Miriam nodded. 'And at my great age I might be stricken with deafness, all of a moment.' Despite their growing intimacy she would still tease her young friend over the Susan Jones misunderstanding.

'At your age?' Susan, restless in gumboots, was indignant on Miriam's behalf. 'You're not five years older than me!'

'And both of you so nimble as ninepence,' came the voice of Sam Farley, 'back and forth with buckets as you were – Angela too, of course.' He favoured her with a long, approving look. 'It's thanks to you things didn't get further out of hand. Talk about start in a place as you mean to go on! Well done, midear. We'm all grateful to you.'

Jan Ridd and his wife Tabitha didn't begrudge the expense, but they were relieved when their guests began at last to drift homeward. Jan planned to be awake early so that he could let the vicar know the truth of what had happened before anyone in Ploverton told him the situation was even worse than it was.

Like many parish priests in rural areas, the Reverend Theodore Hollington had more than one parish in his cure. His vicarage was situated in Combe Ploverton. Over the years he'd grown accustomed to the small commotion whenever the fire engine was called out, and beyond sending up a quick prayer that the outcome would be happy paid little heed to what went on in the middle of the night.

Next morning the telephone call from Jan Ridd put him wise.

The two stood in thoughtful silence among other by-standers sadly contemplating the wreck of the Jubilee Hall. A few enterprising citizens with more curiosity than sense had squeezed past the fire brigade's safety barriers for a closer look and come back, sniffing, with muddy ash clogging their boots. The conscientious Revd Theodore and former Police Sergeant Ridd stayed as intended at the edge of the car park. The air was grey, dull, damp; reeking of smoke. Even Mickey Binns, retrieving the Hockaday taxi from the end of Hempen Row, found no jokes to crack with his cousin Jerry, who drove the minibus.

'An uncommon melancholy sight,' said an unexpected voice at the vicar's elbow.

Theodore and Jan turned to find Barney Christmas beside them.

'Yes, it is.' Mr Hollington achieved a smile. 'Nevertheless, we have cause for rejoicing. Things could have been so much worse. It's truly a blessing that nobody was on the premises when the fire started, and that there were no injuries even among those later fighting it. We should be thankful indeed.'

'Amen to that,' said Jan Ridd.

Barney touched the hat he wasn't wearing, and all three men stood together, saying a respectful nothing while they thought how much worse things might have been.

It was Mr Christmas who broke the silence. 'And thankful to know the place was properly insured we should likewise be. If we can.' He coughed. 'The old queen's jubilee – a hundred and twenty years back if a day, and two world wars since the foundation stone was laid... Keeping up to date idn so easy as folk may suppose.' It was the voice of property-owning experience. 'At a guess there'll have been short cuts took unbeknown to the insurance – and even if not, or if such skimping be already known and took into account, they'll still drag their heels over payment. They always do. Trust me on this.'

The vicar sighed. 'I wish I didn't, but I fear I do. We must simply hope, and pray.'

'Hope for the best,' agreed Jan Ridd, 'and pray it won't take too long.'

Barney grunted. 'Oh, they'll play a waiting game. Trust me on this, likewise.'

Jan bridled. 'I phoned first thing, soon as I'd spoke to the vicar, and they said they'd be sending an assessor—'

'—but they'd not say when, would they? Well, did they?' Jan was silent. Barney grimaced. 'A waiting game,' he insisted, 'while we here in the parish can do nought that's needful for the parish all the while they damned – beg pardon, vicar – London paper-pushers stay in their grand offices iffing an' anding over what to do, and when to do it. And when they do decide at last, then it's only half what's wanted – if that!'

'Oh, dear,' said Mr Hollington. He could find little fault in this reasoning.

'I tell you,' said Barney Christmas, businessman. 'Why else do 'ee suppose I stopped work on the old school yonder?'

There was a further silence.

'Regarding the school,' said Barney at last, 'I've had a thought about that. Now, the skittle alley's not so very big for parish doings, I'd say—'

'Big enough for most,' snapped the landlord of the Anchor.

'Oh, most,' agreed Barney. 'Most, but not all.'

'Enough,' retorted Jan.

Barney ignored him. 'And there's the school. Didn work out as planned, the financial downturn being so sudden in nature – though I'm a patient man, and a tourist hotel can wait – but it's stood empty a while now.'

'Needs work doing,' said Jan. The Anchor's skittle alley was in excellent condition. 'You'd have it all fixed up for us, would 'ee, Barney?'

Mr Christmas shrugged. 'The parish council might just care to take it for a month or so, in such an emergency. No doubt we could come to a suitable arrangement—'

'Reckon money d'grow on trees, do 'ee?'

The vicar raised a hand. The bickering subsided. 'If you're thinking of the legacy from Prudence Budd, the proceeds from the sale of Clammer Cottage have been put in a special account to give her executors time to consider how best it might be used for the long-term benefit of the village. As she wished.' He dared them to say anything. They didn't.

'As for the shorter term,' he went on, 'there must be other options for parish activities, when the skittle alley is in use. Combe Ploverton, remember, has its own village hall. The pub also has a skittle alley—'

'But that's cambered!' Jan and Barney spoke as one. The vicar was no skittler, or he would have remembered that while most pub alleys have a level floor, some are constructed with a gentle side-to-side curve. This changes the very nature of the game if players aren't used to it; and non-players can find a cambered surface uneasy walking.

'Cambered,' reiterated Jan. 'The Anchor's far better suited of the two.'

Skittle matches between Tollbridge (flat) and Ploverton were always warmly contested. Tossing for who played the first match of the season in which alley could be tricky for the captain who lost the toss.

'We must hope all can be settled before the season starts,' said Jan.

'Ah,' said Barney. 'And pray.'

While casual matches can occur at any time, the official season runs from autumn to spring. When days are longer than nights the rural south-west finds other occupation, but in the darker months skittles can be a thrilling league sport.

With nine pins rather than ten, like the ball they are all heavy, being made of solid wood. Into the floor of the alley is set a long wooden 'plate' or board on which, in some leagues, the ball must be pitched before rumbling at speed towards its target. Miriam Evans had been right to warn her young cousins about headaches, and the risk to their hearing. Those who follow a skittles team take the sport seriously... and, often, earplugs.

'Hope and pray,' said Barney; then, with the hint of a twinkle: 'The school might need no more than a lick of paint, perhaps.'

Jan frowned at him. 'Paint, and the plumbing checked, and doubtless the electrics too, you old devil.' He hesitated. 'You'd renew the insurance, would 'ee? I heard you cancelled full cover after locking the gates.'

Barney shrugged. 'Easy enough to renew, in a worthy cause. But it's plain you've a hard heart, Jan Ridd, so I'll not press the matter of paint nor plumbing, considering it's to my own benefit. Too long neglected, and any building suffers.' He grinned. 'Worth a try!' Then he sobered. 'But it's in my mind, vicar, that with so old a building as the hall, the insurance might require a new one built to the modern standard, fire alarms and sprinklers and such. My cottages, now. Folk just aren't let by the law to take such risks as we grew up with, for all we *did* grow up to tell the tale.' He was now very grave. 'It worries me that any replacement hall will have to be... well, a sight smaller for our purposes than before, if sufficient money's not forthcoming – where and whosoever that money comes from.'

'I've been thinking the same myself,' said Mr Hollington.

And again the three fell silent.

Chapter Ten

'…half Tollbridge by my reckoning up there at the hall, stood all agape.' Louise Hockaday, rather later than she'd planned, was in Farley's General Stores telling Olive about the fire and its aftermath, filling in such details as the twins might have been expected to miss and elaborating as far as she thought credible. 'A sad sight of ruination, and a smell you'd never credit! And the vicar, poor man, with Jan Ridd and Barney Christmas in a right quandorum over what's to happen now, and how much it will cost.'

'At least nobody was hurt, for which we should give thanks.' Olive shivered to think of the risk her daughters, and everyone else, had run. 'Doubtless Mr Hollington will have extra prayers for Sunday.'

Debbie looked at her mother. 'Today comes first. Louise, did you see any sign of our delivery truck? From the wholesaler,' as Mrs Hockaday looked puzzled. 'Twice a week, remember, and today one of his days, and as a rule much earlier than this.' For the third time she checked the post office clock. 'I thought maybe he'd stopped to look at the fire, same like everyone else.'

'There were all sorts looking on, but so far as I recall that truck would block the greater part of the road if he stopped to gawp. He'd surely know better, with you waiting.'

Debbie frowned. 'Towards the top of the village there's more room than down here – but if you didn see him then he's late, is all. At least today's idn chilled, or frozen, being mostly tinned stuff and paper goods. Loo rolls and handwash will come to no great harm, if they have to sit on the motorway waiting so long as a week!'

They were laughing together over past shortages when Debbie broke off. A shadow darkened the shop's main window. 'And here he comes at last – oh no, tidn he. Why, that's the bakery van. What can the man be thinking of, to stop right outside here?'

'Never mind a greater part,' said Olive. 'It's the whole road will be blocked if our lorry turns up now to find his normal place took. The Widdowson's delivery usually goes down Bridge Lane to the end of the alley, and wheels the flour from there. Oh!'

'That's not him.' Neither Debbie nor her mother recognised the man who dropped nimbly from the driver's seat and strode to the rear of the van. 'He must be new.'

Olive nodded. Tilda stood on tiptoe but couldn't see clearly over the shield of the post office counter.

'I'd best go and ask him to move.' Olive, official postmistress and proprietor of Farley's General Stores, gripped her walking sticks in resolute hands.

'I'll go and *tell* him.' Debbie was faster on her feet. 'If our lorry should turn up now, Louise is right, the whole road will be blocked.'

As she hurried from the shop, Louise spoke with the confidence of the mother and wife of semi-professional drivers. 'This new man would do best driving on down a bit and then backing up into the Legger, if it's Widdowson's he wants.'

As Debbie approached the van there came a loud, unmelodious clang. She jumped. A heavy sack-truck landed on the ground, lurching rather too close for comfort to her toes. The driver, stiff and clearly displeased at being accosted by a stranger, reached inside his van to drag forward a large plastic crate.

'He'll not want to do that,' said Olive to Louise. 'It's crowding even for them that knows the Legger corner – which is why, in the normal way, they never do it.'

It was evident, from the brief exchange observed through the shop window, that the van driver had no intention of moving. His body language implied that he was in far too much of a hurry. While Debbie attempted to explain he loaded a second crate on the sack-truck and, paying her no further heed, trundled his decided way towards the narrow Legger entrance to make the latest delivery to Widdowson's Bakery, at the far end of the crooked lane.

When the bell jangled at the door it was not Debbie, staring wrathfully up Stickle Street in search of the missing lorry, but Rodney Longstone who entered, in search of his peppermint fix. He didn't like to ask how many Captain's Twists remained, but he knew it couldn't be long before the supply ran out. He smiled with relief as Olive nodded a thumbs-up that for today, at least, his sweet tooth would be satisfied.

'Men!' Debbie, still wrathful, marched back in the captain's wake. 'And of course our lorry's nowhere to be seen – but I wish he might turn up this minute while that man's along to the bakery, and do his paint a mischief! Said he don't know this route yet, and the satnav's playing tricks and he's running late, and never give me the chance to explain.' She glared at the hapless Captain Longstone, innocently pocketing peppermints. 'I'm sure he'd have listened well enough if a man had asked him.' Unlike her tragically widowed twin, Debbie Tucker was acrimoniously divorced. 'I've a mind to call Evan Evans at the bakery this very minute and say he's to set that young fellow straight about how things are done in Tollbridge, if he's going to be coming here regular. Men!'

Louise was still keeping watch. 'Save yourself the trouble, young Deb. Seems likely Evan's had a word already – leastways, I'd say someone has. Your friend don't look too pleased.'

Everyone except Tilda (at the counter) and the captain (bashful on behalf of his sex) peered from various vantage points. The van driver was once more flinging doors open, wrestling crates and sack-truck into the back, closing doors with unnecessary force and using even more force to secure the closure. Mid-clang he stopped, and turned to scowl over his shoulder. He shot Farley's a darkling look and mouthed something his audience guessed it was as well they couldn't hear. He stamped to the front of the van, tugged open the sliding door and vaulted into the driving seat. As the door slammed shut the engine fired, and with a jerk he moved off down Stickle Street...

But didn't then head towards the Harbour Path, at the breakwater end of which the turning area would have eased him safely into the route back out of Combe Tollbridge. His post office audience wondered if Evan Evans had informed the new delivery man of this practical arrangement—

And decided he probably hadn't. The van had not reached the Harbour Path corner before, with a squeal of rubber, the driver braked and began reversing jerkily into the Legger to execute a three-point turn.

Perhaps it was inevitable that the wholesaler's truck should now arrive at Farley's.

Summing up the situation, the truck sounded its horn. The flour-delivery van ignored the hint and kept reversing. The truck likewise went into reverse, manoeuvring a short way up Stickle Street to widen the van driver's ultimate line of sight. One nearside wheel bumped up the kerb, then slipped harmlessly down. With so much of Tollbridge in attendance at the scene of last night's fire there were few pedestrians within range.

The doorbell jangled and one of those few appeared. 'Talk about being in a tight corner,' began Angela Lilley—

And stopped. The post office exclaimed as one. From outside had come a very audible crunch, all the more audible because Angela hadn't finished closing the door. There followed a long, rumbling patter of falling debris – a pause – and an explosion of loud cursing.

Captain Longstone's tone was dry. 'More than tight, I'd say.' He glanced at the others. 'I'd hope there were too many witnesses for the culprit to deny responsibility, but a gentle reminder wouldn't come amiss. Just in case.'

A chorus of agreement accompanied a general surge towards the door. The captain spoke quietly. 'Miss Lilley, if you have your mobile phone with you I think Mr Christmas – I believe he owns the damaged property – and his insurance company would be grateful, if you're in the mood for taking pictures.'

Angela nodded. 'I'd thought of going up past the hall during my walk.'

'Good. Mrs Farley,' as he saw Olive move with obvious effort to follow her daughter and the others, 'could you oblige me with a small notebook and a felt-tip pen? Full details should be taken down while memories are fresh – and then perhaps you, or Mrs Jenkyns,' with a bow for Tilda, 'could phone Mr Christmas to let him know what's happened.'

The walls of a cottage built from cob (which is well-puddled clay, mixed thoroughly with chopped straw) can safely rise to a second storey if sufficient time has been allowed for the mixture to dry before the next layer is added. The walls are of necessity several feet thick; and they are sturdy. If properly maintained they can last for several hundred years. If improperly associated with a motor vehicle they can be repaired by local experts (at a suitably expert cost) but make a considerable mess during their initial collapse. In a cob cottage the fireplace and chimney are usually of brick, or local stone. These chimneys are huge: they stand with their feet firmly on the ground and their heads often higher than the ridge of the roof. A poorly-drawing chimney will have its efficiency further improved by the addition of a terracotta pot.

Terracotta smashes with a highly dramatic effect on the metal roof of a delivery van.

The van driver, any thought of escape thwarted by a small but growing crowd of residential indignation, was blustering his way through the feeblest of excuses – the satnav said Harbour *Path* and he didn't trust it – as Angela set to work with her mobile phone. Captain Longstone left her to it and headed with his notebook for the wholesaler's lorry, whose driver gave every sign of wishing to be well away from the whole situation.

'Your name and address, please.' The captain had already, with a flourish, noted the number of the truck and the company name emblazoned on the side. 'It will help with the insurance claim if we can supply as many details as possible.'

The driver shrugged. 'Mine won't help. Didn't really see what happened – too busy trying not to run up on the pavement, reversing like I was. When everything went smash I had to look frontwards instead of back, but until then...' Once more he shrugged.

Captain Longstone favoured him with a look Angela might have envied. Years of presiding over Requestmen-and-Defaulters had hardened Rodney Longstone's heart against the most inventive of excuses, though if his sense of humour was tickled he'd always been willing to soften a little, within the confines permitted by *Queen's Regulations and Admiralty Instructions*. There was nothing now, however, to amuse him in the truck driver's evident wish to Keep Out Of It in solidarity with his fellow delivery man. 'This won't take long,' said the captain sternly. The driver met his eye, and yielded to a superior force.

Matilda Jenkyns popped out to say that Barney Christmas wadn answering his phone and when they'd tried Jan Ridd instead, Tabitha said he was up to the Jubilee Hall with the vicar and Barney doubtless there too, wondering if he could buy the wreckage at a knock-down price. This made locals smile, even as Louise Hockaday confirmed the guess to be correct.

'So nobody to take a message,' she added. 'Cause for why, they're all at the hall who might otherwise answer the phone.'

The Royal Navy trains its officers to make swift, intelligent decisions. 'I'll go and fetch him,' said Captain Longstone. Apart from Angela he must be the youngest person present. 'Mr Christmas should be here – and,' to the truck driver, 'thank you for your assistance. No doubt you'd now like to get on with your delivery to the shop.'

'He'll get on with it,' said Debbie. 'We've been waiting.'

The captain soon found his quarry, and briefly described the incident. He and Barney were promptly escorted back down Stickle Street by a group of blatant eavesdroppers who'd found that, after a while, smoking ruins lacked excitement. They came downhill in search of action, which a tumbled chimley pot and a brick chimley stack all to smithereens across the highway must surely afford. And there'd be some fun with shovels, brooms and buckets to work off the fidgets, having stood looking on for such a length of time at the Jubilee Hall.

Once Mr Christmas had withered the guilty van driver with a darkling look he ignored him, turning with a smile to Angela. 'You've picture-proofs to show, I understand. I'm thankful to both yourself, midear, and the cap'n for thinking of it. When you own property there's already a sight too much paperwork, even in the routine nature of ownership – and when accidents befall, there's a whole heap more. But,' and he withered the driver again, 'there's nobody will be able to maintain any argument on who's to blame when there's photos of the occurrence set before them.'

As Angela produced the evidence it became clear that Mr Christmas, especially in daylight, was unaccustomed to pocket-sized television screens. His old eyes (he said) were indeed too old for newfangled gadgetry so small he'd be fearful to take hold lest he should drop it. Angela tilted the phone to and fro, which certainly helped, although a retreat with Barney into nearby shadow helped rather more. He blinked, and nodded, and was pleased to admire the work of her swiping forefinger as the pictures scrolled slowly past.

Then he sighed. 'Tidn that I'm ungrateful, midear, for that would be far from the case. It's a good turn you and the Cap'n have done me, I know – and doubtless I'll be able to see and understand still better, once there are proper printed photos a man can hold, and keep in a file, and study at his leisure.'

'It's very easy to download—' Angela began, then realised she must be talking a foreign language to someone at least half a century behind her modern times. 'Yes, of course you can have printed photos if you want them. I imagine the insurance company will accept them as an email attachment, but don't worry about that now. Once I get home I can easily do you some prints from my laptop…' She saw his look of disappointment. 'Mother's place is closer, but I don't like to disturb her when she's using her computer. At this stage in the book she's almost bound to be.'

Barney brightened, and winked. 'Safer to leave her be. Mickey Binns says our Susan can be terrible in her wrath – as doubtless you'd agree – when it's a case of work for money, not for love.'

Lightbulb! 'I know who lives close and would be far more convenient – and she's sure to have the proper glossy paper, which I haven't, because she often turns her pictures into greeting cards, or sells them as prints: Jane Merton.'

'Ah.' After a moment's thought, Barney's eyes gleamed. 'Ah, yes! An easy trot along the Harbour Path and no hills to climb, me having gone up Stickle Street once already this morning, which at my age should suffice… Let's go!'

He took firm hold of Angela's arm, and she was whisked from the scene of the cottage collapse by a cottage owner who was nowhere near as frail as he liked to pretend, though it would have worried her if he'd become involved in the clearance work now being organised by Jan Ridd. It must be some years since Barney Christmas handled a shovel, or wheeled barrow-loads of rubble about. When repairs were needed at any of the properties he owned he always paid someone else to do them, unless it was work so light it could be fixed with no more than a hammer, a screwdriver or a small spanner. 'He says,' Angela heard from more than one of his tenants, 'he's worked harder than most for longer than most, so it's time and beyond he put his feet up. And no blame to the man. What be the point of making money if tidn put to good use once made?'

The unofficial turning area at the breakwater end of Harbour Path was overlooked by Trendle Cottage, set snugly under the impassable cliff that also served as the garden wall. Trendle was another property owned by Barney Christmas, and was currently rented by the Mertons as they waited for Prue Budd's old home to be remodelled to their requirements. Angela hoped one or other of her friends would be in. Barney had seemed polite but was obviously dismayed that she couldn't produce 'proper printed' photos on the spot: the very old, like the very young, wanted instant gratification and didn't always understand why they couldn't have it. Well, at least he hadn't thrown a tantrum! Or rather, he hadn't yet. She wondered what would happen if they found nobody at home when they reached the end of Harbour Path – but so far, so good. He was chatting in a perfectly reasonable way as they made their way past Harbour Glim Cottage, home to Miriam Evans.

On automatic conversational pilot Angela pondered Miriam, who seemed very far from being in any second Difficult Age. Not spinning, nor weaving, nor dyeing could happen in a hurry, but never once did she express impatience over time wasted. As to Miriam's best friend... Angela was still uncertain. It had been some years since she and her mother shared a home: long enough to grow a little strange to each other. For both, life had developed a new focus; was still developing. Angela knew her removal to The Old Printery had given them a welcome chance to catch their breath, relax – and think.

'Shall I knock, or will you?' The Mertons were Angela's friends, but Barney Christmas was their landlord.

Barney was older than his companion and untroubled by niceties of etiquette. 'Ring the bell will do.' It was a brass bell, hanging by a brass chain from a neatly-bent nail hook on the door frame, and with a weathered pull-rope of elaborate braid, knotted in plain white cord by Mike Binns. Mike charged tourists extra for fancy ropework in coloured cord because that wasn't the way he'd been taught by Ralph Ornedge. Barney had long ago chosen to forget all the ropework he'd ever known, and paid Mike in cider for his expertise. Now he wanted to be sure he was getting his money's worth, and pulled mightily on the braided rope.

A burst of clanging, an opened window, an open door, a greeting; the situation explained, and the phone handed over. An invitation to Mr Christmas to come on through – Angela needed no invitation – to the workroom, to take a seat, to watch the technology do its stuff. 'You can choose which photos you think give the best idea of what happened.' Jane produced a box of photograph paper to reload the printer. 'Jasper will run through them all with you first, on the laptop. I'll put the kettle on.'

They all agreed that the insurance company would find it hard to blame anyone but the delivery man for the accident. Chimneys, even those massive ground-to-sky vernacular stacks that stand square and proud on local streets, are not often known to make suicidal leaps from their appointed place into the path of a moving vehicle.

'They'll try to argue,' gloated Mr Christmas, 'but there it is.' He nodded at the screen. 'That's evidence, cleared away though now it be. That's proof – and again, midear, I thank you and Cap'n Longstone for this.'

'I'm glad I was able to help.' Angela slipped the phone into her pocket.

'I'm glad we are able to help.' Jasper was scrolling again through the photos. 'Maybe it would be easiest to print all of them. Certainly it would be quicker.'

'All of them in monochrome,' said Jane, 'plus representative shots in colour to give the overall idea. Details often show up better in black and white,' she explained to an interested Barney. 'Your eye's not distracted or misled by seeing what you expect to see.' Then she sighed. 'I'd meant to paint that view one day, only I never found the time even for photos. And now it's too late. You'll rebuild, I suppose, but it won't be the same.'

'Ah.' The gleam had returned to Barney's eye. 'Rebuilding. Yes. Tidn safe, is it, to leave that cottage of mine to joggle his-self to the ground causing a hazard next time a lorry is minded to drive past. Suppose a mother had a baby in a pram!' Gravely, he shook his head. 'Only, we've a cruel lack of skilled men in these parts for setting to prop up they walls – always excepting them as you two have got so hard at work on Cousin Prue's place...'

Angela choked, and smothered a grin. She knew now why the old man had been so keen to drop in on Trendle Cottage.

The Mertons understood, too. They glanced at each other, faintly smiling.

Jane, though an artist, had a ruthless streak shared only sometimes by Jasper. This turned out to be one of those times.

'Of course,' he said at once. 'Health and Safety – not to mention the police, and the insurance – wouldn't like it if you had to delay starting the necessary repairs.' Barney began to nod, as if at a bargain concluded. 'Of course,' said Jasper again, 'it would mean we might have to extend our stay here,' waving a casual hand, 'depending on what the builders find when they have to stop work at our cottage to start work on yours.'

Mr Christmas looked at him.

Jasper looked back. After a pause: 'Jane and I once had the builders in. Once. We know all too well how even the simplest job can end up taking far longer than it was meant to – which would be inconvenient for us, to say the least.' Then he smiled. 'Of course,' for the third time, 'in the circumstances I'm sure we could come to a suitable arrangement.'

Barney opened his mouth. Jasper forestalled him. 'How about a fifty per cent reduction for any full week we have to stay on beyond the end of our original lease?'

Mr Christmas stared, then began to laugh. 'Worth a try,' he said, eyes bright. 'What would 'ee say to three parts of four, instead?'

Jasper laughed with him. 'How about two thirds?'

Mr Christmas regarded him with growing respect. 'Final week free,' he suggested. 'Tidn so unreasonable. You said you'd be glad to help.'

Jasper countered this with a demand for a fortnight. Barney offered ten days.

Jane and Angela realised the two were enjoying the exchange so much it was likely to continue beyond the patience of most normal people. Jane beckoned to Angela, telling her husband that while he and Barney were making up their minds, the two girls would check things out at Hempen Row because it was all theory, so far, and a progress check on Clammer Cottage would give both parties the full facts, and a sensible position from which to negotiate.

'We'll go past the Legger on our way, to see what's what – and we'll ask Jan Ridd, or someone else who ought to know, how long they think it might take to put things right. Then we'll see who's working up at Clammer Cottage today and ask them to speak to Mr Christmas just as soon as they can.'

The two friends giggled together for most of their subsequent walk…

Until they joined the excited group clustered at the entrance to the Legger.

Barney had been wrong to say the rubble was cleared away. Clearance had certainly begun – was almost complete – but work had been halted near the base of the fallen chimney. A disorderly heap of broken bricks seemed to shelter something of great interest. Jane and Angela drew close. A crude metal hook protruded from a small, leathery globe that was partly covered by a pale brown membrane dotted with dark specks…

'It – it can't be… a shrunken head,' breathed Angela. Jane was speechless.

'No,' said Louise Hockaday. 'It's an ill wish – only, we don't know whose.'

'We can guess.' Warily, Olive Farley leaned across on her sticks to examine, without touching, the dark and shrivelled shape. 'The two sides of that family never did agree.' She shook her head. 'But I'd no notion the trouble went back so far. From the looks of it 'tis a hundred years old, if it's a day.'

'Two hundred, more like.' Louise, conscious of Olive's proximity, prodded bravely with the ferrule of her thumbstick but then stepped back, as the little sphere rocked and metal clinked. 'Two hundred years.' She did her best to sound confident; she almost achieved it. 'Who – whoever would have thought of such a thing?'

For a moment or two, nobody said a word.

Then there came a tentative suggestion from among the onlookers. 'We did perhaps ought to fetch Captain Longstone?'

'No.' On this, at least, the two old ladies could agree. They spoke as one. Their eyes met. Who would blink first?

Jane still could not speak. Angela cleared her throat. 'Why should the captain know anything about this… ill wish?'

'Lives in old Conjuror Baker's house, don't he?' someone said. 'But nobody's ill-wished him – meaning, if harm should be directed against anyone, well, tidn Captain Longstone.'

'It might be best—' ventured Olive.

'Conjuror?' asked Angela.

Louise sniffed. 'Superstition,' she said, firmly. Too firmly? 'No more.'

Olive was undeterred. 'It might be best for Barney Christmas to be fetched, being as he's the only one of that family left, to take up the charmed onion and… deal with it.' She looked a challenge at her old friend. 'For why? For 'cause, even if it was a – a true magic, whoever's name be writ on that paper is long gone and can't be harmed. There's no need for the spell to linger.' She didn't sound entirely sure of this. 'But Barney, now he owns the place outright he could well think it bad luck to have – to have even the memory of an ill wish lingering.' Again she caught Mrs Hockaday's eye. 'As would anyone,' she added.

Louise said nothing. Olive turned to Angela. 'Anyone know where Barney's gone? Went off with you, didn he, some while since?'

Jane at last found her voice; it shook a little. 'He and – J-Jasper are talking terms for – for a rent reduction if we agree to delay the b-building work at Clammer Cot—'

Sudden laughter silenced her. The crowd seized this opportunity to lighten the mood. Why, such behaviour was no more than to be expected from Barney Christmas! They wished Jasper success in the negotiations, but doubted he would win. Barney would doubtless be here any minute, and could then deal with… what remained once the tidying of the road was safely done. They must get on with the job before he arrived.

They did so. They swept and shovelled neatly round that disconcerting sphere without once getting too close. Jane's quick eyes fastened on the metal hook and what it held in its sinister grasp.

'Pins,' she said with a gulp. 'A piece of paper pinned to – an onion, did someone say?'

Olive nodded. 'And the name of the ill-wished spelled out by the ill-wisher.'

'Not a curse,' put in Louise hurriedly. 'An ill wish is all – and superstition, these days.'

'From long ago,' said Olive. 'As the onion withers and fades in the chimley heat, so is it – so was it – for the one bearing that name.' She looked again at Louise. 'Not that there's anyone holds such beliefs these days.'

'Nobody,' affirmed Mrs Hockaday. 'Such ideas belong to the past.'

One of the sweepers looked up from his shovelling. 'I'll warrant Captain Longstone has good fortune these days, living as he do in the conjuror's house.'

Angela looked a question. 'A seventh son,' said Louise, 'means – used to mean – a conjuror. A white witch, some might say.'

'Never black,' agreed Olive. 'No evil eye, no overlooking – oh, no.'

'No,' said Louise. 'Always magic for good, never for bad. If the one pinned and named in such a way was to suspect an ill wish but have no idea who or where it might be, he'd ask a conjuror to speak a more kindly charm to undo the mischief – in days gone by.' She and Olive gazed down at the onion, still without touching it. 'I wonder if they ever did so?'

Olive said the sooner Barney Christmas turned up the better it would be for all concerned. Not, of course, that anyone believed such things these days.

'Of course not,' murmured Angela and Jane together.

'We'll go back and fetch him right away,' added Angela; and they went.

The two erupted into Trendle Cottage in a breathless confusion of bricks, pins, paper and onions that had Jasper begging them to make up their minds which was to tell the story, and would the other please keep quiet while it was told.

Barney was struggling to his feet. 'Seems I'm wanted.' He nodded to his host. 'Finish our liddle chat later. No peace for anyone till this affair's sorted.'

'We'll come too,' said Jasper, his curiosity aroused. 'Safety in numbers, you know.'

Back at the fallen chimney the sweeping and shovelling was done. Neat but bulky piles of rubble made irregular waves along the cottage wall that faced the road. The ill-wish onion lay, a silent menace, in the middle of a dusty patch of tarmac. An uneasy, slowly growing crowd muttered at a safe distance. Even the Farley twins had abandoned all pretence of work and left the shop to join the mutterers.

The crowd gladly parted to allow Mr Christmas through.

'Ah,' was all he said, at first. 'Like that, is it?'

'It is,' said Louise.

'Ah,' he said again. There was a pause. Feet shuffled; throats were cleared.

'So what do 'ee reckon to it, Barney?' asked Olive at last.

As all attention focused on him, Mr Christmas savoured the moment.

During the walk back from Trendle Cottage, Barney had been able to think. Explaining the situation to his townie escort had wonderfully concentrated his mind. He was glad now to find that Olive Farley was still among the onlookers.

'Ah, well, can't leave that-there there, can us?' he drawled. 'Untidy. If you'd give me a lend of your wedding teapot, Olive Ridd, I'd be obliged.'

'My teapot?' Mrs Farley stared.

'The silver teapot kept for best?' Tilda was visibly upset.

'That's for why,' said Barney. 'Silver. No charm gets past true silver.'

Debbie was quicker than the rest of her family. 'And a spoon. I'll fetch them.'

'With a long handle, mind!' Was Mr Christmas quietly laughing at his less well-travelled friends? It was hard to tell. 'And then you, Louise Hockaday, you'll fetch out the key to the old meeting house and we'll lock it safe away inside. If that museum's ever opened—'

'My wedding teapot?' cried an indignant Olive. 'That's no museum piece!'

'It's got a lid,' said Barney. 'For now, it must serve.'

Debbie Tucker reappeared in triumph, bearing a gleaming teapot and a tablespoon. Tilda moaned softly and fumbled for a handkerchief. Olive looked helplessly at Louise.

Barney considered the walking stick he used more for dignity than for support; and the teapot; and the tablespoon; and the onion. 'Need three hands,' he decreed. 'And bending, besides.' He turned to Jane. 'If you'd take my stick, midear…'

It was a reassuring performance, and by the end had everyone smiling. Jasper allowed Barney to balance on his shoulder as the old man instructed Angela to take more photos 'for history as well as the insurance'. Jasper was handed the tablespoon, and knelt awkwardly to guide the withered onion into the mouth of the teapot where a stooping Mr Christmas held it open. Barney made great play over aches, pains and advancing years, and said he was tempted to ill-wish his ancestor himself, for causing so much botheration, but would save his threats for the van driver who'd started this whole nonsense in the first place.

The onion once in the teapot and the lid safely down, Barney told Louise it was time to make for Hempen Row and the key of the meeting house. Mrs Hockaday began to raise a protest on behalf of Mrs Farley, but he cut her short.

'For now,' he reiterated, 'it must serve.' He took back his stick from Jane, returned the spoon to Debbie, and handed Jasper the teapot. 'You come with me, young man. May as well check on Clammer Cottage while I'm up there. Talk to the builders...'

Barney and his entourage set off. Those who stayed behind returned to their own affairs, and tried not to show their profound relief that Mr Christmas had taken such masterly control of a problem of superstition that nobody, these days, believed in.

Nobody!

Chapter Eleven

It was far later that day when, with everything finally resolved to general satisfaction, Jasper settled down to research what he could about seventh sons, white witches, and ill-wishing spells. The more he read the more intrigued he became, and the further from his original subject he was led.

'If Prue Budd was born a Christmas, we should ask where her side of the family lived. Nobody seems to know why the two sides didn't get on – but imagine, Jane! There might be something in one of the Clammer Cottage chimneys for ill-wishing Barney's ancestors just the same way the other ancestor, whoever it was, tried to ill-wish them.'

Jane, sitting nearby with her sketchbook, was shocked. 'From what I remember of Prue she'd never be so – so mean.'

'Well, I'm with you on that, but her ancestors could have been right whatsits. After all, someone must have thought Barney's were, if it was one of them whose name was written and put up the chimney – or if it was his name pinned and put there by someone else... I'm not exactly sure just yet how it worked.'

Jane doodled a cascade of onions spilling from a chimney to fill a handsome wrought-iron grate. She added a set of fire-dogs, a pair of bellows and a toasting-fork, followed by a bulging bag of chestnuts. Feeling hungry, she thought of toasted cheese, and Ben Gunn.

She turned to another page and sketched a desert island with a distant sail approaching. Closer to the island she drew a small boat, tossed by rough water as it drifted too close to a coral reef. Would it capsize – or struggle on safely to the shore?

Jasper interrupted her train of thought before she'd decided between wreck and rescue. 'We might find a child's shoe up the chimney, or animal bones – perhaps the skull of a horse – or a bullock's heart pierced by three iron nails—'

'Ugh,' said Jane. 'Why?'

'To protect those in the house against evil spirits entering when they're at their most vulnerable – like, asleep. Without sympathetic magic the bad guys could come down the chimney or through the doors or windows even when they're shut. If they can't get past the talisman they have to go elsewhere.'

'Seems rather hard on the people living elsewhere.'

He read on. 'You sometimes find a mummified cat in—'

'Shut up,' said Jane.

'Or a witch bottle. That wouldn't be so bad. Full of mysterious dark liquid, the cork studded with pins – iron again, you see…'

Jane stopped listening. She sketched a sharp-featured hag flying a broomstick through the night, a bottle in one hand as she guided her broom with the other. She drew a crescent moon just where the point of the witch's hat would catch it; she added a cat, very much alive, balanced on the witch's shoulder, smacking with its paws at the stars.

'…we might find something of the sort right here!'

Jane surfaced at once. 'We're finding nothing. Think of the soot.'

With decision, Jasper closed his laptop. The romantic in him was fully awake. 'I'll get the flashlight. Don't worry, my love. There are such things as dry cleaners—'

'Not in Tollbridge there aren't.'

'—and washing machines, and showers—'

'And face masks, and goggles – and scrubbing brushes, I suppose. Oh, all right.' Jane shook her pencil at him. 'But don't you dare make a move towards that fireplace until every single inch of the floor has been covered with newspaper.'

Jasper's raid on the Trendle Cottage recycling yielded insufficient protective acreage for Jane's peace of mind. The Mertons took their news updates from online sources, from television and from radio. Combe Tollbridge, deep in its English valley, received signals from Wales more easily than from England: Jane and Jasper could have gone bilingual if they'd wanted. Most of their leisure reading was in the form of periodicals and magazines, which Jane at once rejected. Broadsheet or nothing, she ruled. Tabloid pages would require paperweights, and someone was bound to trip over them. Meekly, Jasper went to Farley's and was surprised to find just how few broadsheet daily papers were still printed.

'So I bought dust sheets.' With pride for his quick thinking he flourished a bundle of folded fabric. 'Debbie Tucker asked if we'd done a deal with Barney to redecorate this place, and would I like brushes and paint as well, but I said we hadn't, and no thanks – and everyone laughed. I'm surprised they didn't ask why I really wanted them.'

'Now you've gone the speculation will run riot.'

He grinned. 'They probably think I'm planning to do away with you. These sheets will save the price of a coffin when I bury you in the garden.'

'Not until we're living in Clammer Cottage, with a much bigger garden. Barney's next tenants after us might grow vegetables the same as you want to, and they'd be sure to dig in just the right spot to find my mouldering corpse. The finger of suspicion would point immediately to my wicked spouse.'

'Oh, by the time we're able to live there I'll have worked up the world's most unbreakable alibi.' He sighed. 'I'm glad we sorted things out with Barney and the builders, and being incomers of course I'd hate to set people's backs up – but I do hope it won't take an age for us to get out of this place and start living in a place of our own.' He looked at Jane. 'I wonder... It wouldn't be tactful to drop hints about bringing in outside help – would it?'

'No idea. We could always ask Susan, or ask Angela to ask Susan in a tactful sort of way.' Jane was as keen as Jasper to start on the new life they'd planned. 'After all, she bought Corner Glim Cottage and had it completely remodelled for herself—'

'—which is why Angela couldn't stay there very long—'

'—but I've no idea who did the job, local or otherwise – or whether local people minded if it was otherwise.'

'We'll find out later.'

When the dust sheets were spread to Jane's satisfaction over the rented carpet it was frustrating to discover the batteries in Jasper's flashlight had died. He returned to Farley's and, together with spare batteries, bought a second flashlight. Combe Tollbridge had for years (apart from the blackout) routinely carried torches of various sizes at night. After the war the fishing village resisted all suggestion that street lighting might be installed. Street lighting cost money! Eating fish improved the brain; the brain controlled the eyes; therefore, eating fish was good for local business, and cheaper than extra taxes. Why, curtains were easy enough to pull open, if needful!

Sketchbook in hand, Jane withdrew to the kitchen as Jasper pursued his investigations. The kettle was filled and set ready to boil; mugs and teabags waited. The coffee machine had been one of those items sent to storage before the move from London, when Jane began to wonder if it was more than city life that was making them restless. Might it be their daily fix of high-quality caffeine? Neither of them cared for herbal tea, though they could enjoy Earl Grey at moments of stress.

She feared such a moment would shortly occur. Brooding again on building delays, and on Barney Christmas's fallen chimney and what had fallen with it, she'd suddenly remembered that Barney had in passing mentioned paying good money for 'another ole chimley' to be swept – just before he put Trendle Cottage on the rental market. 'Oh, dear,' said Jane, as through the dividing wall she heard scuffling, and muffled oaths.

At least Jasper wasn't going to fire the vicar's borrowed shotgun up the chimney in order to dislodge the soot. Lord Peter Wimsey's vicar had tried this, and look what happened.

'Thank goodness there isn't a cellar,' said Jane.

'Who are you talking to?' demanded a voice from the next room, after a pause.

'Me,' she called back. 'Don't worry.'

Another pause. Jane felt guilty.

'How's it going?'

A lengthy pause. Jane made sure the sink was empty, the soap dispenser ready and the kitchen towel to hand.

'Jasper, are you okay?'

A short pause.

'Yes – and no.' She heard stamping, and the rhythmic thumps of someone dusting himself down. 'But it could be worse.' Jasper appeared in the doorway with a smeared face, blackened forearms, and empty hands.

'No luck, then.' Jane made it a statement, not a question.

He shook his head. Quickly she turned on the hot tap, picked up the soap dispenser, and prepared to squirt.

He stared at her as he held out his hands. 'You remembered he'd had the chimney swept!' He lathered with great energy. 'I do think you might have told me before I started poking about in there.'

'Sorry. I only remembered after you'd started, and then it seemed a pity to spoil your fun just in case they might have missed... anything they might have missed.'

'But didn't miss, more's the pity. There's nothing there – but I've had a thought. Now the builders aren't working at Clammer Cottage, we can have the place to ourselves whenever we want!'

'Tomorrow,' said Jane, and handed him the towel.

Saying *tomorrow* committed the Mertons to a night's rest before the next stage of the adventure, but to her surprise Jane's night held little rest. She'd never entirely forgotten the pony phase of her childhood, but she hadn't expected her thoughts, and later her dreams, to be as troubled as they became at the prospect of finding the skull of a horse – or finding any bones at all – in the chimney of a home where she hoped to spend many happy years. She hadn't been greatly bothered by Jasper's investigation into the Trendle Cottage chimney: Trendle Cottage was rented from Barney Christmas. As Louise Hockaday and the others had said of the ill-wishing onion, if it was anyone's problem it belonged to Barney. Jasper had carried the silver teapot and its contents without hesitation...

But now Clammer Cottage belonged to Jane and Jasper Merton.

Therefore, Jane did not sleep particularly well. She knew they'd have to investigate that chimney now, or spend the rest of their time in Tollbridge wondering... But she was fond of cats! She had no particular antipathy towards cows – or bulls! If only Jasper hadn't researched so far beyond the matter of the ill-wishing onion. If only she and Angela had never seen it in the first place – had never encouraged him in any way to fire up his imagination...

Angela.

'I've been thinking.' Jane stifled a yawn as she sipped strong tea and nibbled a thin slice of Widdowson's celebrated carvy cake. Jasper, busy with a rather more robust breakfast, was eager to be up and away. 'I bet Angela would like to come with us. When it's okay to talk to Susan again – more than just pass the time of day, I mean – if we find anything of interest, she can tell her about it properly. She might want to use it in one of the Lorinda Doone booklets.' Susan's tentative pseudonym had been approved by Tollbridge as a rather clever notion. 'I'll take my sketchbook and the camera, if you like, but I'm hardly an impartial witness, the way Angela would be.'

Jasper cut low-fat-fried bread into chubby soldiers, which he decorated lavishly with scrambled saltmarsh eggs from Miriam Evans. 'Toss you for who climbs Meazel Cleeve to fetch her.' When Sam Farley departed The Old Printery for the other side of the harbour he'd taken with him, along with his goods and chattels, his telephone number. While the telephone connection remained, Angela was still waiting for the landline to be allocated its new identity.

'Oh, I'll go.' He could then start without her; might find whatever there was to find before she joined him.

'Sure?' He was savouring the last of the scrambled eggs, gulping tea, glad to reach the bottom of the mug. 'My legs are longer than yours—'

'So, you'll reach Clammer Cottage much faster on your own than with me, and I know you're keen to get started. Angela and I will be as quick as we can, but if you want to start without us feel free. Just make notes of anything Susan might find useful!'

Having thus neatly deflected inconvenient questions, Jane settled to her tea and cake with an improved appetite. If Jasper didn't spot the flaw in her argument…

He didn't. He was keen to be up and doing. He went.

Angela was coming down Meazel Cleeve as Jane, having delayed as long as she realistically might, turned the corner from Harbour Path to start climbing.

The two greeted each other. Jane issued her invitation.

'But,' objected Angela at once, 'if he's gone on ahead to poke about by himself and gets covered in soot he won't find it easy to make notes, will he?'

Jane enlarged on her reasoning. Angela nodded. She'd gone through a horsey phase, too: most little girls did. And although she preferred dogs to cats, she nevertheless classed herself as an animal lover.

'I'll just let Miriam know I won't be along till later.' The "Tiffler & Thrums" name had been approved, but any website was for the future. Angela was having too much fun learning, and Miriam too much fun teaching, the basics of handwoven textiles to think about much else.

Jane felt almost cheerful. This second delay, legitimate and not wilfully manufactured, must surely save her from the grim discoveries with which her imagination had filled Clammer Cottage. Just because she'd never had any creepy experiences when she visited the Budds all those years ago didn't mean there was nothing creepy to experience. She'd been young and innocent; the Budds had been kindly and protective of the liddle maid who heard their stories and ate their sweets and, clearly, couldn't have her innocence corrupted.

'Did he remember something to cover the floor?'

Jane stopped in her tracks. She closed her eyes, envisaging her husband's hurried and enthusiastic departure from home. 'Yes,' she said, with an artist's certainty.

'Good,' said Angela. 'He won't be too popular with the builders if he makes a mess of whatever they've done so far.'

So far – and no farther. Jane could have groaned as, turning into Hempen Row, she saw Jasper, dust sheets under one arm, exchanging pleasantries with Louise Hockaday near the old tin tabernacle. She'd evidently encountered him while heading out for her regular give-and-take with Olive Farley in the shop. All the delaying tactics had been wasted. Jasper hadn't yet gone anywhere near Clammer Cottage.

'Too bad,' said Angela. 'You did your best.'

'It can't be helped.'

'It could be worse. If you'd missed me you'd have been on your own when he found – what he finds. If,' finished Angela, as brightly as she could, 'he finds anything at all.'

They hailed Louise, who looked pleased to see them. She greeted Angela in particular with a knowing smile, though she said little beyond a brief exchange on the stirring events of the day before. The party soon dispersed: Mrs Hockaday to stump her way down to the post office, no doubt to sympathise with Olive on the appropriation of her wedding teapot, and the three younger ones to the end of the road where Jane, uncluttered by impedimenta, opened the gate.

Jasper marched through the gate and up the short path. At the front door he dropped the dust sheets, fumbled with the key and went inside. Jane and Angela exchanged silent but speaking looks, collected the dust sheets, and followed him.

'Not until these are down!' cried Jane as she saw him lean into the fireplace, flashlight in hand. 'Don't you dare!'

He retreated, a guilty grin on his face, his eyes bright. Angela held out one edge of a folded dust sheet – 'Miriam says it's furdled' – and urged him to assist in unfurdling the fabric in order to spread it on the floor.

'Furdle, twirdle, tiffler and thrums. You're picking up the local lingo, all right.' Jasper chuckled as he helped with arranging the dust sheets. 'From Miriam, I think you said?'

'And others.' Angela ignored his evident amusement. 'My mother finds all sorts of dialect words in her researches, you know. She was the one who told Miriam about "tifflings" – it wasn't the other way round.'

'How's the book going?' Jane asked quickly. 'Or doesn't she say?'

'I don't ask.' Angela hadn't forgotten the kitchen timer, the indoor sunglasses, the onion skins and similar bars to mutual understanding. 'I don't see that much of her at the moment, anyway, but when I do I don't want her to think I'm checking up on her. From what Miriam says she's getting through the second draft okay, so it probably won't be too long before she surfaces properly again.'

'Which is sure to please Mickey Binns.' The dust sheets down, Jasper vanished into the fireplace before either Angela or Jane could quell him with a look. His spirits were high, spurred on not only by the thrill of the chase but also by the part he'd been allowed to play in the previous day's adventure. The girls glared at the only part of Jasper they could see – his rear view – and then together rolled their eyes, and sighed.

'There's a hollow – a hole – built into this side of the chimney,' he said, bending down to peer. 'A bit like a chimney pot on its side.'

'A cloamen oven,' said Angela at once. 'Or cloamen, as Miriam calls hers – there are still quite a few left in this area. Barnstaple's not that far from here, and they were exported all over the world in the days before someone invented the kitchen range.'

Jasper backed out of the chimney to join Jane in staring at her. 'Say what?' he demanded, pointing the flashlight like an inquisitor giving the third degree.

Angela blinked at the light, turned her head, and waved an airy hand. 'Miriam told me, then I looked it up. Mother knows about them, too. Cloam equals clay, equals terracotta. Barnstaple and Bideford were the main pottery towns on this coast for years. I'll bet Barney Christmas's chimney pot came from there...' She glanced at Jane. 'The ill-wish onion was probably hidden in a similar hole in the brickwork of the chimney, which is why nobody will have noticed it earlier.'

'A smuggler's cache,' gloated Jasper at once. 'I've read about them, but I didn't know about your cloamen ovens. There's nothing like that in Trendle Cottage.'

'It's been remodelled over the years,' said Jane. 'There's a kitchen range, remember. Once they could stop using the pottery oven they'll have bricked it up to make the chimney draw better, or something. Barney might know.'

Jasper's upper half was vanishing up the chimney. 'Apart from cobwebs there's nothing much in here.' His muffled voice was regretful. 'There's no soot worth speaking of, either. I expect Prue Budd had it regularly swept.'

'Or the neighbours did.' Angela smiled at Jane. 'She sounds to have been a lovely, jolly old person everybody liked. If she'd wanted the garden bridge repaired—'

'The clammer,' said Jane, smiling back.

'The clammer,' Angela agreed. 'If Prue had made enough fuss I bet the village would happily have got it sorted for her to cross to the vegetable patch again...'

'Jasper's not crossing anywhere until we've had it fixed,' said Jane, 'which is hardly our first priority. It can wait until—'

'Hey!'

From inside the chimney came a clatter and a bump. A heavy, unadorned earthenware tile with a crude handle fell to the ground, breaking in three uneven pieces. Jasper, his face pale, without another word emerged into the fireplace.

All Jane's apprehensions came surging back. Even Angela felt nervous.

'I didn't...' Jasper spoke with an effort. 'It – it was a joke, really. I never...'

Jane licked her lips, but it was Angela who managed to speak. 'What is it?'

He brandished the flashlight. 'There really is another hollow in the brickwork – to one side and higher than the oven, blocked off with that pottery shutter gadget...'

'Which you removed.' Angela forced herself to be brisk. 'And dropped.'

He nodded. 'You wouldn't spot it at first – it probably was once a smuggler's cache.'

'Brandy for the parson,' said Angela at once. 'Baccy for the clerk.'

'Not brandy,' said Jasper slowly. 'There's a bottle, all right, but no, I don't think it's brandy. Brandy hasn't got – shouldn't have bits in it.'

There was a long, uneasy pause.

'Bits,' echoed Jane, sidling towards Angela without meaning to.

'What sort of bits?' Angela patted Jane on the shoulder.

Jasper had done far too much research for comfort into ill-wishing, curses and witch bottles. Dumbly, he held out the flashlight, inviting Angela to see for herself.

Would Andromeda Rosemary Marsh, proud exemplar of Girl Power, have hesitated? Angela thought not. She took three resolute steps, the flashlight and several deep breaths, before vanishing in Jasper's wake up the chimney.

The Mertons moved closer together. In silence, they waited.

'It isn't too dusty,' reported Angela from the chimney. 'No cobwebs. But it's hard to make out exactly what's inside.'

She reappeared, flashlight in one hand and the mysterious bottle in the other. 'We're in broad daylight,' she said firmly. 'We'll set this on the window sill and take a proper look.'

They stood, at a safe distance, round the previously concealed bottle three-quarters full of a dark green, sinister liquid that contained…

'Ch-chicken bones?' faltered Jane, in a near whisper. 'Legs – wings? Miriam keeps hens. Would she know? And those… little knobbly loose bits on the bottom…'

Jasper turned accusingly to Miriam's weaving apprentice. 'Could they be the bones of a – a chicken's spine?'

Angela, having once dared to handle the bottle, was now peering far more closely at the contents than either of her friends cared to. First she read the label, which neither of them had taken the time to do. Light began to dawn. She peered even more closely at the contents of the bottle of…

'Crème de menthe,' she said in triumph, and straightened. 'Prue Budd was famous for her peppermint creams, and everyone agrees they never tasted the same once she went into the home and had to rely on other people to arrange the ingredients for her. I bet,' said Angela with glee, 'this is her secret ingredient she didn't want anyone to know about. These aren't bones from any chicken – they're cinnamon sticks, and cloves!'

She produced a paper hankie and dusted the bottle, then held it out. Jane and Jasper read the label, peered inside, and exchanged very sheepish looks.

'Peppermint liqueur.' Jane began to smile. Her childhood memories were once more untarnished. 'I always *knew* old Prue couldn't – wouldn't…'

Jasper mopped an exaggerated brow, and Jane giggled. Angela nodded vaguely but showed more interest in the bottle, which she turned as she held it to the light.

'I wouldn't fancy using this myself,' she said at last. With the stopper in her hand, she sniffed. Her nose wrinkled grotesquely as she recoiled. 'I've no idea how long your Prue used to let it all pickle before adding it to the icing sugar, condensed milk, whatever – but if she made as many sweets as everyone says, my guess is it won't have been more than a few weeks. This has been here for months, from the dust, plus it's got a terrific kick. Far too violent for a humble peppermint cream.' She chuckled. 'But I'd love to play around with the general recipe. Will you want this? May I have it?'

'Decant the contents into another bottle and you're welcome to keep them,' Jasper said with no more than a glance at his wife. 'But we'd like the empty bottle back, please. We'll keep it as an awful warning not to let our imaginations get the better of us.'

'Pride of place in the display cabinet,' agreed Jane, laughing.

'If we ever unpack it.' Jasper sobered. 'Half a home is almost worse than none at all.'

'You keep thinking of the might-have-been,' Jane explained.

'Frustrating, yes, but your builders have got a lot further than I expected.'

'Barney's builders,' corrected Jasper, but Angela ignored him as she set off on a tour of the ground floor.

'You weren't going for all-singing all-dancing electronic gadgets, were you?' she called from the front of the cottage. 'No slick, streamlined, built-in furniture or underfloor heating? Well, then, from the look of it there's the wiring almost ready for things to be plugged in, and most of the basic plumbing. A lick – okay, a few cans – of paint and you're as good as there, if you don't mind leaving some of your stuff in storage a bit longer.'

'But we do,' said Jane. 'Mind, I mean. We had everything planned – and if we accept the situation as it is, and move in here, they'll only think we're not really bothered and keep finding more urgent jobs that must be finished first. We don't want to end up renting Trendle Cottage until we qualify for the old age pension.'

'You could renegotiate terms with Barney Christmas,' said Angela, though she took the point. 'You'd enjoy that,' trying to lighten the mood, to Jasper.

He smiled. 'He may have done the place up for rent, but there are still things we'd have tweaked to suit us, if it was really ours.'

'Which Clammer Cottage is,' said Jane. 'On paper, anyway.'

'Give it time,' said Angela. 'Just, not too much – otherwise it'll be a case of wily inhabitants taking advantage of innocent townies.'

'Miriam wouldn't let them,' said Miriam's loyal cousin and god-daughter.

'You've read too many books,' said Jasper, recalling the Binns accusation. 'You've watched too much television.'

Angela laughed. 'You're right, she wouldn't – and perhaps I have. Or it might have been seeing *The Wicker Man* at an impressionable age.'

Jane laughed with her. 'Nobody's been murdered or disappeared in these parts for yonks, as far as we know.'

'Except the lord of the manor's son,' said Jasper. 'Tell your mother to hurry up with her second draft, Angela. We want to know the full story. Susan's about our only hope.'

'She might be our only hope about the builders, too.' Jane frowned. 'Look, Angela – if we don't hear from Barney by the end of the week, could you ask her who she used when she bought Corner Glim Cottage, and where they came from – and if anyone minded, if it was from outside? Just in case another chimney falls down.'

'Or if any windows need unsticking.' Jasper winked at Angela. 'No more problems with paperweights for you, right?'

'It was only the once, and now I've collected a rather fun assortment from the harbour, it's problem solved. And if you'd only gone ahead with your pebble polishing scheme...'

'Not until we're living here and can rig up something over in the old hemp garden.'

'Not until we've had someone look at the clammer,' said Jane, 'and at least fitted better handrails. I'm all for authenticity and keeping the original character, but there are limits.'

'Ah.' Jasper looked pleased. 'A bit of a lightbulb moment regarding the clammer.' His initial venture from the 'mainland' side of the Chole to Elias Budd's vegetable patch hadn't at first particularly troubled young Mr Merton: as a prospective purchaser he'd been kept going by the adrenalin of curiosity. Then the realism of hindsight, coupled with his wife's genuine concern, gave him cause to reconsider the likely dangers of the crossing. 'Jane's right, we do want to keep the authentic touch – and the clammer. Our very own bridge! But it's our land, on both sides of the river. Who or what's to stop us putting in a second, stronger – safer – bridge right there beside the first?'

'If you're having trouble now with the British workman,' said Angela, 'I shudder to think how you'll get on with special-ist bridge builders. It's not the sort of thing just anyone can do, is it? A tree trunk dropped from bank to bank won't cut it, these days.'

But Jane, who'd been rapidly thinking, now gazed at her husband in admiration. 'The willow-pattern people!' she cried. 'Jasper, that's brilliant!'

Angela was puzzled, and looked it. Jasper apologised.

'You wouldn't know, sorry. One of my lucky breaks. A while ago, Packlemerton's was brought in to help with the launch of a hotel makeover. The original owners went bust after a flood drowned the whole site. They'd cut corners for years, and didn't have adequate insurance cover. The new owners had pots of cash and bought up half the surrounding countryside as well. They had water engineers for drainage, garden designers, landscapers to build a golf course – result, from flood plain to island paradise.'

'Islands, plural,' Jane chipped in. 'They did a wonderful job. There's Treasure Island – a scale model of the Canaries in a huge artificial lake – and a Chinese pagoda garden with the full willow-pattern story, including the bridge, though at first they couldn't guarantee a pair of lovebirds in exactly the right place when people wanted to take photos, and Jasper knew someone who knew somebody else—'

'Movement sensors and holograms,' said Jasper. 'You know the sort of thing.'

Angela nodded. 'Not like wind-up clockwork models with invisible wires, at the mercy of high winds and idiots with fishing rods and a warped sense of humour.'

'And rust. Right! So, Jane and I were invited to the grand opening and got chatting with the people who supplied the willow-pattern bridge. Fascinating! Any not-too-difficult distance that needs spanning, they span it. I forget how far it's possible, but over the Chole should be a doddle after hotel grounds and golf courses and country parks.' He laughed. 'And St Trinian's, which is what they tactfully called the girls' school where a Monet bridge was burned to ashes on the last night of term. An unauthorised moonlit picnic by the lake… One of the prefects doctored the fruit punch with vodka, and things got out of hand.' He laughed again. 'Skinny-dipping and smoking, though what they smoked is anyone's guess. They tried to blame everything on the fireworks, but as these were unauthorised too the entire sixth form would have been expelled in a bunch if they hadn't been leaving anyway.'

'My school was never so exciting.' Angela sounded almost regretful.

'Nor mine.' Jane sighed. 'A leaving party to remember, all right.'

'But it meant they had just seven weeks to get it fixed before the start of the next school year. The governors insisted on an exact replica, for looks at least, only made of something the little dears would need high explosive or – or a bulldozer to destroy.'

'St Trinian's indeed,' said Angela.

'Girls will be girls,' said Jane. 'The happiest days of your life.'

The two giggled together. Jasper looked reproving. 'They work in fibreglass, and from a distance you'd never know the difference, they said. They can design to imitate most likely materials – brick, wrought iron, stone. Even concrete, if you insist. We could ask for a wood lookalike, to maintain local character, but stronger and safer so that Jane can have a studio built over there, near my shed, and not have to worry about it – or about me.'

'Sounds pricey,' said Angela.

Jasper winked. 'I'll try the quid pro quo approach first. Packlemerton's will suggest a big boost on my website about the quaint office I now work in, and what an unusual route I take to reach it – and how reliable the bridge is, and who supplied it. Two birds with one stone, if I'm lucky!'

No other hidey-holes were to be found in the main chimney, and Jasper's might-as-well investigation of loose floorboards in the sitting room, and some irregular tiles on the kitchen floor, yielded nothing. For completeness he peered up the second chimney, but said it was of much later date than the first, by which time smuggling had gone out of fashion.

'Hmm,' said Angela. Once or twice in her midnight wanderings she'd caught the distant chug of an engine out at sea, or the crunch of heavy steps on chezell when conditions were, perhaps, not altogether favourable for fishing. Captain Longstone had explained to her the mysteries of tide tables and, from the same online source that supplied the astronomy book, she obtained a nautical almanac and approved its methodical approach to life. Angela's own life, while far happier than it had been, still held uncertainty about the future. She liked the way star movements and phases of the moon could be accurately predicted for years, if not centuries, ahead.

'There might be something upstairs,' suggested Jane, without conviction. Prue Budd's old home was, once again, the comfortable cottage where as a child she'd listened to local gossip and swigged illicit cider. 'We may as well look – it shouldn't take long.'

'I'll leave you to it.' Angela was keen to begin her analysis of Prue Budd's peppermint liqueur and had already decided where to start. 'Let me know what happens.'

'If anything does,' Jane promised, hoping it wouldn't.

Jasper was furdling dust sheets, and didn't really notice as Angela said goodbye. She grinned at Jane, and headed for Hempen Row.

Just past the old meeting house she encountered a Father Christmas figure leaning on his gate, white beard ruffling in the breeze.

'Good morning, Mr Hockaday! If you're looking for your wife, Jane and I were chatting with her not so long ago. I think she was going to the post office.'

'Ah,' said Gabriel. 'Well, I thank you for the information, but I wadn after my Louise.' He stood upright, and rubbed the small of his back. 'Bin turning over part of my vegeble patch,' he explained. 'Not so spry as once I was.'

Angela was about to make a polite rejoinder when he went on: 'No, it was you I was wishful to see – me or Mike Binns, whichever seed you first, only Mike's out in the boat with Mickey today. My Jerry's driving the bus,' he added, in case she should think his son less attentive than Mike's, 'not that Jerry's much of a gardener – but,' as Angela looked puzzled, 'that's neither here nor there. Only, overhearing that wife of mine pass the time of day with young Jasper, it did cross my mind his missus might be along soon, and you with her.'

'Er… yes,' said Angela.

'Yes, and when I heard the pair of you go by I knew I'd but to wait – and here you are.'

'Er… yes,' said Angela again.

He laughed. 'Yes. Well, we've talked it over together, all us older ones – Jan Ridd and Tabitha, too – and we'd like to ask how you'd feel about taking on the museum.' He waved towards the shabby corrugated iron building that housed the Octopus, the air raid siren, and everything else Tollbridge deemed too good to throw completely away just in case, one day, someone found a use for it.

'Me?' Angela stared.

'And why not? It needs someone with book-learning – someone able to know what's important for keeping and what's not, or at any rate one that knows how to decide which is which, if not from books then from computers, the way your mother does with those tales of hers.' His eyes gleamed. 'But our Susan's a busy woman and – well, midear, you've not found your time overfilled with work just yet, have you?'

Angela had been so thankful to surface, even slowly, from the worst of her break-up gloom that the gradual depletion of her savings was the least of her worries. Tollbridge, for generations so remote from the world, retained its faith in the currency of barter. Both Susan and Miriam had explained that to run a neighbour's errands, help for a while in house or garden, or bake an interesting cake in exchange for free-range eggs, fresh vegetables, or some faded curtains 'to keep you going while you settle in' was an excellent system; and so Angela had found. Tabitha Ridd spoke of bar work, Evan Evans dropped hints about bakery prospects, and Miriam promised that as Angela's weaving skill increased her mentor might sub-contract some of the less demanding work in the interests of efficiency.

'But I manage,' said Angela. 'And I'm enjoying myself, too.'

'Did I say otherwise? Only, high time the place was sorted properly. There's been talk and nothing but talk for years – same like they pamphlets of Sam Farley's, and look at how long that's a-tookt. More-and-so, somebody young would find tidying less wearisome to the body.' Once more he rubbed his back. 'We've talked to the vicar, and he's agreeable.'

'But—' she began.

'Says he always meant to do something, only he never has, living as he does up to Ploverton and with his other parishes, too – and now here's you, right on the spot, with all the modern understanding besides being Susan's daughter, not to mention Miriam's friend. An orderly mind, they say you've got. Bookshop, library, museum – where's the difference?'

'Just because they all arrange things in order on shelves?' She wanted to laugh, but she'd been well brought up.

'That's right,' he told her, straight-faced. 'You'll give it a go, then? Every vessel needs a skipper, no matter how willing the crew. Any one of us would be glad to help if and when asked, only we'd not know where to begin – beyond the name,' he hurried on, silencing any protest. 'The vicar says we could paint its name as the Budd Memorial Museum, and there would likely be something from Prue's will, once the matter's been further discussed among the trustees.'

The refusal that had been hovering on her lips died away. It wasn't so much the idea of monetary reward – Angela was a realist – but hadn't she moved to Combe Tollbridge to start a new life? An entirely different life? And she did, she knew, have a more orderly mind than either her mother, or Miriam Evans.

On the night of the fire she'd had a glimpse inside the museum and wondered what might be hidden among so much dusty clutter.

'I could certainly give it a go,' she found herself saying.

Father Christmas chuckled richly, reached into his back pocket, and gave Angela the present of a set of keys.

Chapter Twelve

In the village shop Louise, in a desperate attempt to divert Olive from brooding on the loss of her silver teapot, theorised idly on the state of the Mertons' marriage. There was no malice in Mrs Hockaday, but she grew impatient of what she thought her old friend's excessive lamentations, and thought a hint of possible scandal might cheer everyone up.

'You say he didn tell you why he wanted the dust sheets?' She shook her head as Debbie said he hadn't; nor had he wanted paint, or brushes. 'Well, of course, he never said a word to me just now, but if I'm right, it's a crying shame.'

Olive looked doubtful. She didn't care to commit to any point of view on such flimsy evidence – dust sheets could be used for all manner of purposes – and if it did happen to be true then Louise was showing very little sympathy.

Tilda's sympathy was plain. Her eyes began to brim with ready tears. 'Miriam will be sorry. Coming down from London to start a new life and already gone wrong '

'I blame Barney Christmas,' said Louise. 'If he'd not took the building work away from Prue Budd's place it would be finished by now, and them able to move in. Moving house is one of the hardest worries in life, they say.' Louise had lived at the same address since her marriage. 'If they could only have come straight from London into Clammer Cottage and not had to rent from Barney.'

'There was no forcing of them to rent,' said Olive. 'Nought wrong with staying on at the Anchor, if they'd wanted. Only they didn want.'

Debbie voiced her own objections. 'Better to blame the van driver. If he'd but listened to me from the start, and moved his van the way I told him, he'd never have struck the chimley in the first place – but there's no telling a man once his mind's made up. Only makes it up more, and sets him in a temper.' Mrs Tucker had experience of bad temper: it was the main reason for her divorce.

'Carrying quite enough for bedroom curtains,' said Louise, 'and enough over to lay on the floor rather than carpet, or a rug. She'll stay in Trendle Cottage, no doubt, him being the gentlemanly sort. Polite enough while we were chatting – *Good morning, Mrs Hockaday!* easy as you please – and not a word, of course, about why he was there alone and no sign of her, when always before they've been out and about together.' She didn't add that Jane and Angela had joined them before the chat was finished. Why spoil a good story? Olive had found something else to interest her – for a while, at least.

'I thought I saw Jane go past with Susan's daughter—' Olive began, when the doorbell jangled and Susan's daughter came in.

Angela wore jeans, a scarf (woven by herself under Miriam's tuition) and a casual jacket of loose, flowing style with deep pockets. The bottle of crème de menthe fitted neatly inside. 'Good morning,' she cheerfully greeted the little group.

The greeting was returned. Everyone looked at everyone else to see who would be first to ask a question. Louise won.

'And how are 'ee settling in, midear? All going well? Still after a job?'

Angela acknowledged this with a smile, saying that life in Tollbridge suited her very well indeed, and she felt sure something would turn up before too long.

Louise nodded, but said nothing beyond: 'And your friends? All well with them, too?'

'Oh, yes. They'll be glad when the building work's over, of course, but Trendle Cottage is very comfortable and I know they're happy there.'

Louise saw Olive brighten at the thought of her old friend's error.

'That's good,' beamed Olive. 'Nought to trouble them, then.' Her voice had a triumphant ring. Louise hid a smile.

'Oh, no. Just a bit fidgety because it's taking longer than they'd like – but that's how it goes with builders, isn't it? My mother told me she was afraid Corner Glim Cottage would never be finished. She said in the end if you doubled every estimate of time and added half again, it made it easier to accept the delays. She told Jane and Jasper to do the same sums and not to get their hopes up, so they didn't.'

'That's good,' said Olive again. 'Such a nice young pair.'

'An asset to the village,' said Louise. 'Young Jane so clever with her pencil, too.'

Angela nodded. 'Anyone can doodle, but Jane's a real artist.'

'Your mother says you're a better cook,' consoled Tilda. 'Says you've done some right smart things with Miriam's eggs – well, so does Miriam.'

'Evan Evans will need to keep an eye on you,' said Louise. 'Set up in competition with Widdowson's Bakery before you know it.'

Angela shook her head, but felt a glow of satisfaction that her modest culinary achievements should be spoken of even by those who hadn't tasted them. 'I hardly think so – but you've reminded me. I know stocks are running low, but would you be willing to let me buy just one Captain's Twist? I'd like to try if I can work out the recipe, and of course I'd need to sample one of the originals.'

'But we promised the captain,' cried Tilda.

'I'm not sure we should,' said her sister.

'Next time he comes in we'll ask if he's agreeable,' said Olive, the ultimate authority.

'Which is tomorrow,' said Debbie, 'most like. Keeps to his routine, does the captain.'

'You could ask him yourself,' put in Louise. A quiver of intuition prompted the thought that Angela might welcome a credible excuse for something more than idle conversation with a quiet, but undeniably personable, man.

'I could,' was all the reply Angela felt like making.

'Your mother, now.' Olive, quietly amused at the gentle snub offered to Louise, was in a mind to prolong the exchange. 'Much more to go with her book, has she?'

'She says it's going as well as can be expected.' Angela flashed a general smile, and advanced to the post office counter. 'Two first class stamps, please.' She rummaged for cash in the other pocket. 'And some air mail stickers.' That would give them something else to think about! She hadn't sent an overseas letter since coming to Tollbridge; she didn't need to send one now, but she'd seen the sly glint in the eye of Mrs Gabriel Hockaday and guessed the old lady to be in playful mood. That remark about job-hunting hadn't been casual; she might have thoughts of matchmaking, too. Angela Lilley, formerly Jones, had had quite enough of being manipulated, even by those with the kindest of motives.

Emerging from Farley's with a smile inside, Angela spotted Jane and Jasper in the distance, but didn't try to catch them up. She wanted to think. Her mind began to turn over schemes for improving – no, for establishing – the Budd Memorial Museum: it might be fun, and would certainly be rewarding. She wondered what her mother and Miriam would think.

Jasper was impatient to be back at his laptop. He wanted to pursue the matter of the willow-pattern bridge, but didn't yet wish to commit himself to a phone call to the designers. Internet research was the first step.

Jane wanted to get to grips with her new project, a series of seaside cottage vignettes based on photos she'd rushed to take after the chimney incident. Though preferring to draw from life she was a realist, and accepted that photos could spare her the worst of the English weather; now, unwilling to risk the loss of another West Country vernacular scene to twenty-first-century traffic, she had spent most of one day prowling the lanes and narrows of Tollbridge, intent on photography.

In Harbour Glim Cottage, Miriam began showing Angela how to use a drop spindle.

In Corner Glim Angela's mother sat back with a thankful sigh, and stretched. Milicent Dalrymple had at last typed *The End* for the second time; Susan Jones was limp with relief. Now the manuscript must be rattled into a block, shoved in a drawer for a week and for that week be right at the back of the author's mind. There were notes for that historical mystery she'd suddenly found she wanted to write that must be turned into something more coherent than scribbles on random bits of paper – once she could find all the bits of paper.

After a mug of hot chocolate and a banana, Susan was in part restored. Her eyes were still tired, her back and shoulders ached: not a driving day, but a day for being driven. She'd added Angela to her car insurance but Angela, she knew, was busy with Miriam today. One of the Hockaday drivers might be available.

Gabriel answered the phone, a little out of breath from working in the garden to warm his elderly bones on a less than sunny afternoon. 'Change of scene, midear? Jerry? Minibus into town, today. Easy to see you've lost track of time, working so hard. Daresay young Mickey would oblige.'

Susan, revelling in brisk air and exercise, found Mickey Binns where his uncle had told her to look for him, on board the *Priscilla Ornedge* making preparations for another fishing trip on the morrow. 'Word about that conger's got round,' he told Susan with a grin. 'Won't be so very long before I'm a millionaire.'

'Every little helps. How much to drive me over to Minehead for an hour or two?'

'You've finished the second draft.' It was the logical deduction. 'Well…' He shoved his hands in his trouser pockets, leaned against the deck railing, and adopted his best bait-the-tourist drawl. 'Well, now. Us peasants living in so small a village, there's many a time our liddle shops can't provide what the grand folk from upalong these days demand…'

'Mickey, it's wasted on me.'

He laughed. 'I'm not really kidding – about stocking up on a few extras for tomorrow's lot – and we can call it a business trip. Tax deductible.' He caught her exasperated eye. 'Okay, we'll call it a treat – a favour – for the celebrated author who deserves a change of scene. I'll fit my errands in around yours.'

'You really do need to go shopping?'

'Farley's can't provide everything, midear.'

'Then, thank you. And you're right about Farley's. Before we go I'll phone Angela at Miriam's to ask if there's anything either of them wants, though I can't imagine there is. They're both better organised than I am, especially Angela.'

She was right that Miriam needed nothing, but Angela surprised her by asking for a bottle of crème de menthe (specified by brand), two bags of icing sugar (unbranded), four tins of condensed milk (two full-fat, two semi-skimmed) and an assortment of spices.

Susan heard Miriam laugh in the background. She herself guessed that Angela had aspirations to the confectionary throne of Prue Budd, but said only that it sounded rather too much for her to carry at her advanced age; she would ask Mickey Binns to help with the shopping bags. 'And I'll swear him to secrecy,' she added.

At which Angela laughed, too, and the conversation ended on a cheerful note.

Susan and Mickey were soon on their way, Mickey teasing her about the fact-finding mission he was sure she intended while he bought his humble necessities. 'There's the department store doing silk sheets on special offer,' he informed her helpfully. 'Saw it in the local paper, which at a guess you've had little time for reading these past few weeks. Drop you at the door, shall I? You could claim it as your own tax deductible expense.'

Susan found herself blushing. 'Mickey Binns! Don't tell me you read Milicent Dalrymple!' She thought of peacock feather fans, and blushed still more.

'I don't *buy* them,' he said quickly. 'Libraries, second-hand bookshops – us poor fisher-folk can't afford to buy what you, I've no doubt, would call—' he coughed – 'spanking new.'

Susan choked as she thought of one particular heroine with a spirited take on modern courtship rituals.

'I like to keep up with the times,' continued Mickey Binns, straight-faced. 'I like to know what's going on: an enquiring mind, that's me. Ask, and it shall be told.' Susan hoped he would never ask where she got her ideas from. She'd find it hard to persuade him it was all imagination. 'Did I ever say why my first wife walked out? True as I sit here beside you. She had a persecution complex. Just because I showed an interest, she kept saying I spied on her all the time. Not true, of course.'

'Of course.' Everyone in Tollbridge knew about the scholarship he'd won, the mining expertise he'd acquired, and the wife who wanted to travel the world while he preferred staying at home. 'A persecution complex must be very hard to live with.'

'And very unfair.' Mickey waxed indignant. 'It wasn't me doing the spying, and I told her so! No, I hired a private detective, which is why I've no money now. Twenty-five dollars a day plus expenses comes hard on a poor fisherman.'

'Poor indeed, if you've no money now.'

'Nor no adulterous first wife, neither.'

His audience was happy to play along. 'And your second wife?'

'Big mistake. Didn't know each other well enough before we tied the knot.'

'Look before you leap,' said Susan gravely.

'Ask before you pop the question.' He adopted the extravagant accents of a Regency dandy. 'Why, I found out too late that the lady actually ate cabbage. What else could I do but cut the connection?'

Again Susan choked. 'Oh, poor Mr Brummell! And do tell me, Mickey, what became of your *third* wife.'

'Took herself off in a huff the seventh time she had bailiffs on the doorstep. Said love in a cottage with a handsome fisherman was all very well, but it just wadn true that two could live as cheap as one and she'd not bargained on kippers for every meal. Such terrible indigestion, poor girl. Can't honestly blame her, I suppose.'

'Angela told me that if you spread marmalade on kippers it somehow helps reduce the effect. I've never tried it myself, but—'

'Got to be able to afford marmalade in the first place, which I never could.'

'You being a poor fisherman,' said Susan. 'Of course.'

Mickey Binns chuckled, and drove on.

The Ridds were delighted when yet another stranger rang to book a single room for a single night, with an option for a second night should it become necessary. Business had been looking up. Repeat visits by double-checking insurance assessors had done wonders for the Anchor's recent profits. Tabitha, grumbling about her feet, recruited Angela as a part-time barmaid; Jan said there was nought anyone could tell a policeman about fallen arches, and that they must make plenty of financial hay while the sun was properly shining.

Human nature is human nature, especially in families. It surprised nobody that Combe Ploverton should laugh over what had been going on lower down the valley: in similar circumstances Combe Tollbridge would have been just as happy to laugh at its upland neighbour, though the two villages would have united as one against any third party poking fun or casting aspersions. Richly quizzed by Ploverton, Tollbridge adopted philosophy. Let it be borne in mind that nobody had been hurt in either incident! True, to have two insurance claims being assessed at the same time by two different insurance companies might look bad: but looks weren't everything. Too many folk found it hard to accept that in real life, coincidences could happen. To be sure, the Jubilee Hall fire and that tumbled chimley stack so close together might be thought unlucky, but – unlucky, who for? You couldn't deny it had brought good business, and not just at the pub! Money made money, no argument. Spread it like manure and watch things grow. Combe Tollbridge – so much smaller than Ploverton, so much farther off the beaten Exmoor track – would welcome a little expansion.

The attractive young woman who checked into the Anchor said she'd been advised that everywhere in Tollbridge was within easy walking distance. Where would be the best place to leave her car?

'Depends, midear.' Tabitha eyed her thoughtfully. 'Big, is it?'

'A small hatchback,' said the attractive young woman, who had signed the register as J.B. Franklin. 'But plenty of space when you fold the back seat down.'

Tabitha tried to hide her surprise. Miss Franklin had booked for one night. Needing to fold down the back seat suggested a lot more luggage than most visitors would bring for even a week's stay in a village where there wasn't much to do.

'My husband will help with your bags,' said Tabitha. Jan could use his judgement as to whether the guest was directed round the back of the Anchor to park, or down Harbour Path to the breakwater, where a modest slipway gave access to a bank of chezell the tide reached in only exceptional circumstances. The Watchfield car park on the opposite headland was mainly for day trippers.

Jan, arriving in answer to his wife's shout, escorted J.B. Franklin back outside so that he might judge both the size of her car and the quality of her driving. Both met with the former policeman's approval. After collecting her one modest bag he gave directions on how to find the Anchor's restricted parking area among assorted sheds and essential outbuildings, within earshot but not sight of the sea.

'What do you do if people turn up in Chelsea tractors?' enquired Miss Franklin, having manoeuvred her little hatchback into its space with efficiency and skill, and emerged to find a smiling Jan beside her wearing a look of approbation. It had been a tight fit, but that's why modern cars had mirrors, sensors, and alarms.

Jan explained about the breakwater, the slipway, and the chezell bank.

'Harbour Path?' She beamed. 'Isn't that where Trendle Cottage is? I'm here to see a Mr and Mrs Merton – Jane and Jasper. I suppose it isn't far?'

'Nought's far, in Tollbridge. Your bag's in your room, and Tabitha has the key waiting. If you're wishful to pop along there now you'm more'n welcome.'

'I'll phone first, to make sure they're in.' She was opening a many-pocketed handbag when she saw his doubtful frown. 'Oh yes, I forgot. Jasper told me mobile reception wasn't too good here. Worth a try, he said, but I'm not to be surprised if I find it quicker to walk straight there and simply knock.'

'Or ring the bell,' said Jan.

'He said that, too. A real ship's bell, right beside the sea! Your village sounds like a cool place to live. And the cottage they're buying sounds ace!'

'Buying? Bought, now.' Jan nodded at the red-and-white surveying poles in the back of the car. 'Reckon that's why you're here today. Only t'other night they were all talking about 'ee in the pub...'

It had been a night to remember; a night that spilled over into morning as the Anchor's official opening hours vanished in a celebratory blur of which the licensing authorities would not have approved. Susan Jones, learning from Mickey in the middle of her manuscript-put-away free week that spectacular lobsters had been caught by himself, and bought by the Ridds, said she would treat Angela and Miriam to a devilled lobster supper. The recipe for Tabitha's devilish tasty sauce had been handed down through several generations of the Evans family, as well-guarded a secret as the recipe for the gingerbread her cousin Evan made at Widdowson's bakery.

Angela was delighted to accept her mother's invitation and the unspoken challenge; like Susan, she had cause to celebrate. The telephone (with broadband) had at last been reconnected to The Old Printery, registered in Angela's name; now she could start serious job-hunting – if she wished. The vicar had been in touch to thank her officially for taking charge of the museum, and proposing a modest honorarium payable from parish funds. Prue Budd, he felt sure, would have approved.

Miriam was naturally one of the party as Susan's first friend in Tollbridge, and Mickey Binns invited himself (as originator of the feast) to come along later. His father came along to make sure his son didn't misbehave in the presence of ladies; Gabriel Hockaday just came. So did his son Jerry and, in due course, Sam Farley. Angela began to worry as the trio grew beyond a quartet, but Sam sat beside her to whisper reassurance, and pointed to Jan Ridd behind the bar, energetically ciphering with chalk on a blackboard. Angela smiled her thanks to Sam, and to Jan, as she raised a cheerful glass.

Mickey Binns unfolded the remarkable tale of his fifth wife ('Best not talk about Number Four, right, dad?') and Susan expressed due sympathy. Barney Christmas arrived to thank Susan formally for the silver hat-pin she had found during her recent Minehead trip: an idle comment, long forgotten, from Angela about vegetarian kebabs had suddenly inspired her.

'Took the words from my mouth, turning up at my door with a surprise present,' he told the company at large. 'And my birthday months away!'

'There's talk of a drone for *my* birthday,' said Mike Binns, fixing his son with a pointed stare. 'All manner of extras you can buy for them, I understand.'

Mickey ignored him. 'That all the thanks she gets?' he flashed at Barney. 'I'd buy her a box of chocolates, at the very least. Better yet, some Turkish delight.'

'It was a kindly gesture.' Mr Christmas jutted his jaw. 'Neighbourly. You'm expecting Olive Farley to buy drinks all round, no doubt.'

'Oh, dear.' Susan blushed. 'I meant it for the best, but...' A visit to the village store had seen Tilda burst into tears as she walked in, while Debbie embraced her heartily before wiping her eyes and sniffing. Their mother told her that she couldn't, just couldn't think how to thank her and stumbled, sobbing, from the main shop back to the private quarters.

Now Susan looked helplessly round. 'It was only a hatpin,' she excused herself. 'From a little antique shop I happened to pass. Mickey reminded me in the car about the ill wish, and I've read enough to know... I thought it would give Olive back her wedding teapot and – and might make the museum exhibit more interesting, when the time comes.'

'If it ever comes.' Sam Farley winked heavily at Angela. 'If it ever comes!'

Mickey, knight errant, continued to brood on the wrong apparently done to Susan by Mr Christmas. 'Silver hatpins don't come cheap,' said Mr Binns. 'And they're sharp.' He turned to Susan. 'Did the old skinflint pay you so much as a penny?'

'Superstition,' snapped Mr Christmas, before Susan could say that, rather than the modest coin required by tradition, Barney had offered a cheque and fifty pence (she accepted the coin) and argued at her refusal, until she explained she would be claiming the cost of the hatpin as tax-deductible research, which he naturally understood at once.

'Superstition like the onion,' Mickey snapped back.

'Yes, he paid me,' said Susan quickly. 'We can still be friends.' It was known that no friend should give as a present a knife, scissors or anything sharp without due payment received, lest the sharpness should sever the friendship. This made good sense, though she'd never understood why a similar penny must be involved in the giving of a handbag. Handbag – sandbag? Was a penny the price the giver paid for not being bashed over the head?

'So all's well that ends well.' Mike recalled his son to order. 'Hello there, you two!'

Jane and Jasper Merton, greeted next by Angela and her willing mother, were soon absorbed into the party. They drank as much cider as anyone and began elaborating on their plans for Clammer Cottage, as Barney gave his solemn word – before witnesses – that the chimley repairs were almost complete.

'—a workroom shed, and a separate studio for Jane, see?' Jasper was felt-tip doodling on a paper napkin.

'Once we've done something about the clammer,' Jane reminded him.

Everyone had views on what should be done. Barney said twadn right to be unmindful of history. That old clam had sufficed for the needs of Cousin Elias seventy years or more.

Gabriel Hockaday said they shouldn forget even oak didn last for ever, which the handrail wadn anyway. Small wonder young Jane here might be anxious!

Mike Binns nodded. 'Heart in her mouth, that day you first come to see the place.'

'Me, too,' admitted Jasper, with a grin. 'Afterwards.' He smiled a general apology. 'I was so carried away I – well, I didn't think, before.'

'You're thinking now,' said Jane.

'I've thunk.' He hadn't meant to tell her just yet, but general exuberance and a second mug of scrumpy had changed his mind. Perhaps there was a hint of slurring in his sibilants, perhaps not: the bar was a noisy place. 'I've spoken to Horatius, that's the firm who build made-to-measure bridges, and they shed – *said* – they said if I could give them a reasonable indication of dishtance, if it was one of their standard lengths it wouldn't be so long to wait. Cheaper, too.' He blinked slowly over the rim of his glass.

Susan, entranced by the name of the bridge-building company, would have put the obvious question, but Jane forestalled her with a question of her own.

'With a handrail? Each side?'

'If we want.'

'We want.' Jane had no doubts. 'Of course we want it safer, even though we want it to look as much like the original as possible.'

'Side by side,' agreed Jasper.

Here, Mike Binns favoured the company with tuneful thoughts on barrels of money, being ragged and funny, and travelling side by side. He had a full-bodied voice, and wetted his whistle with enthusiasm at the end of the second chorus.

'Side *to* side, you mean.' Mickey grinned at his father, then addressed Jasper. 'From one bank of the Chole to the other. So, how flexible – how far out could the measurements be? How easy for these Horatius – nice one! – people to accommodate, say, a few inches – a couple of feet – a yard or two into their original designs?'

Jasper opened his mouth, but Mike spoke first. 'Like riding a bicycle.' He winked at Jasper. 'You never forget.'

With growing suspicion, Jasper contemplated the scrumpy left in his mug. He glanced at the mug just emptied by Mike Binns. Mickey provided a swift translation. 'The old man means I was a surveyor of sorts, back in my mining days. If you'd like any help getting a few advance measurements for your Horatius – Horatius! – friends, you've but to ask.'

Gabriel Hockaday drained his own mug and began to recite from his schooldays, long ago. 'Lars Porsena of Clusium / By the nine gods he swore…'

As he hesitated, Miriam tried to recall the poem's next line and found she couldn't. She sat back with her eyes half-closed, and pondered.

'A cricket ball,' said Mike, 'thrown across with an attachment of string.' He sighed. 'Of course, if my birthday wadn so far ahead we could have sent up my drone—'

'—if anyone was giving you a drone for your birthday,' Mickey broke in.

'Why shouldn they? Chris Hockaday has a drone,' said Sam.

'I thought he was a bird photographer.' Angela frowned. 'Doesn't the noise—?'

'Oh no, not for birds,' said Sam quickly. 'Wouldn want to upset his precious birds nor any other wildlife, now would he? He says it's just a bit of fun, no more.'

'Fun,' echoed Mike, glaring at his son.

Gabriel abandoned recitation of a poem he couldn't remember as well as he'd thought he could. 'All such discussion is to no purpose,' he announced, 'seeing as young Chris idn here nor his drone, neither. Nor he don't play cricket,' he added with a withering look for his brother-in-law. 'And it's dark outside.'

'Never said he did,' said Mike. 'Said you could throw a cricket ball across and pull it back on a bit of string and measure the string and then you'd know – leastways, roughly.'

'Or a stone,' suggested Barney Christmas, but nobody was listening.

'So you might.' Gabriel tried to be fair. 'Roughly.' He sat up. 'Or a cannon-bullet – now, there's a thought. Hey, Jan!'

'Never mind,' called Jerry, as the landlord looked across. Jerry knew the famous relic of the Battle of Sedgemoor would stay in its display case no matter how fervent the cider-fuelled pleas for a loan might be, but there was no point in stirring up trouble.

Jan saw Jerry's expression, and decided to keep a closer eye on the group.

'A laser beam would be easiest by far,' he heard Mickey say, 'if only some people hadn mislaid mine and tried to cover up the loss with bluster.'

'A long time ago,' pleaded Mike.

'And so? You borrowed without asking, and you lost it.'

'If it mattered that much you'd have bought another before now.'

'Wouldn have been the same. Halfway round the world I went with that liddle gadget and you only went and dropped it upalong to the moor—'

'Excelsior!' cried Gabriel. Their squabbling had taken him back to school again.

This silenced everyone, until Susan giggled. Angela shot her an anxious glance. Cider – or something more sinister?

'Gadget? A – a strange device,' said Susan, and Angela relaxed.

Mickey laughed. 'Strange or not, that device did the business all right. Dad will swear he took a line from a molehill half a mile away, though I'm inclined to believe a quarter of a mile at most, but mine was an early model. Jasper's bridge people will be slap up to date.'

'Horatius,' Mr Merton prompted.

Susan simply had to know. 'Name of Macaulay?'

'No, Franklin.' Jasper wondered why she looked amused. 'We met a while back.'

'Josie and Tom Franklin,' nodded Jane.

'A cricket ball, with string.' Mike frowned. 'Who said a stone? Not a stone. A ball's more regular in shape and easier to wrap, same as you'd wrap a glass float in netting.' He sighed. 'Old Ralph could have done it in no time.'

'So can you,' said his son. 'He taught you well, like you taught me – and you've the patience, which I haven't so much these days.'

'So all we need's a cricket ball,' said Sam.

'Or a stone.' Barney Christmas had, like Gabriel, gone back to the past; he thought of his youth, and collecting chuckle-stones to sell to his schoolfellows. He glanced at the clock, trying to recall the current state of the tide. 'Tidn so far to throw, at that point in the river – and chezell stones of every shape and size free on the beach for the asking.'

It had, reflected Susan as at last she tumbled into bed, been an evening – and morning – of conviviality not soon to be forgotten.

Chapter Thirteen

J.B. Franklin made her way along Harbour Path at a brisk, efficient pace. She arrived at Trendle Cottage and prepared to ring the ship's bell.

She hesitated, which seemed out of character. She was still standing on the front step when Jasper opened the door.

'Thought I heard somebody,' he greeted her. 'Josie Franklin, we meet again!'

'Jasper, hello.' She pulled herself together, and released the bell-pull she'd been so closely examining. 'That's a seriously cool piece of work. You can't have made it yourself?'

'Neither of us could. Jane! Come in,' to the new arrival. 'She's upstairs – no, she's here. Everyone remember everyone else?'

They did. 'I told you we're just renting from one of the locals while the builders fix up our new place. Another of the locals is a ropework genius – doormats, sea-chest handles, customised netting for anything you like...'

He broke off to join with Jane as she spluttered into laughter. 'Sorry,' he told the visitor. 'But the other night in the pub one old boy challenged another to fit a made-to-measure net round a pebble...'

'The old boy who made your bell-pull?' Josie deduced.

'Right. He's way past eighty, but bright as a button. Wants a drone for his birthday, would you believe? He'll be part of your audience while you're working, I'm pretty sure. He's fascinated by technology. Semi-retired fisherman and part-time inventor.'

'An enquiring mind.' Josie nodded. 'You get used to an audience, but I'd love to meet him anyway. I wonder. Would he make something for me along the same lines as your bell-pull, but in aqua, or teal? I'd find the cord – and pay him for the work, of course.'

'He charges extra for coloured,' said Jane. 'He says it's not the way he was taught, but first there was a war on, and afterwards the shortages went on for years. Still, these days if people want it he'll do it, if you insist.'

Jasper chuckled. 'And he won't ask for cash up front, unlike some.'

'That's a bit unfair to Barney,' began Jane, then recollected herself to smile at Josie.

Ms Franklin smiled back. 'You two seem to have settled in nicely. That big chap at the pub knew all about you – and me, and your footbridge.'

'Clammer,' said Jane. 'Or clam. Local term.'

'We've studied the photos and sketches you sent.' Emails and attachments had zinged many times between Trendle Cottage and Horatius, Limited. 'It doesn't look like there'll be much of a problem. We need to get exact measurements, of course, and to check ground conditions where the footings will go – but you're doing that yourselves, yes?'

'Once you've told us exactly what's required,' said Jasper.

'We want to shop locally, as far as we can,' said Jane. 'Mickey Binns – he's the son of the man who made the bell-pull – and his cousin Jerry have volunteered for that job.'

'Keeping it in the family,' said Jasper.

'And keeping an eye on us,' said Jane.

As the Mertons accompanied Josie back to the Anchor, and the assorted equipment she'd left in the hatchback boot, they did their best to give a brief summary of Combe Tollbridge notables, and to explain why Elias Budd's vegetable patch held such importance. They also explained, as far as they could, the lost silver mine, and asked if she would need someone to hold poles or set reference sights on the opposite bank of the Chole.

'If you do, then I'll be heading off,' said Jasper. 'We tossed and I lost, so I'm the one who climbs the rough ground on the other side while Jane takes you up the nice smooth tarmac of the main street. We must keep away from the Silver Wood, you see.'

'An outsider might be tempted to take a tactless detour?'

'It could happen.' He grinned. 'We don't want to run any risks – of upsetting the village by stirring up the ghosts, or anything else.'

'The witches, for example,' said Jane. 'Tell you as we go,' to Ms Franklin as various bits and pieces were shared out for carrying; whereafter, waving Jasper on his way towards the former toll bridge, she regaled the bridge designer with the tale of the Clammer Cottage witch bottle, and loudly sang the praises of Prue Budd's peppermint creams.

'Synchronise watches,' she ordered as they turned the corner into Hempen Row.

'Why?'

'Aren't you curious about how long it will take people to know you're here – they know why, already – and how long it will be before the audience assembles? Jasper and I have a bet on. You're an independent witness.'

'Too late already, if you ask me.' Josie had spotted a twitching curtain, an opening door – 'A yellow walking stick! Is that cool, or what!'

Jane waved to Louise Hockaday. 'It's a thumbstick,' she murmured. 'Check for glugging noises when she's close enough: there's a flask of brandy inside the handle.'

Ms Franklin could barely contain her enthusiasm for the inhabitants and general atmosphere of Combe Tollbridge. She greeted Mrs Hockaday with delight, confirmed who she was and what she planned to do at Clammer Cottage, and went into further detail when Mike Binns was discovered leaning on his front gate, waiting for them.

'Jan Ridd said you'd be along.' Mike joined the party. 'Mickey's on his way. He's – he was a mining engineer. Knows how to use them poles and trapments you've brung with you. Young Jasper on the other side, midear?' to Jane, his grin wide and bright against his ginger beard. 'Can't have him worrying you again, can we, walking over on that-there old clam?'

Jane smiled at him, then told Josie: 'Mr Binns, here, is the ropework expert who made the bell-pull that impressed you so much.'

'Ropework, yes.' Mike adopted a modest attitude. 'Expert – well, tidn for me to say. Thought I'd found a way for you to save carting everything up and down the hill, only we must have used the wrong sort of string when we tried it. Went for best of three five times, and never got the same answer twice.'

'The whole boiling lot of you were seeing double before you even started,' Louise reminded him. 'What's more, that was the morning after!'

Josie Franklin rushed to deflect the squabble she could see developing. She addressed Mike Binns with proper deference. 'Jasper Merton tells me you're interested to see how modern laser technology compares to the old theodolites. Is that right?'

'Well, now, I do like to keep my brain active, but it's more Mickey wants to know than me. He's the one with the education to understand the jargon.' Mike uttered this disclaimer in tones that invited protest. Josie duly shook her head at him, and smiled. Mr Binns winked. 'All I can do is go so far as common sense will get me. Beyond that, I proceed slow and steady to find out what happens next.'

'It seems to work,' said Josie. 'I've heard how your Octopus pump saved the village hall – or very nearly – and all about your loudspeaker system for the church, and the air raid siren. For a self-taught engineer you do a remarkable job.'

Mike preened himself, and ignored the gently mocking laughter from his sister-in-law Louise as the four continued to the far end of Hempen Row.

Outside Clammer Cottage the builders were discovered at the back of their white van, enriching a tea break with meat pasties from Widdowson's. Like Mr Binns they expressed great interest in Josie's plans. They finished the pasties, drained their mugs and tramped after the little group into the garden, cheering as Jasper arrived in the vegetable patch opposite and paused to catch his breath at the end of the clammer. Mickey Binns manifested himself alongside his father, asking if anyone had brought a camera. The younger generation produced mobile phones; he said they were better than nothing, and by the way did Josie know taking photos was about all a mobile phone was good for, in Tollbridge.

'Yes, thanks, I've been warned. To be honest, it will make a nice change being able to get on with my work knowing there won't be too many interruptions.'

Mike nudged Mickey in the ribs. 'That's you told, my lad.'

Josie gasped. 'I'm so sorry! I didn't mean—'

"O'course not,' snapped Louise, glaring at father and son and also the builders, who were smirking. 'No more'n Mickey meant talking down to you. Slip of the tongue can happen to anyone – but,' she added, 'being fair, there's some from outside who do take it amiss if they can't be checking every five minutes for fear they've been tweeted – twooted – whatever the comical name might be.'

'Twoot,' cried Jane, as Josie choked and exchanged smiles with Mickey. 'Love it!'

'Twit,' suggested Mickey, laughing along with Josie. 'Ping. Now, if it's too far for you to shout, midear, you've only to ask. A fine voice, my dad's got.'

Ms Franklin glanced across to calculate by eye the distance to be bridged. Thirty feet? Nine, ten metres? She giggled. 'Or we could semaphore. Over such a wide valley, though… Perhaps I should have given Jasper a telescope.'

Mike was about to send his son home for theirs, but got the joke just in time. 'Sign language,' he said. 'Left, right, up a bit, down a bit – who needs modern technology to wave their arms about?' He megaphoned his hands. 'Can you hear me, young Jasper?'

'You don't have to shout.'

'Anyway,' said Mickey, grinning, 'you know full well sound carries over water.'

Josie edged forward to peer warily over the steep bank to the rushing Chole below. 'I think the theory applies more to calm, open water than to a torrent like this,' she ventured. 'Especially when it's so far down.'

'Tidn always that way,' said Louise. 'Should there be heavy rain on the moor then the Chole will rise – and rise. Hadn burst above the bank that any of us has ever heard, but it's been close enough for regular concern, when blocked on its way to the sea. Has nobody told you of the mine yonder, gone these five hundred years?' She brandished her stick towards the distant trees of the Silver Wood.

'We've given her the basic history,' said Jane, 'but I know Mr Binns could tell it far better, if he'd be willing to spare the time.'

Josie flashed the old gentleman another smile as bright as his own. 'I'd love to hear it,' she said. 'Once we've finished the job.'

The job (as so often happened) had become a common enterprise, and everyone gathered round to offer advice for Josie to ignore. This she was well able to do, explaining in detail what they needed to know only to Mike Binns, who was enthusiastic, and to Mickey, who listened. He soon realised that he hadn't lost his former skill, and allowed Mike to play his part, but delivered a stern warning first. 'Should this gadget here go the way of mine, there'll be no birthday drone for you.'

Mike made a point of moving to stand exactly where Ms Franklin directed, and stood there rock-steady until she sent him to another spot.

Jasper, likewise, moved from spot to spot as directed, positioning reflective poles for laser beams to be bounced. Mickey hovered in the background, ready to grab anything vital if it fell; but his father dropped nothing, and relished every moment of service. Josie made detailed paper notes of critical readings in case a battery went flat, or modern technology failed in any other way. Mike talked approvingly of belt and braces; Mickey recalled his early days with a theodolite, and told Josie about cross-hairs and Vernier scales.

They all enjoyed themselves very much. Time passed quickly. In due course Josie called her thanks to Jasper, and graciously acknowledged the builders; Jane pointedly consulted her watch. The builders returned to work on those final touches necessary for the cottage to be ready for the Mertons to move in. Louise took the hint and made her excuses, keen to be first in the shop to tell Olive what she'd missed. Jasper gathered up the survey poles and challenged Mrs Hockaday to a race back down the hill.

Josie, packing away her share of the equipment, invited Binns *père et fils* to the Anchor that evening, when she would be pleased to buy her assistants a drink and learn the history of the lost silver mine. Mike was glad Louise hadn't heard, because she'd have been sure to tell Gabriel, which would mean sharing any tips.

'And you behave yourself,' Mickey warned his father, as they escorted Jane and Josie to the corner of Hempen Row and waved them on their way. 'Young Josie tells me she's after some fancy ropework. No charging twice the price because she's from the city.'

'As if I would, now we've worked side by side together!' But a gleam of mischief hinted that it was as well for Ms Franklin's bank balance that the younger Binns had spoken.

The Anchor enjoyed another convivial night, with Jan Ridd suffering fewer qualms of conscience about after-hours drinking because Josie Franklin was a paying guest.

'And I guess,' she told the Mertons, when everyone was saying goodnight, 'you want it yesterday, if we can manage it? I can't promise that, but – hey, I can see why you'd want it! Over the sea to Skye? Over the bridge to work! How many people can say that?'

'And how many can say they have such a good advertising opportunity?' asked the owner of Packlemerton's Publicity.

'Okay, I can take a hint. I'll talk it through with Tom when I get back, but now I've seen the set-up I know we can sort something out. Talk about a quid pro quo. I didn't know I wanted one until I saw yours, but if I hadn't come to Tollbridge for your clammer I wouldn't be getting a teal-blue bell pull made by an expert, would I?'

Angela climbed Coastguard Steps in an almost absent-minded manner, no longer needing the concentrated effort of a few weeks ago. Like Jane and Jasper she could now reach the top without pausing to catch her breath. She then strolled along the headland, and happily checked her mobile phone for text messages: cutting the majority of ties with her previous life had shortened this to just a few minutes' efficient scrolling.

She deleted at once what she didn't wish to recognise, but was pleased to see Andy Marsh was again in touch. It dimmed her pleasure, however, to learn that the bookshop's new owner's cards-and-posters plan had indeed morphed into the stationery-and-assorted-trivia gloom of Angela's own worst case prediction. Having been right from the start was poor compensation for the idea of *plstic tat n wndow stickrs* replacing those infinite riches in the civilised little room where she'd worked for so long among few but honest friends, and had enjoyed herself so much until everything changed.

'Cheerful, aren't you?' Sam Farley emerged from the Coastguard Printery in time to hear Angela's deep sigh. 'A day for sunshine, this is.'

'Hello, Sam.' She pocketed her phone. 'You're right, it's a glorious day. Just some news from a friend – but it's not important. That was then. This is now! You look pretty cheerful yourself.'

'Come along in and I'll show you why.' He beamed. 'Not a word to your mum, though, as it's early days. Nor Jane neither...'

'The booklets are ready?'

'The dummy for the first one – the silver mine – is. We're on the way at last.'

Lorinda Doone had written a vivid account of the toll bridge, the Ankatell greed and the Exmoor cloudburst. Jane's thumbnail sketches, one per page, were in the same spirit. They showed each step in the disaster, from the king's revenue men sternly detailing to a reluctant lord of the manor his fiscal duty, to the lord's fury as what remained of Combe Ankatell's populace confronted him in a body, the parish priest at their head, when he arrived too late to pay his respects to those lost in the destruction of the mine.

The centrepiece was a Chris Hockaday photo of the stone obelisk that was the Silver Wood memorial. The four highlight sketches, one to each corner of the cover, had (after a lively week) been selected by self-appointed critics in the Anchor. None of the regular drinkers admitted to knowing anything about art, but they knew what they liked. They liked Jane's sketches, which had been displayed as numbered photocopies down one wall of the skittle alley; they couldn't settle on which four they liked best, and they kept saying this and changing their minds repeatedly as they stood arguing at the bar, trying to reach a decision.

Two evenings of this was enough. On the third day after the pictures went up Jan Ridd spoke to Gabriel Hockaday, who said better ask young Angela because, while he himself knew what to look for, he couldn't rightly say where it was. Angela rummaged with enthusiasm in the former meeting house and, that night, an old wooden ballot-box, former property of the long defunct Tollbridge and Ploverton Friendly Society, appeared in the skittle alley beside the sketches. With it was a coffee mug of pencils and a pile of paper slips to be dropped, once completed, through the circular hole into the green baize drawer below.

'All to be signed, or they'll not count,' warned the ex-policeman. Would-be humourists took note and grew serious. There was further discussion and much scratching of heads, but in the end, after a vociferous recount, Tollbridge's four favourite drawings were chosen and the choice was conveyed to Sam Farley. Sam insisted it must be put in writing and, with this confirmation on file, he carried on the good work with much enthusiasm.

'I like it.' Angela leafed through the pages to admire the overall effect. 'You've used just the right paper. It doesn't feel too smooth and weigh too much and scream "self-published" the way so many limited-run productions often do.' Even the smallest bookshop has had dealings with authors whose work, deemed uncommercial by the mainstream, can from its modest shelves reach out to a wider readership. Or so it is hoped. Angela had learned that the smaller the bookshop, the kinder the heart and the greater the optimism – for there is always the possibility of a 'sleeper' word-of-mouth success that can bring cheer to author and bookseller alike.

'Mother will be impressed, and so will Jane. I wonder if Farley's could find room for a revolving stand? Mike or Mickey Binns could make one...' She laughed, shyly. At Sam's encouraging look, she blushed. 'You know, I've been thinking. Once the other booklets are back in print, it might help with sales to have the whole series numbered, and set out in a proper display. If you could persuade shops in other tourist areas – reasonably local, to start with – to stock them, too – sale or return, probably...'

Sam looked at her. 'Numbered just like a proper book, you mean?'

'Yes, an ISBN.' Having an International Standard Book Number – and a barcode for scanning at the till – gave a certain cachet to anyone who self-published a book. 'Then the author can register for Public Lending Right. If nothing else, you'd know how many readers were borrowing from the library rather than buying outright... You need a name, of course.' She gazed thoughtfully around. Sam knew better than to break her train of thought. 'Coastguard Publishing? No, could be anywhere on any coast... The Tollbridge Press? Yes, nice one. Jane Merton can design a snappy colophon for the spine and the title page – a bridge might be too obvious, perhaps a silver coin for paying the toll – a groat, or something... The house colours could be silver and black and grey...'

She emerged, with a start, from her thoughts. 'I'm sorry, I got carried away!'

'Don't matter. I think it's a grand idea. Needs some thinking about, but I'd say you'm on to something there. Give the whole thing a professional touch, right? I like the notion of all the booklets on a revolving stand, I must say.'

'If there's room in Farley's.' Angela felt a note of caution should be sounded; but she was pleased. 'We – you could ask

Mickey Binns to get busy with his graph paper again. Look how well he helped arrange your move here from Meazel Cleeve.'

Sam smiled for her discretion. 'So he did. Your own move settling down okay now?'

Angela smiled back. 'Rather slower than expected because there's so much else going on, but getting there, thanks.' She tapped the pocket where she'd put her mobile phone. 'That message from my friend was partly her inviting herself down for the weekend. She says her bike needs another detox—'

'Oh, the girl with green hair! A Triumph Bonneville, right?'

'Right. Well, she doesn't know it, but she's just decided me to buy a flat-pack storage unit for the main room downstairs. She can help me assemble the thing.' Angela thought of the Mertons, and the expert from Horatius, Limited. 'A quid pro quo, you could say.'

Then she wondered if Sam Farley of Combe Tollbridge would ever say anything of the sort – then wondered if she was being an intellectual snob – and, before she could start to blush for her bad manners, was relieved to hear him chuckle.

'You drive a hard bargain, young Angela. Come all that long way and be handed a screwdriver when you've barely walked in the door?'

'I might even ask her to do some sorting in the museum! She wouldn't mind.'

'That's the one as got your stuff out of storage and hired a van and drove it down here with her pals to sort it all out for you?'

'That's Andy. And by the time she comes I'll have done some baking. She's a pushover for marshmallows, and I've found a new recipe for a rocky road cake. She'll love that. She loved Widdowson's gingerbread, too. I'm still trying to work out that recipe, so I'll buy one from Evan Evans and we can compare and contrast at the same time as building up our strength for our flat-pack exertions.'

He laughed. 'Bribery, corruption and industrial espionage all in one! So, what's it worth if I don't tell Evan? Can I come to tea, too? Never met anyone with green hair afore.'

'With a pink streak, or it was pink when I saw her. By now, it could be purple! You'd be more than welcome to join us, but there isn't much left on my phone so I'm ringing her from home, later, on the landline. I'll have to let you know.'

'Nice to hear you call it home.' Indeed he looked pleased. 'We need folk in Tollbridge to settle, not just pass through a few days and never stay more'n a week...'

'Better than nothing,' she suggested.

He nodded. 'True enough, but it's sad to see the changes there have been even in my lifetime, and I'm no great age, midear.' He was at most five years older than Angela. 'Oh, I know Barney's hotel plan for the old school still wouldn bring folk here to settle, but it would have meant jobs in the village, and then some. Never mind how he's sometimes talked of, they mean nothing by it really. Everyone knows old Barney always tries first for local workmen – stonework, carpentry, roofing – or decorating. Has Miriam never told you he did his best to talk her into weaving carpets?'

Angela laughed. 'I hadn't heard that one! I imagine the technique's basically the same, but I should think it's far heavier than weaving cloth.' No mention of Miriam's age: she'd learned her lesson. 'He might have done better to ask for curtains, or cushions, or tapestry wall hangings.' The Mertons had told Angela, with her growing interest in weaving, of Miriam's splendid wedding present and how they looked forward to retrieving it, with other valued possessions, from storage to be installed in Clammer Cottage.

'The smells don't seem to bother you when you'm dyeing?'

'Perhaps a bit, but you get used to it. I tell myself I'm cooking an unusual curry, or one of those exotic pickles that will strip varnish off the table if you drop the spoon.'

'Any luck yet with Prue Budd's peppermints?'

Angela had lived in Tollbridge long enough to be unsurprised that her every ambition was known. Sam's remark about industrial espionage had missed its target: the baker himself had asked, the last time she bought gingerbread, how she was getting on, and said if she cracked it he might think of offering her a part-time job. 'It's pure guesswork,' she said now, 'because it's hard to know exactly what they ought to taste like when I haven't tasted them. I know the basic ingredients, and what *I* like, but that's not at all the same thing.'

'Cousin Olive and the girls won't even let you have one liddle twist?'

'They promised Captain Longstone, and somehow I don't care to ask him – deprive him, I should say, when there are so very few left.'

'I could have a word for 'ee, if it would help.'

'Not with the captain!' Angela would hate him to think her a spineless featherhead who couldn't put a straightforward question without getting a man to ask on her behalf.

'No, with Cousin Olive. She'd be glad, maybe, should anyone start making them again. They sold well to others besides the captain, I know. I could put it to Debbie, if you'd rather. She's the one with the best business head.'

'They did say they'd ask him,' said Angela. 'If he'd mind them selling a few to me, that is, when I said I wanted to try to make some more. But they've never mentioned it since and, well, I don't like to pester people.' She didn't want to be told that Rodney Longstone's answer had been a flat refusal.

'Worried they'll think you an incomer throwing her weight around?' He shook his head. 'You're Susan's daughter, midear. They know you'd not do that, no more than Susan done from the day she come to live here. My guess is, they've plain forgot, what with the onion and the silver teapot and suchlike disturbance. What's more, wadn from Farley's you bought the icing sugar and condensed milk and all the trimmings, was it? Would have jogged their memories nicely, that would.'

No secrets in a village was one thing, but how could he possibly—

'Mickey Binns,' said Angela.

Sam grinned. 'Told us in the pub one night how Susan made him carry the bags. Said his arms had grown a yard at least, and his back would never be the same.'

'My heart bleeds for him,' said Angela, who only that morning had watched Mr Binns stride easily across the chezell, snatch at the side of MV *Priscilla Ornedge* as she lay aslant on the tide-free beach, and swing himself on board with no effort whatever.

'Tell the truth—' Sam became confidential – 'Mickey's always glad of the chance to do Susan Jones a favour. Been sweet on her for years, but never likes to speak for the risk of having her say no. How would 'ee fancy a stepdad, young Angela?'

Angela might feel herself to be going through an anti-man phase, but that wasn't the reason she hesitated. 'I like Mickey, of course, but… I don't remember my father. He died before I even went to school, but it was a terrible shock to my mother. She was left to bring me up alone – she wouldn't put me with a childminder, and writing meant we could be together in the house all the time. She kept trying and trying to get published, and suddenly she got an agent, and a contract, and she never looked back – but while she was so busy trying I think she sort of got used to concentrating on me, and her books, and nothing else. And it went on like that – and on. After so many years I think it's become a habit.'

'And hard to break, specially now you've come back.'

She didn't remind him she'd never lived in Tollbridge before: it would be churlish to correct what was no more than a convenient shorthand. 'I can hardly move away again on the off-chance she'll accept Mickey if he ever brings himself to propose. I like living here.'

'Glad to hear it,' said Sam.

'And she might not fancy being Wife Number Six,' she added. 'Or do I mean Seven?'

He laughed. 'Never tells the tale the same way twice, he don't – but I do see your mum might see our Mickey as another Bluff King Hal. That's a deal to ask of anyone.'

'His beard's the wrong colour for Henry. If you'd said *Mike* Binns I'd agree with you.'

'Ah. Mike. Well, he's of a mind to sympathise with Susan, of course.' He saw her look of bewilderment. 'You not heard that one, neither?'

'I don't believe so.'

'Nobody talks much about it, but tidn forgot by any.' And Sam told how the young Mike Binns, having escaped his London slum, had gone to school in Tollbridge and made a shaky start when he winked at a pretty little girl. A slightly older, but larger, boy who had until then considered the pretty little girl his own, punched his nose for presumption: but Marguerite Jerome could think for herself, and she winked back. It was Marguerite who held Mike's jacket, while her sister Louise held that of Gabriel Hockaday, when the two boys squared up to each other behind the block of earth closets. Gabriel was inevitably the victor, but swore eternal friendship with the loser. The oath, to this day, had not been broken.

Gabriel grew up to marry Louise Jerome in a double wedding with Mike and Marguerite who, like her sister, had been pretty and popular. Her unexpected death plunged all Tollbridge into mourning; the newborn Mickey Binns, left motherless, became living proof of the old saw that it takes a village to raise a child. Ralph and Priscilla Ornedge were doting grandparents; every neighbour pitched in to help. Cockney Mike Binns became as much a son of the West Country as he could ever have hoped to be.

'That,' said Angela, 'is even sadder than my own – my mother's – story. At least she had my father for three years, I think it was, before he died, and there are photos of him with me even if I don't remember. Poor Mike.' She gently shut the dummy booklet. 'Mother knows, I suppose?' Sam nodded. 'Then I'll tell her the next story to write up really should be the one about Bran the little black dog. Mike would like that.'

'Yes, he would. The silver mine did by rights have to come first, because that's about all for which we're really known in Tollbridge these days – nor we're not very well-known, neither. But a shipwreck makes a good tale. And there's the memorial in the churchyard for a photograph, not to mention snapshots in the family albums.'

'After Bran, what about smugglers?' Angela smiled. 'Or would that be telling?'

Sam looked her straight in the eye. 'What's to tell?' He smiled back. 'No doubt Susan will look in some of her old books and find something to write, but there's nothing so remarkable about smugglers along this coast.'

She tactfully made no mention of unusual activity sometimes glimpsed on moonless nights, or faint gleams out at sea that might come from muffled torches.

'Widdowson's Bakery,' said Sam. 'That's another tale to be rewrote. Evan Evans idn in the direct line, but he took over from my cousin Farley Ridd – who *was* direct, through his mother – after being prenticed to him. Evan's likewise by way of being my cousin.' He looked sideways at Angela. 'He's told you the story, no doubt.'

She said that he had, and she'd also been shown the booklet. A storm, a sunken boat, a fisherman's young widow with a small child; a plea to the Ploverton miller for a sack of flour on credit, to be paid for once the bread she planned to bake had all been sold.

But the miller, as plump and greedy as tradition, was perhaps less greedy than he might have been – or perhaps he had designs on the young widow, nobody knew: but he told everyone the poor soul could never make a success of such a business on her own, and he refused to take advantage. He allowed her credit for but half a sack of flour, laughed, and told her to try her best; he promised to take back what remained at no extra cost, when her bakery failed as it was sure to do.

The miller had no need to redeem his promise.

The young widow stayed true to the fisherman's memory.

Their son grew up to inherit a highly successful little bakery, and gave it a new name in honour of his mother.

'Plenty there to keep Susan busy,' said Sam Farley. 'And young Jane, with her clever sketches – but from what I've been hearing they'd best make haste in the work.'

Angela looked a question. He laughed. 'Oh yes, looks like the wait's nearly over. Your friends could be living in Clammer Cottage by the end of this very week!'

Chapter Fourteen

His guess was close enough. It was eight days later that the Mertons thanked Barney Christmas for the use of Trendle Cottage, returned his keys, and at long last asked Sam Farley to print the change of address cards.

Of the young couple it was Jane who had the more practical streak. Jasper, his mind on building a business, accepted that in non-business matters he could sometimes let himself be distracted. Jane it was who'd made the final choice as to which possessions should follow them to their new home, and which were no longer required; it was Jane who sternly packed cardboard boxes for Jasper to deliver to selected charity shops.

It was Jane who, contemplating the far end of Hempen Row, voiced her doubts on the state of this non-through road less travelled by. Her future neighbours had fewer qualms. True, the tarmac might be a touch iffy, but twadn as if the underneath was riddled with brock-holes or rabbit-burries. More-and-so, surely the removal van would have insurance?

Jane and Jasper didn't want to start their life in Combe Tollbridge being sued by the local council – or by the storage company. 'Definitely not a pantechnicon,' decreed Jane. 'We'll ask for two smaller vans. On two consecutive days.'

Jasper hesitated. 'Why?'

'We mustn't block access to anyone's front gate, which one large van *might* do and two smaller ones almost certainly would. People would be polite and say they didn't mind, but you can bet they'd grumble behind our backs and we don't want that.'

Two days running, an audience of interested gossips watched from a distance as the contents of a London-based removal van were carried into Clammer Cottage. Once the men in overalls had finally gone, neighbours retreated to their homes, but friends knocked at the door to ask if any help was needed. The Mertons preferred to trip over each other's feet with no extra complications, kindly meant though these extras might be. They'd see everyone in the pub later on, and would have a house-warming party in due course.

And so it came to pass.

The telephone, cut off when Prue Budd went into the home, was reconnected two days after the party. The Mertons were glad to have communications with the wider world available between their own four walls as well as on the breakwater, at the end of the pier, and at the top of Coastguard Steps.

'Once we have our bridge, if anything goes wrong with the landline we can take our mobiles across to the headland far more quickly than if we had to go all the way down to the harbour and climb halfway back up the other side,' said Jasper.

'We can start planting vegetables, too.' Jane wasn't fooled by his apparent indifference to the possibilities of the former hemp garden. 'Once we have our bridge.'

Emails had continued to fly between the Mertons and Horatius, Limited. Having agreed that the necessary concrete footings should, to save time, be arranged by Jasper, the biggest decision to make became whether to have a gate at each end of the clammer, or at one end only – and if so, which end.

Josie Franklin had asked on measuring day the purpose of the original clammer gates.

'The gates? The goats.' Mike Binns chuckled richly. 'Might not stop them, nothing can do that, but it makes 'em think twice.'

Mickey saw his father was getting above himself. He grinned apologetically at Josie. She was almost encouraging the old man to be outrageous.

Louise Hockaday became the voice of reason. 'They come from upalong after shelter, when the weather's bad,' she explained. 'Mostly they live apart in the woods or on the cliffs, but they can cause powerful havoc in a garden, rampaging over walls and eating anything that grows. They're every bit as bold and mischievious as them across to Lynmouth, same like they cashmere goats in Wales.'

'Llandudno,' supplied Mike. 'Some of *them* was took away for conservation, if memory serves. Supposed to eat all the wrong plants in awkward places so the right ones can grow there properly, the paper said, but how anyone can tell a goat what to eat, beats me.'

'Two gates, then,' said Jasper.

'Better safe than sorry,' said Louise. 'As Prue and Elias would ever maintain.'

On Josie's return to the Horatius premises, research was duly undertaken into Britain's various colonies of feral goats. Ms Franklin promptly phoned to ask about metal spikes.

Jane raised the spectre of Health and Safety. Jasper said that what had been good enough for Elias Budd should do perfectly for them. 'Two gates, one each end, no spikes,' he said. 'Otherwise, we might as well install an electric fence and have done with it! Everyone agrees it's only a serious problem in really bad weather.'

Jane shivered. She had, for atmosphere, re-read *Lorna Doone* before undertaking the first of her sketches, and remembered the bitter fight in Lynton's Valley of Rocks between the 'fine fat sheep with an honest face' and the lean black goat that tossed its victim five hundred feet to the sea below. Small consolation that

Girt Jan Ridd had then caught the goat by his right hind leg and hurled him after the sheep! It had been, as Jan Ridd wrote, a wild March day with a piercing wind.

'Fingers crossed the weather stays fine,' was, however, all Jane said aloud.

'But not too fine.' Jasper thought only of the bridge. 'They'll deliver it on a low loader and swing it into position with a crane. They expect, some time in August. If the day's too hot and the tarmac gets too soft…'

In the event it was just after noon on a warm, very humid day when the little cavalcade arrived from Horatius to install the fibreglass clammer that would link flower garden to vegetable patch. There was more than a hint of thunder in the air. Clouds of flying ants began to swarm from their nests, erupting in eager clouds into the sky for queens to find and mate with males who, having fulfilled their destiny, would in a day or two be dead.

Jane began closing all the windows she'd previously opened in search of even the weakest current of air. 'Talk about muggy.' She repositioned an electric fan. 'I don't remember anything like this when we lived in London.'

'We were always too busy to notice,' said Jasper. 'And most offices had air con – but we live in the country, now.'

Angela, appointed by Jasper the Back-Up (Phone) Photographer – in case Jane, with her camera, became distracted – volunteered a childhood memory of walking through the park with friends one late summer's day and counting half a dozen or more places where the ground was alive with crawling black ants opening flimsy wings to harden in the sun before flying to meet their doom.

'At least they don't bite,' said Jane.

The Franklins' car came first. They checked in with the Mertons, then drove down to the harbour for Josie to decant Tom and his crew, with Jasper, near the old toll bridge. She drove back up again and cast an expert eye over the concrete footings Jerry Hockaday and Mickey Binns (supervised by Mike) had built to industry standard on the cottage side of the Chole. Jasper led the way up the other riverbank, and Tom was able to report favourably on what the construction team of Binns & Hockaday had achieved in the vegetable patch.

The crane then rolled down the ramp from its modest low-loader to advance slowly to the low stone wall at the far end of Hempen Row. None of the neighbours even tried to ignore it, though it seemed likely their front gates would be blocked by the Horatius vehicles for some time to come. A small crowd of spectators grew bigger by the minute as others drifted up from the main village, including a breathless Debbie Tucker. Olive wouldn't close the shop under any pretext, the twins tossed a coin, and Tilda Jenkyns found herself volunteered to keep an eye on things from behind the post office counter.

Jane sighed with relief that the caterpillar tracks of the crane hadn't chewed up the tarmac any more than weather and removal vans had already done.

Debbie fanned herself with a straw hat that had seen better days, but still had a wide, useful brim. She flapped away several near misses from heat-drugged ants. 'Wish the weather would turn,' she muttered. 'A clap or two of thunder and a burst of rain would sort they dratted emmets out, sure enough.'

The second, larger low loader, carrying the bridge, moved into position within grappling range of the crane. Jane again eyed the tarmac. It held firm.

Jasper had been correct in supposing his wife would become too distracted for photography. Angela was pleased she'd put her phone on full charge that morning, and had warned her friends to do the same: if hers ran out of steam while filming she could borrow theirs, for neither was in action. The Mertons were far too intent on what was going on.

The crane wasn't one of the self-build tower structures found on construction sites: it was all-in-one and ready for action as soon as the driver pushed the right buttons. The first push drove a pair of steel arms horizontally from each side of the body, with a metal plate under each end. These outriggers fully extended, another button was pushed and each arm grew a leg, directing the metal plate of its foot down to the surface of the road. There was some jiggling and manoeuvring. The outriggers were still. The crane was stabilised.

Josie smiled reassurance at Jane. 'He used to work with much bigger stuff, building skyscrapers. This should be a doddle for him.'

Jane thought of the insurance, tried not to think about tempting fate, and smiled bravely.

The crane driver called through an open window: 'Ready to go when you are!' Josie and her small team double-checked everything again, exchanging careful signals with Tom, doing his own double-checking opposite. The go-ahead was given.

Jane watched the driver wipe a steaming brow, and wasn't happy.

The boom of the crane unfolded: up... and over... and down. The heavy metal hook at the end swayed on its pivot. There was some skilful byplay on the part of the crane driver, and the hook linked neatly into the chains wrapped around the bridge. The Horatius workforce stepped back. Jane held her breath as the chains clanked and tautened.

The bridge rose from the back of its low loader. Suspended in mid-air, it swung slowly up and over the garden wall, then out over the Chole; and then as slowly swung down.

Tom Franklin signalled and shouted; the crane driver closely followed his instructions. The chained bridge swung lower, and still lower... slower, and more slowly, until it came almost to a halt. Josie checked the position at her end; Tom checked at his. Extra shouts and signals were exchanged; guide ropes were tugged. The crane driver mopped his brow again, but nobody seemed concerned. It was, after all, a hot August afternoon.

There came a judder, a clunk, and the rattle of collapsing chains as the clammer settled to its designated spot on the concrete footings. There were sighs of relief all round.

The hook swayed free; the boom of the empty crane rose at a steeper angle as it began to swing round and down to its original position.

The driver let out a yell – his hands flew up – the boom slanted to one side. The angle grew steeper. The boom shuddered – shot out, and up – and the sudden weight of twice its working length dragged the body of the crane right over, away from the two extended outriggers that now gave no support as they began to swing up from the ground.

For one paralysing moment, the whole crane seemed to hover in the balance.

Gravity won.

While the body fell with creaks and groans, the boom came down with a crash.

It missed the wooden clammer once maintained by Elias Budd. It missed the fibreglass clammer made and installed by Horatius, Limited. By inches it missed the horrified Tom and Jasper, whose yells outdid the crane driver's as he flapped his hands in the overturned cab.

It became a third, metal bridge across the Chole to the old hemp garden.

Josie Franklin was white and shaken; Tom sank to the ground, his head in his hands. The crane driver could be heard cursing. Other members of the Horatius team cursed him back.

Combe Tollbridge hadn't known so much excitement for years.

'Send for Jan Ridd,' was the general recommendation, once it had been established that nobody had been hurt even if everyone was in shock.

The crane driver was trying to scramble from his cab: as the main body buckled, so the door had jammed. Onlookers rushed to help him squeeze through the open window.

'What,' demanded everyone as he reached the ground, 'happened?'

'Bloody great hornet in my cab.' He was visibly shaking. 'Bright blue!'

'A blue hornet?' Tollbridge had encountered visiting experts who hunted for rare ferns and unusual trees, but...

'Wasn't having a monster like that sting me, was I? Huge great wings, buzzing – came at me from nowhere!'

'From the river, at a guess,' said Mike Binns. 'You're a city lad, right? I remember the first time I saw a dragonfly close up. Scared me half to death, being London born meself.'

'A dragonfly. Of course.' Once more there were sighs all round, several of regret that Combe Tollbridge wasn't about to rewrite England's natural history. 'After the flying ants.'

'The insurance,' said Jane, 'is going to be a nightmare!'

Angela smiled at her mobile phone. She'd caught every moment of the drama on film.

'If I'd only had my birthday,' Mike Binns lamented. 'Make a good picture, that would, from the air.' He grinned. 'Unusual's hardly the word. Side by side – by side!'

'Chris Hockaday's got a drone,' someone said. 'Louise, know where he is today?'

The photographer's grandmother shook her head. 'Could be anywhere in these parts. The boy's got his way to make in the world. He idn tied to anyone's apron-strings – but Mike has the right of it. I'll go home and try to find him: he'd be sorry to miss such a spectacle.'

'Phone Jan Ridd first,' the crowd advised her. 'He'll know what's best to be done.'

Josie was busy directing those on her side of the Chole to dismantle the chains, coil the guiding ropes, and generally tidy things up. The bridge had been correctly positioned before the accident: with installation complete, it would be safe to cross to inspect any damage done by – or to – the crane in its collapse. Tom took charge on his side. 'Who's Jan Ridd?' he asked. 'Why does everyone keep saying he ought to be here?'

Jasper explained. Tom was unconvinced, and said so. 'It's going to take rather more than an outsize ex-policeman to sort out a mess like this.'

How the news spread nobody knew for certain, but nobody was surprised that it did. Louise had spoken to Tabitha Ridd, which might well explain why, in due course, even Captain Longstone came to learn of recent events at the end of Hempen Row.

Angela was reluctantly showing later arrivals what had happened, a little anxious now that so many wanted to watch. If her phone went flat... Her mother, anticipating another historical pamphlet, must be the last until the movie had been safely downloaded.

The captain arrived. They exchanged smiles, and from a courteous distance he listened to her conversation with Susan. He then asked permission of Jane Merton to trespass for a closer look.

Jane laughed. 'Nobody else is bothering! Please, feel free.'

'Half this – this unlucky contraption may have fallen on the public highway, but the other half is clearly on private property.' He turned a calculating eye upon the unexpected metal bridge. 'If you don't mind, Mrs Merton?'

She laughed again. 'We forgot the bottle of champagne,' she said, and waved him on.

'May God bless all who walk on her?' The captain raised his albatross hat in a respectful gesture, bowed, and walked across to join the excited villagers in Elias Budd's vegetable patch. Jan Ridd was there, discussing with Jasper and Tom Franklin various possibilities for action; discussion was still at an early stage. Josie and her team were trying to pack chains and other gear away, with Mike Binns beside them proposing, if they wished, to adapt the Octopus to pump air for the inflation of a giant balloon, would they only wait while he, Mickey and Gabriel fashioned one from a couple of strong tarpaulins.

Captain Longstone stood, thinking. Then he approached Jasper and his companions.

'Mr Merton? Mr Ridd? I believe there may be a fairly simple solution. I can't promise, but I can certainly pursue enquiries, if you'd like.'

Jan beamed, and introduced Tom Franklin as co-owner of the firm that built the bridge. 'If the captain has an idea, it's worth a listen,' he said loyally. 'Fire away, Cap'n.'

'As you know,' began Rodney Longstone, 'I served mostly in submarines, but I've kept in touch with one or two of my term who went into the Fleet Air Arm. I wondered if a heavy-duty helicopter might be what's needed here.'

There was an awed silence.

'It would make a pleasant change from routine training such as shifting gun-barrels from one imaginary battleship to another, or transporting motor trucks across flooded valleys that are in fact bone dry.' The captain smiled. 'Some years ago a model aeroplane enthusiast had his birthday present blown by a sudden gust of wind into the top of a factory chimney, where it caught fast. The birthday present seemed lost for ever, but the poor chap's wife had spent a lot of money on the thing and I don't believe it was insured. Someone proposed an informal rescue exercise and spoke of crates of beer for the petty officers' mess.' His smiled broadened. 'And gin for the officers! The birthday boy and his wife were invited to join the subsequent jollifications, and I understand from my friend that a very good time was had by all.'

The awed silence continued.

Jan Ridd drew breath. 'Bloody brilliant, if 'ee can pull it off!' he said; and looked at Tom. 'What say you, Mr Franklin? The Cap'n refers to HMS *Whirlybird* – a stone frigate, I'm told's the proper term—' the captain nodded – 'being within easy flying distance. Every whip's while, if the wind is right, they fly over us here doing circuits and bumps around the moor – and I recall not so long since, Lynmouth way, them rescuing a sheep tumbled over the cliff when the lifeboat couldn't cope.'

Tom stared, first at Jan and then at Captain Longstone. 'Do you think you could fix it?'

Rodney Longstone raised a hand in warning. 'Remember, I can't promise, but I can certainly call my friend – the commanding officer – to explain the circumstances. He might well be interested in something that's out of the ordinary. It would take a day or two to arrange, I fancy. It's hardly a matter of life and death and they'd have to discuss things with Air Traffic Control, but somehow I don't see there being any strong objections. If you'd like me to phone on your behalf, I will.'

He glanced at Jasper, on whose property lay the fallen crane. 'I don't suppose you or anyone else could arrange to have this sorted much faster,' he said apologetically.

Jasper, founder of Packlemerton's Publicity, was equally apologetic as he replied: 'It would be a godsend from a – a professional point of view, too. There could be drones and television cameras and reporters all over the show.'

The team from Horatius winced. So did Captain Longstone, who understood this kindly warning. His dislike of attracting attention to himself was well known, even to Tollbridge newcomers. He achieved another smile. 'I'll go home now to phone *Whirlybird*, and I'll report the answer to Mr Ridd in due course. I take it,' to Tom Franklin, 'none of you anticipated having to stay overnight?'

'We're staying now,' asserted Tom; and once more Jan Ridd beamed.

Jerry Hockaday, returning from a taxi job, was promptly given another. He took the still-shaken crane driver up to Combe Ploverton, and the doctor.

Onlookers began to disperse now the main excitement was over. Captain Longstone disappeared to make his phone calls; and he wasn't the only one. The Franklins acknowledged their cheek, but asked if Jane and Jasper would be willing to allow access to their landline because mobiles didn't work well if you were in the wrong place, as most of Tollbridge seemed to be. The Mertons were starting to see the funny side, and said by all means – but only after Jasper had finished making phone calls of his own.

Across the electric wire the message came, and went – repeatedly – as Josie and Tom did their best to turn chaos into some sort of order. Jasper emphasised the publicity potential in what had happened; Horatius began at last to see things his way. They cheered up.

They were even more cheered when, on finally checking into the Anchor, they found Captain Longstone's message. The helicopter from HMS *Whirlybird* would be deployed on behalf of royal naval training and Horatius, Limited the day after tomorrow.

Farley's General Stores could supply toothbrushes and paste, but no night attire, though tee-shirts were to be had at a reasonable price. There weren't many, and they sold quickly. The bad luck of the accident had been counterbalanced by the good luck that nobody had been hurt. Anyone who risked sleeping in the nude was sure to find that turning luck would sound the Anchor's fire alarm in the middle of the night. Tilda Jenkyns phoned the Ploverton shop, and Jerry Hockaday's taxi was despatched to collect the few tee-shirts stocked there.

The Horatius team, with the recuperating crane driver, explored both villages briefly and went early into the Anchor's bar. Tollbridge welcomed the visitors and made very merry over recent events; the television set in the bar was switched on early for the evening news, just in case. The news, it seemed, hadn't yet caught the nation's attention, though rumour had outsiders checking into Ploverton's pub when the Anchor couldn't help. Inquisitive strangers were encountered wandering with note-books, cameras and microphones.

This was, after all, August: the silly season. Next morning there were front-page photos (courtesy of Chris Hockaday and his drone) and screaming headlines: *Combe Threebridge!* or *Bridges Trouble Over Water!* were only two of the many. Angela's video had been safely downloaded to her computer; regional television asked permission to share with national channels later that day. After consulting Jasper, she negotiated an acceptable price. More reporters arrived to interview every-one they could find.

Mike Binns and Gabriel Hockaday got carried away as they told their version of the lost mine, the parson's curse, and their fears that the impiety of a new bridge 'so close' to Silver Wood might have been the original cause of the accident. Jasper Merton heard about this and begged them to add a few ghosts, if they could. 'Clanking chains and ghastly groans at midnight should do nicely, thanks. An advertising campaign run by someone who works in a haunted garden? You just can't buy publicity like that!'

As reporters prowled the village, Captain Longstone stayed at home. Angela, who from several sources had heard the story of his comically scandalous divorce, realised that her quiet friend was likely to be suffering withdrawal symptoms. She knocked on his door.

After a cautious moment or two, he opened it. She smiled. 'I wondered how your stock of Captain's Twists was holding out,' she said. 'I think I've discovered Prue Budd's mystery ingredient and I'm trying to duplicate her recipe, but Farley's won't sell me any for comparison because they promised them all to you.'

She knew she could offer to buy some, strictly on his behalf; she felt sure the Farleys would permit such a purchase, but she didn't want him to feel embarrassed that she knew his foolish, guilty secret. She had no intention of offering to buy his daily paper.

'So I wondered,' she went on, 'if you'd care to try a few of my samples and let me know what you think?' She held out a clip-lid box, in which rolls of greaseproof paper could be seen labelled with letters of the alphabet.

'That – that's amazingly kind of you, Miss Lilley.' He reached for the box. Their fingers lightly touched. 'Angela. Amazingly kind. Thank you.'

'That's okay. Rodney.' Smiles were exchanged as she released the box. 'I've always liked cooking; experimenting. Variations on an original theme, my mother used to call it. If Miriam wasn't such a hard taskmaster I'd have sussed out your peppermints ages ago!' She knew when to beat a discreet retreat. 'Talking of Miriam, with all this talk of ghosts she said she'd teach me invisible – no, transparent weaving. I'd better be off. Let me know about the mints,' she added in farewell; waved; and was gone.

On the following day, crowds in and around Hempen Row exceeded all expectation. Locals began to feel overwhelmed. Jasper and Jane thought about boosting parish funds by charging a nominal sum for outsiders to cross by the new clammer to strategic positions in the vegetable patch, but second thoughts decided them that Health and Safety might not like it. A phone call to Captain Longstone suggested the Royal Navy might not like it, either.

The distant growl of engines high in a clear sky heralded the Fleet Air Arm's approach from their shore base twenty miles along the coast of the Bristol Channel. Cameras and microphones turned to focus on a black speck – two black dots – two dark blurs – two grey, whirring shapes that, as one, altered course to fly in line abreast inland from the Severn Sea. They flew lower, and closer; the pilots tilted their craft in salute to those below and then began, in line ahead, a slow and thorough tour of inspection.

Captain Longstone, with Jane and Jasper's permission invited by Angela to join herself, Susan and Miriam in the relative privacy of the Clammer Cottage flower garden, gave an intelligent if limited commentary on proceedings. Submarines (he said) had far less to do with helicopters than other branches of the service, but he owned to a basic knowledge, which he was happy to share.

Jane had her camera and was resolved, this time, to miss nothing. Jasper would do his best with his mobile phone, Angela with hers. Susan simply trusted to note-taking, and to the memory Angela as a child once described as *a sponge with blotting-paper skin*. Miriam Evans simply looked, and marvelled.

The captain of HMS *Whirlybird* knew that Combe Tollbridge had made headlines nationwide, if not round the world as time zones advanced. This must be no routine 'find, collect and fly home' exercise. His men, and the public, wanted a challenge – a display – and a display they should have. He sent no ground crew in advance to put in the preliminary work: in real life, preliminaries had to be decided on the spot, and so it must happen here.

The helicopters ended their inspection, to hover in formation above the stricken crane. Doors were opened. A blue-overalled figure in a hard helmet was winched slowly down from each. Ropes and tackle followed. Nylon strops were passed round the boom of the crane by one blue-overalled pair of sailors as the other pair deployed padded spreaders on the overturned body; then their shipmates doubled across the Clammer to assist them in wrapping the body in a firm nylon embrace, afterwards doubling back to indicate that the waiting tackle should be lowered still further.

Hooks were slipped into eyes. Every connection was checked, and checked again. The senior rating stood where he was clearly visible to both pilots. He raised his right arm, and began to make circles with his hand: 'The signal to hoist,' said the captain.

The engine growl was joined by the descant squeal of a working winch. The crane juddered, and began to move. In mid-air, it swayed. Guide ropes were hastily tugged.

The crane moved again…

And stood, battered but triumphant, on its waiting low loader – upright at last.

The next morning felt very flat. Farley's ordered twice the usual amount of newspapers and sold the lot. Once they'd been read, and relevant pages snipped for scrapbooks – the Farley stock of crafting sticky-sticks ran dangerously low – people looked sadly for further diversion. Everyone had stayed up late the previous night to watch every likely news bulletin; the name of Combe Tollbridge, for a while at least, had been famous from coast to coast.

Never before had Tollbridge seen so many visitors; it was likely there would never be so many again. The Anchor was drunk almost dry of cider; once again Angela joined Tabitha behind the bar, and Mrs Ridd promised her weary feet that slippers, not shoes, would be the dress code for tomorrow no matter what happened.

The rules of skittles were explained, and games were unskilfully played. Jan Ridd, with the eyes of the world upon him, was firm about closing time…

And, next morning, everything felt very flat.

Mike Binns and Gabriel Hockaday were down by the harbour, being picturesque. Mike was mending lobster pots; Gabriel was busy finishing his umpteenth jumper. August might be too hot for woollen beanies, but they wore them anyway. A beanie was part of a fisherman's uniform. A peaked cap was permissible at sea, but on dry land it could look affected.

As the brothers-in-law sat enjoying the bright summer day, a strange voice addressed them. 'Excuse me. We're looking for the bridge.'

Mike and Gabriel had barely begun their routine when the little group was joined by others who had come from the Watchfield car park. In the distance, strange voices could be heard approaching from the same direction.

Combe Tollbridge, it seemed, was no longer being ignored by the twenty-first century.

Also available – the Miss Seeton series

Retired art teacher Miss Seeton steps in where Scotland Yard stumbles.
Armed with only her sketch pad and umbrella, she is every inch an
eccentric English spinster and at every turn the most lovable and unlikely
master of detection.

Picture Miss Seeton
A night at the opera strikes a chord of danger when Miss Seeton
witnesses a murder . . . and paints a portrait of the killer.

Miss Seeton Draws the Line
Miss Seeton is enlisted by Scotland Yard when her
paintings of a little girl turn the young subject into a
model for murder.

Witch Miss Seeton
Double, double, toil and trouble sweep through
the village when Miss Seeton goes undercover . . .
to investigate a local witches' coven!

Miss Seeton Sings
Miss Seeton boards the wrong plane and lands amidst
a gang of European counterfeiters. One false note, and her
new destination is deadly indeed.

Odds on Miss Seeton
Miss Seeton in diamonds and furs at the roulette table?
It's all a clever disguise for the high-rolling spinster . . . but
the game of money and murder is all too real.

Miss Seeton, By Appointment
Miss Seeton is off to Buckingham Palace on a secret
mission—but to foil a jewel heist, she must risk losing the
Queen's head . . . and her own neck!

Advantage, Miss Seeton
Miss Seeton's summer outing to a tennis match serves up more than
expected when Britain's up-and-coming female tennis star is hounded
by mysterious death threats.

Miss Seeton at the Helm
Miss Seeton takes a whirlwind cruise to the
Mediterranean—bound for disaster. A murder on board
leads the seafaring sleuth into some very stormy waters.

Miss Seeton Cracks the Case
It's highway robbery for the innocent passengers of a
motor coach tour. When Miss Seeton sketches the
roadside bandits, she becomes a moving target herself.

Miss Seeton Paints the Town
The Best Kept Village Competition inspires Miss Seeton's most
unusual artwork—a burning cottage—and clears the smoke
of suspicion in a series of local fires.

Hands Up, Miss Seeton
The gentle Miss Seeton? A thief? A preposterous notion—until she's
accused of helping a pickpocket . . . and stumbles into a nest of crime.

Miss Seeton by Moonlight
Scotland Yard borrows one of Miss Seeton's paintings
to bait an art thief . . . when suddenly a second thief strikes.

Miss Seeton Rocks the Cradle
It takes all of Miss Seeton's best instincts—maternal and otherwise—to
solve a crime that's hardly child's play.

Miss Seeton Goes to Bat
Miss Seeton's in on the action when a cricket game leads to mayhem in
the village of Plummergen . . . and gives her a shot at smashing Britain's
most baffling burglary ring.

Miss Seeton Plants Suspicion
Miss Seeton was tending her garden when a local youth was arrested
for murder. Now she has to find out who's really at the root of the crime.

Starring Miss Seeton
Miss Seeton's playing a backstage role in the village's annual Christmas
pantomime. But the real drama is behind the scenes . . . when the next
act turns out to be murder!

Miss Seeton Undercover
The village is abuzz, as a TV crew searches for a rare apple, the
Plummergen Peculier—while police hunt a murderous thief . . . and with
Miss Seeton at the centre of it all.

Miss Seeton Rules
Royalty comes to Plummergen, and the villagers are plotting a grand
impression. But when Princess Georgina goes missing, Miss Seeton
herself has questions to answer.

Sold to Miss Seeton
Miss Seeton accidentally buys a mysterious antique box at auction . . .
and finds herself crossing paths with some very dangerous characters!

Sweet Miss Seeton
Miss Seeton is stalked by a confectionary sculptor, just as a spate of
suspicious deaths among the village's elderly residents calls for her
attention.

Bonjour, Miss Seeton
After a trip to explore the French countryside, a case of murder awaits
Miss Seeton back in the village . . . and a shocking revelation.

Miss Seeton's Finest Hour
War-time England, and a young Miss Emily Seeton's suspicious
sketches call her loyalty into question—until she is recruited to uncover
a case of sabotage.

Miss Seeton Quilts the Village
Miss Seeton lends her talents to the village scheme to create a giant
quilted tapestry. But her intuitive sketches reveal a startlingly different
perspective, involving murder.

Miss Seeton Flies High
On a week away in legendary Glastonbury, Miss Seeton's
artistic talents are called upon to help solve a
mysterious kidnapping.

Watch the Wall, Miss Seeton
Miss Seeton foils a murderous gang of professional
smugglers operating on the Kent coast.

About the Author

Roseanna Hall is the pseudonym adopted by Sarah J. Mason for her new 'Exmoor Harbour Tales' series, to distinguish these books from the seventeen 'Miss Seeton' mysteries she has written as Hamilton Crane, and a further eight mysteries under her own name.

The first Roseanna Hall was Sarah's grandfather's grandmother. Roseanna married John George and, in 1843, gave birth to grandfather's mother, Elizabeth. Elizabeth George might have been a good name for an author, but sadly it's already taken.

When not busy at the keyboard Sarah will relax with craft work. Her current enthusiasm is for weaving inkle bands, but she also enjoys patchwork, tapestry weaving and, from diagrams in a Danish textbook, she taught herself to make 3-D beaded animals. She's especially proud of her peacocks.

She supports her local hospice shop by checking 500-piece jigsaw puzzle donations. Please don't ask about the earwigs.

Note from the Publisher

To receive updates on further releases in the Exmoor Harbour
Tales – plus special offers and news of other humorous fiction
series to make you smile – sign up now to the Farrago mailing list
at farragobooks.com/sign-up